Praise for Dana Marie Bell's
Cynful

"I've adored Dana Marie Bell's *Halle* stories from the very beginning. The characters are fun, imaginative, snarky and could easily pass for someone you might know—minus the fur."

~ *Romance Junkies*

"This is the kind of book that makes you laugh out loud and smile too wide."

~ *Night Owl Reviews*

"I wanted to keep reading so I could find out what happened next."

~ *Fresh Fiction*

Look for these titles by
Dana Marie Bell

Now Available:

Halle Pumas
The Wallflower
Sweet Dreams
Cat of a Different Color
Steel Beauty
Only in My Dreams

Halle Shifters
Bear Necessities
Cynful

True Destiny
Very Much Alive
Eye of the Beholder
Howl for Me

Poconos Pack
Finding Forgiveness

Gray Court
Dare to Believe
Noble Blood
Artistic Vision
The Hob

Heart's Desire
Shadow of the Wolf
Hecate's Own

Print Collections
Hunting Love
Mating Games
Animal Attraction

Cynful

Dana Marie Bell

SAMHAIN
PUBLISHING

Samhain Publishing, Ltd.
11821 Mason Montgomery Road, 4B
Cincinnati, OH 45249
www.samhainpublishing.com

Editing by Tera Kleinfelter
Cover by Kanaxa

First Samhain Publishing, Ltd. electronic publication: June 2012
First Samhain Publishing, Ltd. print publication: May 2013

Dedication

To Mom, who retired recently. How are you liking those Facebook games?

To Dad, who is still deciding if he wants Diablo III or not. Considering how many times my sister has managed to erase his level 60 paladin in Diablo II, I'm thinking it might be a lost cause.

To Dusty, who recently discovered the joys of the Mass Effect universe. I *dare* you to stay loyal to Ashley with Miranda waving her bodacious butt in your face.

And to all the girl gamers out there: Let's show the boys how it's done.

Chapter One

His expression was priceless. She should have come up with this sooner just to see that look on his face.

One dark brow rose in disbelief. "You want to what?"

"You heard me." Cyn shrugged. He could take it or leave it, but no way was she going to let him have a nip until he met her demands. After all, he'd shown up on her doorstep and made some demands of his own, namely that she bare her neck and accept him just because he said so. Pfft. Like *that* would happen. *Okay, maybe if he begs really prettily.* "I want to date." She leaned against the doorjamb and grinned at him.

His jaw dropped. Julian was speechless, probably for the first time in his life.

"You have a problem with that?" Man, she was enjoying this. If she thought things were going to go the way they had for Alex and Tabby, with one date and BAM!, mates for life, he had another thing coming.

"But... Cyn, we are *mates.*"

"You *say* we're mates. You could be a stalker who's in serious need of a depilatory half the time." She crossed her arms over her chest and shot him a saucy look. "You want a piece of me?"

"Dear gods, yes." Tiny, light grey dots appeared in his otherwise dark brown eyes. A thin strip of white ran down his waist-length black hair. "More than you could possibly appreciate."

She wasn't surprised. She'd seen the way Tabby and Alex had instantly bonded, their inner animals forcing them to link their life forces together. The good news was Alex was everything Tabby needed, and it seemed Tabby was everything Alex wanted. Alex would keep her friend safe, give her a home and make sure she was never alone again.

What could Julian give Cyn that she didn't already have? A bigger butt? Prematurely gray hair? "So. Dinner. Movies. The occasional box of chocolates. Jewelry, if you have good taste in it. You're a smart guy. Figure it out."

He sighed and rubbed his eyes. "Why are you fighting it? We can date if you like, but in the end we're just going to wind up at the same place. You, me, a bite and a fu—"

She pressed her finger against his lips. "Do *not* go there."

He kissed her fingertip but didn't move his lips. Those gray specks in his eyes became more prominent.

"Down, boy."

He huffed out a laugh. "That only works on dogs." He managed to get hold of her hand. He toyed with her fingers, his gaze never leaving her face. "Date, huh?"

She nodded firmly. "And don't think you'll weasel your way out of it, Mr. Due Charm." She deliberately mispronounced his last name, but from the grin on his face it didn't bother him one bit. The *ch* in his last name was supposed to be pronounced *sh*, but on first reading it most people got it wrong. Lord knew she'd done so when she first saw his name.

Julian chuckled and brushed a kiss across her knuckles before releasing her hand. "I'll pick you up tonight, then." He turned, his waist length hair brushing against her. She'd always been a sucker for long hair on a guy. "Jeans are fine."

Oh really? "What time?" Maybe she'd still be at work when he stopped by. Or already be gone. She was the boss. She was allowed to take off early once in a while.

"I'll wait at the shop for you." He waved and sauntered off, every inch the confident, sexy man he was. And that terrified her. She shut the door before she could stare any longer than she already had. She leaned back against it and blew out a rough breath. He was sexy and smart and funny and everything she'd ever wanted in a man.

Julian could break her without even trying.

"Huh. That was...unexpected." Julian sat in the front seat of his car and pondered the predicament he found himself in. His mate wanted to *date*. Who would have thought? At least the mate dreams, while hot, weren't driving him crazy. Yet.

His cell phone rang. He studied the caller ID and winced. Shit. Tai Boucher, the leader of the Spirit Bears, was calling him again. Ever since he'd arrived in Halle, Pennsylvania, Tai had called him every week. His boss wanted updates on the visions Julian had left his home to pursue.

He was going to be seriously ticked when he found out Julian was planning to apply for US citizenship. Julian's mate was American; she loved Halle and had no intention of leaving. Her roots, her chosen family, all were here. Uprooting her would kill something special inside her, and he couldn't do it. But no Spirit Bear had left British Columbia since the time of...well, *never*. Tai was going to shit kittens when he found out.

Julian would rather live on his own, without the support of his brothers and sisters, than take Cyn away from here. This was home, and he planned on keeping it that way.

So Julian let it go to voicemail and headed home. He had about an hour to get ready for work at Dr. Howard's private practice. Thank God his work visa was up to date. He'd managed to get the necessary paperwork and certifications pushed through to accept the job in Dr. Howard's office, but Jamie had said he'd take on Julian even without it. He valued the Spirit Bears and all they represented, despite the fact that the good doctor was a Puma.

Julian smiled. So far things were going well, and he had no intention of allowing little things like dates and impatient Bears ruin his good mood.

"What do you think, Doc?" Julian stared at the jagged wound Jamie had just finished stitching up. His fingers twitched. He desperately wanted to heal it, but had been ordered not to by Jamie. The power spread through him, trying to escape his control, trying to force him to do what nature had intended Spirit Bears to do—*heal*. He bet white had already begun to streak his hair from forcing himself to stop.

Dr. Jamie Howard finished cleaning out the wound and sighed. "He'll need a tetanus shot."

Julian watched as their patient, Ryan Williams, turned pale. The big Grizzly began shaking his head like a six-year-old. "No. No, no, no, no. No shots. Uh-uh. Ain't happening."

"You run the risk of getting infected, Ryan. We might be shifters but we're not magically immune to disease. It isn't like the movies where you shift and bam! Severed heads reattach, limbs re-grow and suddenly you no longer have leprosy. I swear, humans think being a shifter cures everything." Jamie glanced over and Julian nodded. Julian could tell with barely a glance that Ryan already had the tetanus virus within him. How the Grizzly had managed to find a piece of rusty barbed wire in downtown Halle was unbelievable, but Ryan seemed to have a knack for getting himself into interesting situations. All Julian had to do was visit Living Art Tattoos to see proof of that. The pixyish Glory had the poor Bear tied up in knots.

Jamie handed Julian the orders to prepare the shot. While Julian could heal something as simple as tetanus in the early stages, Dr. Howard had convinced him to keep his powers as quiet as possible and use them only in cases where simple shots wouldn't fix what was wrong.

Julian prepped the needle. "It's only a pinch, you big baby."

Ryan whimpered. "Hell no, I won't go."

"I'll tell Glory what a wuss you are." Julian held up the needle and shook it, then handed it to Jamie.

"I'll tell Cyn how sexy you look in nurse's tights." Ryan growled.

"Really? You think so?" Julian held out his leg, currently encased in blue scrubs, and gave it a thoughtful glance. "I thought my calves looked a little big in white." He batted his lashes at the Grizzly, trying to distract him. "But thanks, sweetie."

It didn't work. Ryan saw the needle coming and jumped off the examination table. "No." He held up his hands and waved them like a three-year-old.

"Man up." Jamie swabbed Ryan's arm and did his best to hold him in place. "On three."

Ryan eyed the needle with dread. "How about on one hundred?"

Jamie sighed. "Fine. One, two, skip a few, ninety-nine, one hundred."

"OW! Motherfucker!" Ryan rubbed his arm where Jamie had jabbed him.

Jamie disposed of the needle, his face a mask of professionalism. "Was that so bad?"

"Yes!"

Jamie sighed again. He reached into a cabinet and pulled something out. "You'll need to keep the wound clean. No shifting for a day or two." He slapped something over Ryan's heart. "There. You're all done."

Julian was laughing so hard he was wheezing. God, he loved Pumas. They were fucking sadistic.

Ryan peeled the Hello Kitty sticker off his chest. "I hate you."

"Good. Don't get hurt again." Jamie grinned. "I'll bill you." He sauntered out of the exam room, winking at Julian on the way out.

Ryan grumbled something under his breath as he hopped off the table. He dumped the crumpled sticker on Julian's head and stomped out of the room, growling at the desk nurse who asked for his paperwork.

Julian wiped away the tears and tried to catch his breath. "I love my job." He cleaned up the exam room and got it ready for the next patient, all the while wondering whether or not Ryan was going to go show off his boo-boo to his as yet unclaimed mate, Glory. If so, Julian could relax.

Ever since Gary had attacked the girls six weeks ago in Living Art, Julian, Alex and Ryan had made it a point to stop in at least once a day to check on them. All three had good excuses. Alex was mated to Tabitha Garwood, the apprentice tattoo artist. Ryan's mate, Glory, was the piercing specialist, and wasn't it fun when some poor sap came in for a Prince Albert while Ryan was there? Julian's mate, Cynthia Reyes, owned Living Art. They were *dating*, and had been for two weeks.

Julian grinned as he thought about what he had planned for later that night. He was going to wine her, dine her and hopefully convince her to accept a nibble or two for dessert. It was driving him insane, having her so close yet so untouchable.

But she insisted that she had to fall in love with him before he bit her.

Julian didn't need any time at all to fall for Cyn. He'd fallen for her the moment he'd seen her. Cyn was the only one he'd ever want to be with. She was his, and now that the danger was past he was all ready for his mating. If only he could convince his reluctant mate that, come hell or high water or asshole Wolves out for blood, Julian DuCharme wasn't going anywhere.

Chapter Two

"Is it me, or have the boys been by a lot recently?" Tabby tapped her pen against the glass and wood counter, her lime green hair glistening in the bright afternoon sunlight pouring in through the plate glass window. Cyn smiled, glad she'd gone with Emma's suggestion to get rid of the all-glass counter and do something half wood, half glass.

She'd chosen to go all out; instead of veneers she'd done solid wood, something that could be sanded out and refinished if she ever changed the look of the shop. She was pleased with the simple mission style and the dark cherry stain. She'd even gone so far as to reframe the flash, the artwork that represented some of their best tattoos, in the same cherry.

The walls were still bright aqua, displaying the flash to advantage. A huge image of tattooed yin-yang dragons, one red, one blue, hung behind the counter. That had cost a bundle to reframe, but it was worth it. The flash in the windows and on the walls was still in silver frames, making it look even more like art. Their flash books lay open on the counter, bound in brown leather and containing more tattoos.

The floor was wood, a dark ebony stain that would hide spilled ink. She was considering replacing the tan chairs by the plate glass window; with the new countertops and frames, they didn't seem to fit anymore. There were still four curtained-off cubicles where they worked, even though there were only three of them at the moment.

Cyn was still looking to replace the girl who'd left after learning Tabby was a Wolf, but she hadn't found someone who met her exacting standards. At the very end was a last curtained-off area marked "Employees Only". Tacked over the curtain hung Tabby's crooked *De Nile* sign.

She still hadn't found where the bitch had stashed her ladder, or that sign would be toast by now.

"Earth to Cyn. Come in, Cyn. Over. Bzzt." Cyn turned to Glory, her partner in LA, and grinned. Today Glory had her waist length, powder-blue curls up in a high ponytail. She wore one of her floaty outfits, a broomstick skirt in some sort of patchwork design and a peasant top in the same blue as her hair. Bangles graced her wrists and clinked together merrily as she waved her arms. "Tabby's right. The boys *have* been coming by more." She grimaced at Cyn. "We need to get some Bear-Be-Gone."

Tabby snorted, amused. "Yeah, let's all sashay down to the local Save-A-Lot and pick some up. I'm sure it will work beautifully."

Glory crumpled up a blank receipt and threw it at Tabby's head.

Cyn laughed, happy to see her friends playing again. Six weeks ago a maniac with a grudge against Tabby had tried to smash their lives. Now they were back on track and ready to roll.

The bell over the door jangled, and in walked the reason their lives had gotten back on track so quickly. Alexander "Bunny" Bunsun stepped into LA, a huge grin on his face and a bag of sandwiches in his hand. His hazel eyes lit up when they landed on Tabby. "Hungry, baby?"

"Always, sugar." Tabby glided out from behind the counter and let the huge Grizzly wrap her up in his arms. Even in her three-inch heels Tabby barely came to her mate's bottom lip. She looked fragile, breakable next to him.

Today she'd told them she was pregnant. Cyn couldn't be happier for her. Tabby had found something she'd always longed for—a permanent home. Much to Cyn's surprise she'd found that not in Halle, but in the man who held her in his arms. Tabby would go wherever Alex led, and she'd smile the entire way.

Cyn wasn't certain she understood it, but she was happy for her friend.

"You girls ready for the masquerade tomorrow night?" Alex stole a quick kiss from his mate, one that would have been much longer if Cyn and Glory hadn't been present.

No. No, she wasn't. Cyn rolled her eyes. How the hell had she allowed Tabby to talk her into this? She wasn't the one who'd lost the stupid bet, but somehow Tabby had begged and pleaded and offered up shoes and chocolate until Glory and Cyn had agreed to go along with her. Gah. Just thinking about her costume made her butt itch. "I'll never be ready for that costume. Pamela Anderson wouldn't be ready for it."

Alex smirked. "You three are going to look *amazing*. We'll have to beat the Pumas off with a stick."

"Or a well-used ball of yarn." Glory yawned. "Bored now."

Cyn grabbed the bag of food and practically threw it at Glory. "Eat."

"Yay!" Glory raced for the back room, squealing like a teenager who'd just gotten the keys to Daddy's car. "Roast beef, all for me!"

"That's my beef, you bitch!" Tabby tore free of Alex's arms and chased after Glory.

"Who are you calling bitch, bitch?"

"You, bitch."

The two girls began a tug-of-war over the bag, with Alex and Cyn looking on in sheer disbelief. Tabby bared fang and growled at Glory. Glory growled back, snapping her human teeth and making Tabby laugh. Glory actually yapped at Tabby, making the Wolf lose her grip on the sandwich from laughing so hard.

Cyn pinched the bridge of her nose. "*Dios.* It's like watching two Yorkies fighting over a French fry."

Alex shook his head, chuckling softly as Glory won the battle and raced into the back room, Tabby hot on her heels. "You all right?"

"Why wouldn't I be?" She wished people would stop asking her that. It wasn't the first time she'd been punched in the face, and she doubted it would be the last. Gary's idiot sidekick had damaged her ego more than her cheek. She'd been more terrified for Tabby, since Gary was hoping to scare Tabby into leaving with him. If she had... It didn't bear thinking on. "Dude hit like a girl."

That feral *something* that marked him as a shifter peeked out of his gaze, his hazel eyes darkening. "I should have turned him into a pretzel for you."

She hid her shudder. Alex wasn't just saying that. The Grizzly could easily have taken the rogue Wolf and turned him into modern art. "Nah. From what Julian told me he's going to be in enough pain by the time the Senate gets done with him." And wasn't that freaky to learn? It wasn't enough that there were shifters in the world, but they had their own laws, their own government. Their own law enforcement—even their own jails. She was still processing everything she'd learned since Tabby came into their lives.

Someday soon, she might even be one of them.

"I'm going to pick Tabby up tonight. If anything, and I mean *anything* happens that makes you uncomfortable you call me, Ryan or Julian, hear? Gabe told me some unsettling news a few days ago, and I want you girls on guard."

Great. More shit coming down on top of them? Just what they needed. "What news?"

"Gary's main reason for being in Halle wasn't Tabby. It was Chloe."

"Chloe?" What the fuck did Gary have to do with Chloe?

"She was one of the people he was sent to Halle to keep an eye on. We have no idea who else he was here to watch, but I doubt she was the only one. He also told me that Hunters in other parts of the country have found three other bodies, all beaten the way Chloe was. All of them were half-breeds."

"And Tabby is pregnant with a half-breed." Fuck her gently with a chainsaw. This was bad. Alex was protective of Tabby on *good* days.

Alex smiled. It was full of sharp, pointy Bear teeth. If she didn't agree whole-heartedly with the sentiment behind the look she'd be scared spitless.

"Right. Watch pregger-lady, call you if anyone looks shifty eyed." She snapped off a salute worthy of Glory. "Aye aye, sir."

He shook his head again, grinning like the Cheshire cat. The feral, overprotective look disappeared, to be replaced by a mischievous one. "How are things going with Julian, by the way?"

She shrugged, hoping it came off as nonchalant when she was anything but. "We're dating. It's okay. He's not a bad guy." And that was all Alex was going to wheedle out of her. No way was she telling Alex that Julian had to be the best damn kisser she'd ever gone out with.

"Maybe you can convince Glory to do the same with Ryan. If he doesn't claim her soon he's going to lose his damn mind."

She bit back her smile. "He's giving her fits."

"She's giving him hives. Just...talk to her, please? You two are the only ones she listens to, and Ryan's slowly going insane." Alex looked serious for the first time since he entered the shop. "You can't possibly understand what it's like, to have your mate *right there* and you can't touch, can barely look at them before they start running away. It's this itch under your skin, a burning need you can't quench. You start dreaming about her. Your Bear can't even look at anyone else, think about anyone else. She's it. She's the one."

She swallowed hard. "So you're saying Julian and Ryan are suffering?"

He nodded. "Yeah. Bad. You'll never understand, because when they change you, they'll mate you. You won't go through what they are." He held up his hand. "And they wouldn't want you to."

Cyn immediately bristled. "I could handle it."

"I never said you couldn't. I said they wouldn't want you to. Big difference." He leaned in close, his eyes completing the shift from hazel to dark brown. Bear's eyes. "Perhaps you two should think about that."

Cyn didn't back down. Her heart might be racing, her palms damp, but Alex would sooner bite off his paw than hurt her, if only because it would hurt Tabby. "I am."

He blinked, his eyes bleeding back out to hazel. "You aren't afraid of anything, are you?"

"Only one thing."

One of his brows rose, questioning her.

"Losing who I am." And she was terrified the extremely sexy Julian could make her do just that.

Julian pulled his car into LA's parking lot and hopped out. He hoped Cyn was ready to go. He was starving. An emergency at the doc's office had kept him from his lunch, and his stomach was growling louder than Ryan had.

Julian took a deep breath and stretched, pulling his arms taut over his head. The scent of strange shifters, mostly Wolf, drifted through his senses. It wasn't uncommon for him to catch the occasional whiff of other shifters. Halle housed a university on its outskirts, and the students would often come to town, especially this part of town. It was a little bit rougher than the pretty downtown area where Becky and Emma ran Wallflowers. There was Living Art Tattoos, a really great Chinese restaurant, a small bookstore that specialized in pagan books and artwork that Cyn said the students adored, and a few clothing shops that seemed to carry the type of clothes Cyn and the girls wore. He loved coming to this part of town. It was vibrant and fun and suited his mate to a T.

He walked up to the glass front door of LA Tattoos and peeked in, totally unsurprised by what he saw.

Chaos. The place was chock full of it, as usual, only this time the chaos was the fun kind. Julian smiled as he watched Cyn chase Tabby around with a rolled up set of papers. Whatever the Wolf had done, Cyn was ready to bat her nose over it. Glory was holding her stomach and laughing as Tabby skidded in her heels and went down.

Julian was through the door so fast the bell barely had time to jingle before he was kneeling at Tabby's side. "You okay?"

"Ow." She rubbed her hip and grimaced. "Just a bruise to my pride."

Julian brushed his finger over the area, grinning at her sigh of relief. "What can I say? I'm better than Bengay."

That sent Glory into another round of musical giggles.

Cyn swatted Tabby on the head with the papers. "I am *not* tattooing you until after the baby is born. Get over it!"

Tabby stuck her tongue out at Cyn. "Please. The needles are changed every customer, we pour the ink into those tiny little cups and toss what we don't use. It's perfectly safe."

"No, it's not." Cyn tapped her foot. "Unless a doctor can tell me you won't go into shock and lose the baby, I won't tattoo you until after your flabby ass gives birth."

Tabby squeaked and sat up. "It is not flabby!"

Cyn cocked her hip and smirked at her apprentice. "Honey, I've seen you naked."

"Ooh!" Tabby jumped to her feet and grabbed the papers from Cyn's hand. "I'll show you flabby!" She started chasing Cyn around the tattoo parlor, waving the paper and giving a rebel yell that hurt Julian's ears. Glory collapsed into one of the chairs by the window, seriously out of breath from laughing. Tears streamed down her face.

Julian just shook his head. He leaned back on his elbows and crossed his ankles, careful to hold still when the ladies hopped over his legs. "Welcome to the jungle."

Julian blinked as the image of a girly bedroom superimposed itself over the tattoo parlor. He tried to clench his left hand, sighing when it wouldn't close all the way. Damn it, Chloe was looking through his eyes again.

The spiritual connection he'd established with the Fox when he'd saved her life was much stronger than he'd first thought it would be, and this was the result. Ryan's little sister had nearly died when she was attacked and left for dead in the middle of the road.

They still hadn't caught the ones who'd hurt her.

"Chloe?"

"Hmm? Oh! Shit. I'm sorry, Julian. Am I doing it again? I thought I was gleaming."

23

Julian ground his teeth together. *"Dreaming, sweetie. And no, you're not. Could you pull back? Remind me when I visit tomorrow, we need to work on your control some more."*

The problems with her hand and taking over his sight were the least of his concerns. Chloe kept confusing words, often with hysterical—or disastrous—results. The other day she'd told her physical therapist not to let the floor blob hit him in the ass on the way out. It had taken them five minutes to figure out she'd meant *doorknob*.

For someone who'd worked damn hard to earn a degree in veterinary medicine, the fact that she couldn't keep her words straight or use her left hand properly meant her career was dead before it even started. Not one of the doctors knew if the damage was permanent.

Julian did, and the knowledge hurt both of them, because, due to their bond, Chloe knew too.

"Julian!"

He snapped his attention back to Cyn, his double vision fading as Chloe left him. He grinned weakly up at his mate. "Hey."

She was tapping her foot. Not a good sign. "Are you ready to go?"

He got to his feet and wiped his pants off in quick, jerky movements. *Please, let Chloe keep her thoughts to herself while I drive.* "Whenever you are."

She held up her purse as if that said it all.

Julian, not being an idiot, held open the door for his future mate and prayed his dinner for two didn't get crashed by a needy, unhappy Fox.

Cyn studied Julian out of the corner of her eye as he maneuvered the quiet, dark streets of Halle. Something about the way he'd zoned out in her shop had her worried. It was like he wasn't there anymore; his dark brown eyes had taken on that gray-speckled look; his hair had grown a thin, white strip near his face. He was using his freaky-ass powers, but doing *what* she had no clue.

They pulled up outside Frank's Diner and Cyn grinned. "Oh God. How did you guess I'd kill for a burger tonight?"

Julian's stomach grumbled loud enough to startle a laugh out of her. "I could eat a cow or two myself." He grinned sheepishly and got out of the car.

Not waiting for him to open her door she hopped out too, smirking when he rolled his eyes. "You hungry?"

"I've got two words for you. Star. Ving." He managed to open the diner's front door before she could get to it.

She shook her head and headed into her favorite burger joint. Frank's had the best damn burgers in the whole damn town, possibly the whole damn state. She snagged a booth and settled in, waving hello to several people she recognized.

Julian was also exchanging greetings, but his were a little more personal. Cyn hid her grin behind a plastic-coated menu as the entire Bunsun-Williams family descended on her date *en masse*. For once, Julian looked like the hunted instead of the hunter, surrounded by a family chock full of Grizzlies and Foxes.

"Hey."

Cyn smiled a greeting at the shy Fox female who plunked herself into the booth across from her. The eighteen-year-old had made it a point to seek Cyn out whenever they were in the same place. "Hey yourself."

Heather Allen, Ryan and Alex's youngest cousin, bit her plump bottom lip and stared at Cyn's hair like a starving kitten

She twirled a lock of her own bright red hair between her fingers. "You changed it."

Cyn preened. She'd done the dye job just two days ago, and she loved it. "You like?"

Heather nodded so vigorously Cyn was afraid she'd snap her own neck. "I like the blend of blonde, black and pink."

Cyn pushed her hair back over her shoulders. The hair on top was white-blonde, the middle layer cotton-candy pink and the bottom layer that rested on her shoulders was midnight black. It was striking, and she got looks everywhere she went. Cyn gave a mental finger to everyone who disapproved and smiled at everyone who did. "Thanks. Want me to do yours sometime?"

"No, she doesn't." Eric, Alex's little brother, plucked the girl from the booth and scowled at Cyn. "She likes her hair red, thank you."

Cyn's brows rose. As much as she loved Alex she'd come to despise his high-handed brother. "I think that's her decision to make."

He actually shook his finger at her. "You keep your paws off my cousin, got it?"

Heather pulled free of his grip and shrank in on herself. Damn it. Getting that poor girl to open up had been one of Cyn's favorite things lately. Too bad Eric liked to interrupt. Heather closed right back up around him. "I can dye my hair if I ant."

Shit. Heather was speaking in that little mousy voice again. yn didn't know better she'd think Eric abused the poor kid. Eric would sooner cut off his foot than hurt the girl.

My baby cousin isn't going to look like some freak." Eric's rinkled.

A low growl filled the air. Cyn, wide-eyed, stared over at Julian.

That white streak was back in his hair, thicker now. The gray in his eyes had almost completely obliterated the brown. "Stand down, Eric."

The scary part wasn't how quickly Eric obeyed Julian. It was Julian's quietly furious tone that had Cyn stiffening her spine. She didn't need Julian to protect her from bigots.

Eric's lip curled back. His huge fangs were displayed for a split second before his father, William Bunsun, slapped a hand over his mouth and began yelling at him for being a rude dumbass. Cyn tried to blink away the image of those fangs, but it wasn't working.

Okay. Maybe she could admit she needed protection from bigoted Grizzlies.

Julian slid into Heather's vacated seat and winked, the silver streak already faded from his hair. "So much for a quiet meal."

Cyn snorted. "In this town?" She waved over their waitress, who deftly side-stepped the feuding shifters. Thank goodness they remembered they were in a human establishment or Cyn had the feeling fur would be flying. "Two burgers, the works, extra ketchup, make them moo."

"And two chocolate shakes." A baseball hat landed on their table and Julian tossed it back into the fray. William had Eric in a headlock. He was giving his son a noogie and demanding his immediate surrender.

Thank God she wasn't mating into *that* family. She'd go insane inside a week. Every single one of them was nuts.

Julian grinned weakly as the waitress side-stepped one of the fleeing Foxes. Cyn was ready to follow the poor girl right out the door. "Can you make that to go?"

Chapter Three

Julian handed over his keys to the valet and ran into the brightly lit Freidelinde mansion. Tonight was the annual Halle Halloween masquerade. Jamie and Marie Howard had apparently continued a long-standing tradition and agreed to host it at their lavish estate. He entered the building and grinned.

The place was rockin' and it wasn't even nine o'clock at night.

Julian smiled at everyone he met, until his eyes landed on Eric Bunsun. He was still ticked at Eric. Not only had the Grizzly messed with his date, he'd disrespected Julian's mate. He planned on having words with Alex's brother if the boy didn't straighten his ass out. *No one,* especially not another Bear, treated a Kermode's mate that way. Julian might not be as strong physically as Eric, but he could still put the man in his place.

Eric simply nodded and turned away. If he was ashamed of himself he didn't show it. Julian snarled and added Eric's education to his to-do list.

He'd caught glimpses here and there of the Pumas. Emma and Max were dressed in matching gangster costumes, the long coat of Emma's costume giving way to a pair of short-shorts that had Julian's eyebrows rising in surprise. The Curana had some fine legs on her. She and Max were striding through the room as if they owned the place, the Pumas in their path acknowledging them with a discreet tilt of the head to show their submission. Simon and Becky were dressed as Spiderman and Spiderwoman, the spandex outfit striking on Becky's slender frame. Gabe and Sarah had come as Indiana Jones and Lara Croft, an odd yet fitting combination. And Adrian and Sheri were...steampunk vampires? Maybe? He would have said cowboys if it weren't for the brass goggles on their heads and the painted brass Nerf guns at their hips. He was pretty sure the fangs they were flashing weren't plastic. When they passed Max and Emma, they grinned and whipped out the guns, nailing the Alpha and Curana before running away, laughing like little children.

Those two are just too weird.

"Have you seen the girls?" Alex's deep voice startled him. He turned to find the Grizzly behind him, grinning at the fleeing Pumas. Max and Emma had taken off after Sheri and Adrian, vowing Nerfy revenge. Julian stared at Alex's masked face and burst into laughter. Alex had come dressed as Tuxedo Mask, complete with cane and red rose. The man's obsession with Sailor Moon was scary.

"What the hell are you dressed as?" Alex shook his head. "Paul Bunyan? Really? You couldn't come up with something better than that?"

"It's too cold out for a loincloth." Julian shook his head. He'd bound his long black hair in a braid down his back. The bottom of it swung out and hit a nearby partygoer. He waved his foam rubber axe in apology. *Nerf seems to be popular tonight.* "Sorry! Besides, I'm all out of my favorite war paint. It's not like I can order a new supply from Mary Kay." He frowned. "I thought you were giving the girls a ride tonight." Julian immediately sniffed the air, looking for any sign Cyn had made it. It was just too loud to pick her voice out from among the crowd, though he'd been listening for it since entering the mansion.

"They should be here any minute now. Tabby wanted their costumes to be a surprise." Alex gave him a secretive grin.

What the hell had Alex talked his mate into? If Cyn showed up as a stripper—okay. If Cyn showed up in a skimpy outfit, he'd have to yell at Alex...in public.

In private he'd owe him a burger.

Murmurs of surprise and laughter came from the front of the ballroom. Julian turned and there, in all their glory, were Alex's fantasy women come to life.

"This skirt's so short it's a sports bra." Cyn reached behind her and tugged on the bright red skirt with a grunt. The white, satiny shirt gleamed, the huge, sailor-like collar red and white striped just like in the anime. The huge purple bow was draped across her breasts like an invitation, the red gem in the center glittering. Her elbow length white gloves were topped with bands of red in the same shade as her skirt. She'd thrown on a waist-length black wig to go with her white and red Sailor Mars outfit. Julian's jaw dropped at the length of thigh the shiny miniskirt revealed. She was the only one of the three not wearing boots. Instead, Sailor Mars wore red fuck-me pumps.

He was beginning to understand Alex's obsession. Fuck, she looked *hot*. He owed the man two burgers. Maybe even fries.

"That's nothing. Try wearing this wig." Tabby reached under the blonde wig to scratch her scalp. Some of her lime green hair escaped, giving the blonde, floor-length pigtails some really odd highlights. Her outfit was predominantly white and navy blue, with touches of red. She made a stunning Sailor Moon.

"I kind of like it." Glory stuck out her powder blue booted foot to admire it. She hadn't even bothered with the short, blue-black wig Sailor Mercury should have worn. Instead, her blue curls were loosely held back by the gold tiara all the Sailor Scouts wore.

"Oh my God. You got them to dress as the Sailor Scouts?" Julian's eyes gleamed as he took in Cyn's seriously short skirt. "Me likey."

He started forward, only to stop when Cyn plastered a Post-It note covered in *kanji* on his forehead. It was a well-known Sailor Mars trick, but only if you were a fan, which meant she could only have learned it if Alex told her about it. "Hey, it worked!"

Everyone laughed. Julian ripped the Post-It note off his forehead. "Ha-ha. Very funny."

"Ahem."

Glory's eyes widened as she stared at something over Alex's shoulder. He turned to find Ryan, dressed as a sheik in all white, grinning at them. He carried a white rose in his hand. "Someone call for the Moonlight Knight?"

"Oh *hell* no." Alex shoved his cousin back a step with a low, menacing growl. "You stay away from Sailor Moon, you sneaky bastard."

Julian burst into laughter. Ryan must have found out about the costumes the girls were coming in and bought his costume to match, but he'd picked the wrong guy for Glory's Sailor Mercury.

"Your Sailor Scout is safe. I find myself enchanted by the color blue." Ryan held out the rose to Glory. "Sailor Mercury, may I have this dance?"

Glory took off running in the *opposite* direction.

Ryan grinned. "When will she learn that predators love to give chase?" Ryan took off after his errant, unclaimed mate.

When he stopped laughing long enough to take stock he realized Alex and Tabby had also disappeared. Only Cyn was left. She batted ridiculously long, false lashes at him. "Want to dance?"

Did he look stupid? He glanced down at his red-checkered shirt. Perhaps he shouldn't ask that out loud. "Yes, please." He vibrated between the need to take her in his arms and hold her close and the need to cover her skin so no one else could see how fucking sexy she was.

She stepped into his arms and his first need took precedence. God. *Damn.* He had to buy his woman more miniskirts. "You look gorgeous."

"Thank you. You look...lumberjacky."

He grinned. "Thanks. And for the record, I'd love to show you how I swing my axe." He waggled his eyebrows, chuckling when she threw her head back and laughed. That ridiculous wig almost fell off her head. "How did you get roped into this outfit, by the way?"

She scowled and tugged on her skirt again. "Tabby lost a bet."

"And?"

"She talked us into this stupid shit." She glared at him. "Not. One. Word."

He had no idea what she was talking about but he zipped it anyway.

"This skirt is illegal in twenty-five states. The wig itches like a bitch and I look *horrible* in white."

Huh. He thought she looked delectable. He bit his tongue and kept dancing. Was it his fault if his hands just happened to slip down to the top of her ass?

"And then she has the nerve to try and talk me into full makeup! She even wanted me to wear these—*hands!*"

Julian's hands, which had made a very happy foray to her southern hemisphere, moved back up to her waist.

"These stupid contact lenses you can't even buy off an eye doctor. You have to order them over the web. They're the same ones Lady Gaga used in this video—*hands!*"

Julian immediately removed his hands from under her skirt. Damn, she was wearing boy shorts under it. All of his secret fantasies of backseat explorations were dashed.

"Do you have anything to say for yourself, mister?"

Julian pretended to think about it for a moment before shaking his head.

"Jeez. It's like talking to a three-year-old."

"A three-year-old wouldn't be trying to shove his hands down your pants." Julian stopped dancing long enough to rub his shin. Those pointy red shoes were hard on the anatomy.

"Jules!"

Julian stood and grinned at Jamie and Marie Howard. They'd dressed as a cowboy and a sexy cowgirl. Damn, he'd have to buy Cyn a pair of chaps. He wondered how Jamie felt about his mate wearing them with nothing more than a pair of boy shorts under them. "Nice party!"

"Nice kick." Marie high-fived Cyn, the fringe of her short, tummy-bearing vest swinging with her movements. Julian was *definitely* begging Jamie for the name of the shop he got that outfit from.

"What if Julian didn't deserve the kick?" Jamie patted his wife's butt.

Marie shrugged. "Does it matter?" She winked at Cyn and accepted her fist bump.

"Ah. He has a penis, therefore he's the enemy. Gotcha."

Marie swatted her mate's arm. "I'm not *that* bad."

Julian smiled at the love between them. Marie had a strained relationship with Emma and Becky, and therefore Max and Simon, but he had no idea why. She seemed like a perfectly nice woman to him.

"Be good, you." She wagged her finger in her mate's face, but he merely grinned. She turned on Julian and wagged her finger at him as well. "You too."

"Yes, ma'am."

The Howards danced away, already greeting other guests.

"Liar," Cyn whispered in his ear.

He cupped her ass again and braced for impact. "Yes, ma'am."

Cyn tossed the wig in the backseat of Julian's car and sighed. She'd agreed to let him take her home, but only that. The man had barely reached first base, and she had every intention of keeping him there for a while, no matter how good his hands felt. After all, they hadn't been dating long enough for second yet. "God, my feet hurt."

"So does my shin."

She grinned. That should teach him to keep his hands where she could see them. Besides, he was adorable when he pouted.

"Going to invite me in?"

That deep, dark tone always sent a shiver down her spine, but Cyn stiffened it. She wasn't going to give in to him *that* easily. Julian would have to work to earn the right to bite her. "Nope."

"Damn." His hand drifted to her thigh. "Have I mentioned I like your costume?"

"Maybe." She pushed his hand down to her knee. She wasn't opposed to him touching her. In fact, she'd love to do more than touch, but Cyn wasn't easy. It was going to take Julian more than a date or three to get *her* boy shorts off.

That wicked gleam was back in his eye, and she just knew something outrageous was going to pop out of his mouth. "How do you feel about role-playing?"

Cyn bit her cheek to keep from laughing. *Role-playing, huh?* "Well, Rolemaster was a bitch to learn because of all the Companion books, plus you needed a physics calculator just to figure out your stats." The car swerved as Julian jerked, his expression shocked. "Some versions of Dungeons and Dragons weren't too bad, but Star Wars seriously sucked unless you were a Jedi." She tapped her fingernail against her lips. "Wait, did you mean pen and paper or online RPGs, because—"

His expression had gone completely blank. "Oh, my god. You're a geek!"

"Yup." She waited for the usual explosion she got when she revealed her secret life as a (gasp!) *nerd*. Most of the guys she dated either laughed their asses off at her, thus ending any chance they had of getting into her boy shorts, or simply stopped calling. What self-respecting man wanted to date a tattooed geek? If anything were capable of scaring Julian off, this would be it.

"That is so fucking hot." His gaze had turned reverent, those brown eyes sparkling with laughter.

Apparently one freaky Bear did. Cyn's jaw dropped. "I'm sorry. What did you just say?"

He grinned at her and pulled to the curb before turning in his seat to face her. "What online game do you play?"

She blinked. He couldn't be serious. Could he? "Which one do you think?"

"I'd say DDO, but I'm betting it's World of Warcraft. Eve Online would be too boring for you. Not enough action."

She nodded before she could stop herself. "Wait. You play?"

"Yup."

"You."

"Yes." He was looking confused.

Good, because so was she. "Mr. Shits-in-the-Woods."

"Hey! I only do that when I'm fuzzy. And I have high speed Internet in my cave, thank you very much. Why, recently, I installed a dorm fridge right next to my sleeping furs." He crossed his arms and glared at her.

"Fine. Yes, WoW, and I play a paladin."

He blinked, then grinned. "I play a warlock."

"Pfft. Of course. It all makes sense now. You're a *spell-caster*." Cyn sneered at him good-naturedly.

"Oh yeah. Because it takes serious brains to beat the bad guys with a huge metal stick." Julian rolled his eyes in disgust.

Cyn studied her nails. "Oh look, I'm a big, bad warlock. I think I'll give myself a mani-pedi while my summoned pet does all the work."

"Yup. I named my pet *Paladin*."

They glared at each other across the console. "Hmph." Cyn relented first. "Maybe we could group sometime."

"Oh, baby. I am *so* turned on right now." Julian leaned forward and tried to steal a kiss.

Cyn added another bruise to his leg. She was really beginning to like these shoes.

"You're mean." Julian pouted as he put the car in gear and turned down her street.

"Yes. You have a problem with that?" She was fighting off a laugh. God, the man was such a goof! And he liked the same stuff she did, crazy though it was.

She was in *such* deep shit.

"Nope." He pulled into her driveway and cut the engine. "I like it."

She shivered. His deep voice had turned sultry, sexy as hell. She had goose bumps running down her arms. How the hell was she supposed to resist him when he spoke like that?

He leaned over the console and cupped the back of her head. She had learned to crave his taste in the short time they'd been dating. Cyn wasn't one to give in to cravings just for the hell of it, but she was learning that Julian's kiss was more than a craving. It was rapidly becoming an addiction.

Her heart beat faster as his lips drew near. She wanted his kiss more than anything, even more than she'd wanted Living Art. God, what was she supposed to do? Two weeks of dating and the man had her melted into a puddle of mindless goo.

His mouth came down on hers, gentle and patient, his tongue stroking her lips until she parted for him and allowed him inside. His taste hit her, made her shiver. Her nipples beaded beneath her padded bra, a new addition to her wardrobe thanks to a certain sexy Bear. It wouldn't do to let him know that they went hard whenever he touched her. He kept it slow, languid, seducing her with his kiss, his hands staying exactly where he'd put them.

He was adhering to the rules she'd set down, and she'd never been more sorry in her life.

Julian broke the kiss and smiled down at her. His eyes were pure silver. "Let me walk you to your door tonight."

Oh hell to the no. If Julian got to her door she'd invite him in, and she wasn't ready for that. She swallowed hard. "Not yet."

Is that my voice? It was husky and low and, God help her, chock full of a need she wasn't quite ready to fulfill.

Julian grimaced and shifted in his seat. He smiled, and she was once again reminded of why she wanted to take things slow when his fangs poked his bottom lip. "I'll watch for your signal."

She shook her head. Really, the man took overprotective too far sometimes. No one was after Cyn, and the fucker who'd been after Tabby was in shifter jail, hopefully getting his ass reamed by Tony the Tiger. "You're the one who told Alex and Ryan to constantly stop by the shop, weren't you?"

Those silver eyes darkened back to brown. "Why would I do that?" He pulled back until he was back in his own seat. "Alex is the overprotective one, not me. Ryan, on the other hand, just wants his mate." The look he shot her should have melted the dashboard. "I understand how he feels."

She remembered some of the things Alex had told her, about how shifters yearned for their mates until it became almost painful. "Have I told you you're doing a good job with the whole dating thing?"

"It's not like I haven't done it before."

She could practically feel the laugh trying to break free. She huffed and tapped her foot. "Way to ruin a mood, Share Bear."

He froze. "Oh *no* you didn't."

She opened the car door and dashed for her front door. There was a Bear on her tail, and she had no intention of getting caught too easily. She giggled and dug out her keys, but didn't get any farther than jangling them in the direction of the lock before she found herself pressed against the door. One hundred and eighty-five pounds of laughing hunk caged her in, one impressive package brushing against her lower back.

Wait. She *giggled*? Since when? Cyn laughed, smirked, sometimes even guffawed, but she *never* giggled. Pretty soon she'd be in a Martha Stewart apron, learning one hundred ways to cook with honey. "Get off me, you big dork."

"Don't you want to rub my tummy symbol?"

God damn it. How did he *do* that? She was giggling like a loon again! "Go away!" She wiggled, elbowing him right in his symbol.

"But I want to share with you!" He was laughing right along with her, and that made all the stupid giggles worth it. He could have easily gotten pissed, but instead he'd run with it, taking the insult and turning it around on her. She had fun with him, even when they were both wearing the lamest costumes on the planet.

Okay, the guy who'd shown up as SpongeBob SquarePants *might* have the mighty lumberjack beat, but barely.

"I think we're done sharing for the evening." She turned in his arms and stared at him. It amazed her how someone as good looking as him could want someone like her, but according to Tabby, once Julian had gotten a whiff of Cyn's scent no one else would ever do.

"But I'm really good at cuddling." He was doing his damndest to look innocent, but the devilish gleam and silver eyes gave him away. "Especially in bed." He patted her butt. "Just call me Teddy."

"Uh-huh." She pushed against his chest and he took a step back. *Damn.* The boy had some muscle on him, muscle she was dying to see. *Why couldn't he have tried to mate me in summer?* She opened the door and waved good-bye with a cheery grin. "Night-night!"

He sighed and stared at his stomach. "You failed me."

"Are you talking to your tummy symbol or your—"

The look he shot her from under his lashes dared her to finish that question.

She laughed, part of her desperate to invite him inside. Sense won out, but her libido was threatening to never speak to her again. "Sweet dreams, Super Bear."

One dark brow quirked upward and he pressed a soft kiss to the back of her hand. "Trust me. They will be."

She shut the door behind him after one last, lingering kiss. Cyn watched as his headlights disappeared down the road and kicked off the high-heeled torture devices with a sigh.

He'd sounded so strange just before he left, almost sad. Why would he react that way to a simple wish for sweet dreams?

"Shifters are so weird." Cyn yawned and headed for bed, wishing for a few sweet dreams of her own.

Chapter Four

That gorgeous, multicolored hair looked incredible across the skin of his thighs. It was a sight he never got tired of.

Cyn hummed an off-key tune as she fished his cock out of his underwear. Thank fuck he'd worn boxers to bed instead of pajama pants. It was so much easier for her to release him into her hot, waiting mouth.

He hissed in a breath as she licked the underside of his cock with her tongue. He stroked the length of her back, not quite reaching her ass. It was so tempting too, covered in that short-as-fuck skirt she'd worn to the masquerade that night. "C'mon, sweetheart. Suck me."

Cyn hummed and he shuddered. She was good at this, almost too good. He watched, entranced, as her head began to bob up and down, sucking him in. His eyes nearly crossed when she stopped at the crown, the suction intensifying as she tried to get him to come.

He wouldn't climax that easily. He palmed her breasts, thumbing the nipples to aching hardness. Her rhythm faltered as she began to stroke her clit, just as eager to orgasm as he was.

"Come up here." If she was going to come, it was going to be on his cock.

She smirked up at him, her lips still wrapped around his dick, and sucked harder. This time, his eyes did cross. He was close, so damn close.

"Cyn." He wrapped his hands in her hair and held on for dear life. "Gonna."

She nodded, and that was it. Permission given, he gave his mate what she wanted. Pure bliss exploded from the tip of his cock, blinding him.

He blinked, and stared at the dark ceiling above him. Something wet and cool was dripping off his stomach.

"Shit. Fucking mate dreams." Julian peeled the wet sheets from his body with a sigh. The mate dreams were getting more and more intense. If he didn't find a way to get Cyn into his bed soon he'd go insane. He was tired of coming alone, tired of sleeping alone.

And he was damn tired of washing the sheets every night. He stripped the bed, tossing his dirty shorts in the pile. He used the edge of the sheet to clean himself off, grimacing at the sticky mess. His water bill was going to be through the roof at this rate. He put the dirty laundry in the washer and started it. He leaned against it for a moment and wished with all his heart that his mate were waiting for him in the other room.

Soon, Julian. Soon.

"You want a what now?" Cyn hid her grin. Damn, the girl had found some balls.

"I want a tattoo." Heather Allen handed her a folded slip of paper. "This is what I want."

Cyn unfolded the paper and stared at the gorgeous, yet sad, drawing. "Are you sure about this?"

Heather scowled, an expression Cyn was delighted to see. "I'm eighteen. I can do this if I want."

Cyn shook her head. "That's not what I meant." She shook the paper. "Are you sure about *this*? A tattoo is forever."

Heather looked scared and relieved at the same time. She gulped, her green gaze bright and resolute. "I'm positive."

Cyn sighed. "Black and white or color?"

"Yes!" Heather danced a little jig and Cyn laughed. If Eric could only see her now. She stopped and shot Cyn a happy little smile that lit her whole face. "Color, I think."

"Just so you know, color costs more and will hurt more." Heather tilted her head, the happy smile dimming. "You'll be under the needle for longer." Cyn shrugged. "It's still your choice, but you need to understand what's going to happen in the other room."

Heather bit her lip. Cyn could practically see the wheels turning. "How much will it cost?"

Cyn named a price that was half what she would have charged anyone else. "But that's the family discount, so don't go bragging how cheap this was."

Heather hugged her tight, surprising her. The girl was strong for such a little slip of a thing. She *might* weigh a hundred and ten pounds soaking wet, but only if she was in one of those heavily padded parkas. "Definitely color." She kissed Cyn's cheek. "Thank you."

Cyn hugged her back. "You're welcome." She led Heather toward the back room, where she would discuss what colors the girl wanted. Heather had handed her a black and white drawing, but it would look stunning in blues and greens on the girl's pale skin. She took another look at the drawing. "You're going to school for art, right?"

Heather shook her head, her shoulders hunching in that awful protective pose Cyn had noted in Frank's. "I want to, but..."

"But?" Who was stomping on this poor kid's dreams? Cyn would have to have a chat with them. Preferably with a baseball bat.

"The others think I should go to the community college and study bookkeeping."

"Ew." Cyn wrinkled her nose, glad when Heather giggled. "Seriously. Bookkeeping?"

"I know, right?" Heather settled in the chair and bared her shoulder.

"You should be the one to decide what you want to do, not anyone else. You think I'd have this shop if I'd listened to the nay-sayers?" Cyn wiped Heather's shoulder down with alcohol, cleansing the area for the tattoo. "If I'd listened to the people who thought I shouldn't be a tattoo artist I'd probably be stuck in a hideous brown uniform asking people if they want fries with that."

Heather sighed. "All I want to do is paint. Is that so wrong?"

"Nope. Have you applied to art school?"

Heather shrugged. "It's hard to argue with your family when half of them can eat you in two bites."

Cyn rolled her stool until she was face to face with Heather. "I tell you what. You go and apply to art school. See if you get in. If it doesn't work out, you come see me."

Heather frowned. "Why?"

Cyn shrugged. "I could use an apprentice." Tabby was ready to fly on her own; hell, Cyn was considering making her a partner. Cyn, Glory and Tabby meshed together beautifully, even when they bitched at each other. They had become family, the three of them, and she wouldn't have it any other way.

Besides, Heather reminded her of both Tabby and Glory. Both women had been hurt by life. Cyn made sure they had a safe place to land and a willing ear to listen. She was more than willing to do the same for Heather.

Huge green eyes blinked at her, like a startled doe. "Really?"

"I wouldn't offer if I didn't think you had talent." From the small glimpse she'd seen of Heather's work, the girl would make a killing as a tattoo artist. She'd just have to figure out how to rid her of her fear of large men, especially Alex. Maybe she could have Alex dance the Macarena in front of her? Not even Chuck Norris could look intimidating dancing to *that*.

Heather gripped Cyn's hand fiercely. "I'd like to."

Cyn grinned. "So would I." She winked and stood, dragging the Fox up with her. "Lesson one: mixing ink."

Heather followed Cyn into the back room, all eager questions and bright smiles. Cyn mentally patted herself on the back.

This was going to work out just fine.

Julian decided to pay a visit to his favorite Fox. Julian followed Chloe into her tiny living room, watching the weary way she moved through the space. The girl looked like she'd been beaten with a stick, which was a damn sight better than she'd looked the first time he saw her, broken, bleeding and dying in the middle of the road. The rejection by her mate was only adding to the toll on her. If Jim Woods didn't come to his senses soon Julian was going to hunt the fucker down and force the shift on him. Maybe that would show him exactly what he was doing to the poor, injured Fox. "How are you feeling?"

She sighed and rolled her eyes. Her long red hair had been shorn short for surgery, and she missed it bitterly. "The usable."

He hid his wince. The doctors weren't certain whether or not her language problem would clear up, but her hand would never again have the dexterity necessary for surgery. Chloe's scholarship, and her career, had flown out of her grasp. "Yeah." He ran his fingers through her shorn hair and winced in sympathy. He'd cleared up as much of the damage as he could, saving her life and nearly losing his own, but the damage had been severe and extensive. Not even Tai would have been able to do more. Hell, Julian was surprised she'd survived, and he'd been the one to heal her.

One of them should have died that night. He still wasn't certain how Tabby and Alex had helped him, feeding him just enough energy to keep his heart from stopping. He had no intention of ever telling them how close he'd come to walking the Long Road.

"Are you up to this today?" She looked tired, dark circles under her pretty green eyes.

"Yeah. I have to be, don't I?" She flopped down on the old, but clean, sofa. "I don't want to wind up in your brain when you finally claim your bait." She shuddered. "No offense, but I don't want to see Cyn naked."

"None taken." He sat down next to her and held out his hand. "You remember what I taught you last time?

She nodded and, taking his hand, closed her eyes.

Julian watched her closely as she tried to block him from her mind. He threw image after image at her, wincing along with her when her head started to pound from effort. Within five minutes she was gasping like an out of shape marathon runner; within seven, she dropped his hand and moaned from the pain.

Julian spiraled down the healing path and took her pain from her, soothed the inflamed tissues until she sat back with a sigh of relief. He pulled his consciousness from her body. "You're doing better."

"How far did I get?"

"Seven minutes."

The relief on her face was monumental. She needed to control these funky new powers of hers, but the pressure was getting to her. Physical therapy, speech therapy, plus her sessions with Julian were wearing her out, and her savings were almost depleted. She might lose her apartment soon. "Jamie will be pleased."

"Yeah, he will. You're doing good, pumpkin."

She leaned her head against his shoulder and closed her eyes. "I'm so tired, Jules."

He wrapped his arm around her and rested his head against her poor, scarred scalp. "I know." He mentally cursed Jim for ditching her once again. She might be twenty-two years old, but hers was a beautiful soul, one Jim would come to appreciate if only he'd allow himself.

The mental link between himself and Chloe was unusually strong. The side-effect of the spirit healing, their ability to see through each other's eyes, was something he'd never anticipated. "Any unusual dreams?"

She shifted uncomfortably. "Yeah."

"Tell me."

She sighed. "Two becomes one, one becomes three. Bear knows the way, but Fox holds the key."

He blinked. "Oh shit."

"Yeah. It was so freaking weird. One minute I'm in the middle of a mate dream where Jim is being all sweet to me. The next, there's this huge freaking white fox staring at me, grinning. He spouts that riddle, drops a key at my feet and takes off running. What the hell, Jules?"

"Well. Um." Wow. He'd *never* heard of a non-Kermode having that deep a connection with the spirit world. If Fox himself was speaking to her... "Could you do me a favor?"

"Hmm?"

"Shift for me."

Her brows rose. "The doc told me to wait for a bit, that I could damage the unhealed portions of my hull."

He almost smiled. She'd meant *skull.* "I forgot about that. Okay, we wait to check my theory until after you get the okay from Jamie." He tugged his braid and thought about what Fox had told her. "Two become one, one becomes three?"

"Nope. Two *becomes* one. With an s. I got the impression that was significant for some reason."

She was probably right. The person who received the vision usually understood the nuances better than anyone except the person it was intended for. "Who do you think Fox was talking about?"

"I have no idea. Me, maybe? Jim, since I was dreaming about him? Jamie, because he and that rat bastard physical therapist were torturing me a few hours before?" She shrugged. "You, because you're a Bear? I'm not sure, but I have a bad feeling about it."

A knock on the door interrupted them. "I'll get it. You stay put." Julian stood up and answered Chloe's door. "Hey, Ryan."

Ryan snarled at Julian. "Why do I smell my baby sister all over you?"

Julian rolled his eyes. "Welcome to Casa de Luv." He stepped out of the way and let Ryan pass him, shutting the door behind the Grizzly. "Hey, pumpkin. Grumpy's here."

She giggled like a madwoman as her brother picked her up and blew raspberries against her neck. It was good to see her acting like a twenty-two year old girl instead of a wounded old woman. "Stop it, Ryan! Stop!" She began beating him on the head and shoulders, hitting him as only a sibling could and live to tell about it.

Ryan settled her back on the sofa. "How was your PT?"

She grimaced. "The man could give lessons to Genghis Khan." She scowled at Ryan as he settled in next to her. "And what is this I hear about Eric giving Cyn shit?"

Julian's ears perked up. Was the problem with Eric worse than he'd originally thought?

"He can be a real douche where Heather is concerned." Ryan shrugged. "He'll get over it."

"Explain, please." Julian allowed some of his power to seep into his voice, forcing the other Bear to comply.

Ryan winced. "When Heather was ten years old a group of teenage Bears decided it would be fun to force her to change."

Julian blinked. "But the change doesn't hit until puberty."

Ryan just stared at him, a look of disgust and anger on his face.

"Oh."

"Yeah. The fucking pervs terrorized her. Then Bunny showed up and explained to them the error of their ways. The leader of the group refused to apologize to Heather, so Bunny nearly ripped his arm off."

"Good for him." Julian crossed his arms over his chest. "What happened next?"

"Heather had nightmares for years afterward, but instead of being terrified of her attackers she became terrified of Bunny. Apparently he was really fucking scary when he snapped some guy's arm like a twig and demanded his surrender. Bunny began to think he needed to control his rage because of it and started on the whole yoga and tai chi kick." Ryan shrugged. "I have to admit, he's easier to get along with now, but Heather's still afraid of him."

"And Eric is just as overprotective as Bunny. If he thinks even the slightest thing will bother Heather he does his best to make it go away, but he tries to do it where Heather won't see. And it's not just Heather he's protective of." Chloe leaned her head back against the sofa. "You should see what he does when he comes over here. He's worse than Grumpy."

"Hey!" Ryan grabbed the blanket draped over the coffee table and tucked his baby sister in. "He's been here?"

"Who hasn't?" Chloe yawned. "Guys?"

She was fading fast, her energy nowhere near what it should be. He'd have to talk to Jamie about that, maybe have some of her sessions eased until she was a little stronger. "Yeah, I'm going. Ryan?"

"I'll stay here, make her some dinner. She hasn't been eating right."

"*She* is sitting right here. Dork. And pizza is a perfectly acceptable food group."

"Hey, Ryan?"

"Hmm?" Ryan was distracted, already heading for Chloe's postage-stamp kitchen.

"Why would Eric see Cyn as a threat to Heather?"

Ryan shrugged. "Because of the way she looks and how Heather seems fascinated by her. He thinks anybody with ink and funny hair is dangerous. You should have seen the fit he had when Bunny got his tats."

Julian grinned. "Isn't your cousin eighteen now?"

"Yeah, and?"

Chloe chuckled. "Take her to LA, moron. And take Bunny with you."

Ryan and Julian exchanged an evil grin.

"And take me too. I have a tattoo I want to get, and I want Cyn to do it."

"Chloe—"

"Nope. Not talking me out of it, big bro."

"I was just going to ask what you're going to get."

Sure he was. Julian hung by the door and waited to hear Chloe's answer.

"A two-tailed kitsune."

"What the hell is a kitsune?" Ryan was starting Chloe's lunch and sounded distracted.

"It's a Japanese fox spirit. It's said that the more tails it has, the more wisdom it possesses. They could change shape into humans, and were said to have strong magical powers. The legends were probably born of Fox shifters mating with humans, since they could be spouses, lovers, advisors, even guardians."

"Ah. I like that." Ryan grinned. "Why only two tails, though?"

"Because I'm starting my second life."

The two men were silent as they absorbed the implications of what Chloe had said. She was right. Her old life was gone; it was time to start the new one. Damn, she was braver than he'd thought.

"You are wise beyond your years, young Padiwan." Julian grinned when Chloe glared at him. "And on that note, I'm out of here. Take care, pumpkin. Later, Grumpy."

Ryan's snarl was muted by the heavy wooden door.

Chapter Five

Bear stared at him, his furry face inscrutable. Julian stared back.

To Bear, patience really was a virtue.

"'Two becomes one, one becomes three. Bear knows the way, but Fox holds the key.'"

The deep, rumbling voice after waiting for so long would have startled a much younger Julian, but he'd learned the ways of Bear and wasn't surprised by much anymore. The spirit dropped a map at his feet, got to his feet and waddled off, leaving behind one very confused Kermode. Julian picked up the map and tried to study it, but it flared to bright life, flashing in his hands, soaking into his skin until nothing was left.

"Huh." He stood, brushed off his naked ass and turned back down the path that led back to his body. He nodded to the great white Fox on the way, again unsurprised to find him there. Chloe was tied tightly into whatever message the spirits were trying to impart, whether because of their odd bond or because she'd been on the paths and come back. He wasn't sure, but he'd figure it out. Eventually.

There was one thing he was certain of. Chloe had nearly died. That affected a person on deeper levels than most understood, especially after what he'd done to guide her back to her body from the dark paths. She was closer to the spirit world than most shifters would ever be, and the tie between the two of them had only deepened it.

He'd have to talk to Tai, find out what his leader thought about all of this. If his hunch was right, Chloe was changed in more ways than he could see right now. Unfortunately, that meant answering one of Tai's phone calls. Julian was certain whatever Tai wanted to say to him wasn't going to be pleasant.

He followed the path that led back to his body, ready to put an end to this walk through the spirit realm. It hadn't been nearly as difficult as the one he'd taken when he pulled Chloe back into her body, but it still drained him. If his mate had been there, she would have been on the paths as well, lending her strength, borrowing his own. They'd be much stronger together.

He couldn't wait until he could take her down the paths. Once Bear accepted her, their mating would be complete.

There. The veil between this world and the physical, a misty barrier he crossed through easily. He landed in his body with a sigh, pulling his skin and bones around him like a familiar, comforting blanket. He opened his eyes—

—and jumped a foot at the sight of bright blue eyes staring into his.

"Hey, Jules. Went spirit-walkies, did we?"

He tried to get his racing heart back under control. "Fuck, Jamie."

"No thanks. You're not my type." Jamie put his stethoscope back around his neck. "I've never seen that before."

"Seen what?" Julian got up from the chair he'd nodded off in and went straight for the coffee machine. He'd fallen asleep in the break room.

"A Kermode in a trance."

Julian poured himself some coffee. "Yeah, well. I was summoned."

"Could that happen when you're driving?"

"Hasn't yet." Julian added enough sugar to send a six-year-old into spasms. "Bear's usually pretty good about that sort of thing. Now, Coyote, he's a real bitch. When he's got a message, you'd better be ready to hear it. Lucky me, he doesn't like to talk much. He's more a doer." He poured creamer until the coffee was nearly white, just the way he liked it.

Jamie shook his head. "You want some coffee with that?"

"Nah, I'm good." Julian took a sip, moaning under his breath. God, Jamie made some damn good coffee. "How long was I out for?"

"About half an hour."

Shit. There went lunch. "Damn." He glanced at his watch and grimaced.

"Take some time. Eat. Your hair still has some white in it and that will freak the patients."

"Thank you." Julian pulled his sandwich out of the fridge and sat his ass at the table.

"What did Bear have to say?" Jamie sat across from him and snagged one of Julian's chips.

"Two becomes one, one becomes three. Bear knows the way, but Fox holds the key."

"Chloe?"

"Possibly, since she had the same dream." Julian took a bite of his sandwich and tried to ignore the stare Jamie was giving him.

"Since when does Bear speak to Chloe?"

"He doesn't." He took another bite and tried not to smile at the frustration on Jamie's face.

"Then who did?"

"Fox." He took a sip of coffee and arched a brow at Jamie. "Chloe's different now."

"Yeah, but I didn't think she was *that* different." Jamie got to his feet and began to pace, his expression going from friend to concerned doctor. "Will this affect her recovery?"

"Not that I'm aware of. But when I went to visit her last night she was more tired than she should be."

"Hmm." Jamie stroked his chin, his gaze distant. "I want to be kept apprised of her new abilities, even the dreaming. It could impact other areas of her recovery, especially if it drains her of energy."

Julian nodded. "I'll do my best, but if she doesn't tell me there isn't much I can do."

"Agreed." Jamie looked at his watch. "Think you'll be ready in about ten minutes?"

He felt better already and he hadn't finished half his sandwich. "Yup."

"See you out there."

Julian scarfed the rest of his sandwich and headed back to work, Bear's words still bouncing around in his head. What the hell had he meant, and why had he given Julian the same riddle that Fox had given Chloe?

"Aw. How pretty." Glory practically cooed at the glass vase sitting on the counter. The little white envelope dared Cyn to open it, but she refused to touch the damn thing. She kept her nose buried in the magazine she was reading, ignoring the two insane bitches cooing over dead vegetation.

Cyn snorted. What the hell was that moron thinking?

"They are pretty. Two dozen roses, mixed colors." Tabby sighed. "Alex never sends *me* roses."

"I don't think Alex was the one who sent flowers to Cyn." Glory waggled her eyebrows.

"If I remember my flower language correctly—" Tabby tapped the glass, "—red is for true love. Pink is admiration. Lavender is—"

"Frou-frou." Cyn grimaced. "Flowers? At my age?"

"First off, Crabby Patsy, you're only twenty-four. Second, what woman alive hates getting flowers?" Cyn opened her mouth to respond but Tabby cut her off by clearing her throat. "And lavender means love at first sight."

Cyn clenched her jaw. Julian had to have guessed how she'd react to roses delivered at work, which meant he'd done it deliberately. She tried to ignore the girls as they continued discussing the flowers, but part of her couldn't help but listen in.

"What does yellow mean? I thought they meant true love, but there aren't any in the arrangement." Out of the corner of her eye she saw Glory stroke one of the lavender roses, a wistful expression on her face. Maybe Ryan was getting to her more than she wanted to let on.

"Nope. Yellow is friendship, orange is passion." Tabby tapped one blazing orange rose. "Which explains why they're in here but the yellow aren't."

"Friends with benefits sounds nice." Glory sniffed the orange rose. "But there are a lot more red and lavender ones than any other color." Glory flipped her hair back over her shoulder. "Cyndi's got a boyfriend!" she sang, grinning at Cyn.

Cyn flipped her off. Bitch knew how much she hated being called Cyndi.

"Oh, yes, I will read the note, thank you!"

Glory grabbed for it, but Cyn was fast, snatching it away from her at the last second. "Ha!"

Glory waved her hands. "Fine. Now you have to read it."

Cyn held it like she was going to rip it in two. She wasn't certain she'd have gone through with it, but Tabby was even quicker than she was. Tabby grabbed it and opened it, bursting into laughter. "What happened after you two went home last night?"

"Give me that." Cyn took the note, biting her lip at the image of Share Bear. That stupid purple bear with two heart-shaped lollipops on its tummy grinned at her. The note said *Thanks for sharing* in the kind of neat, extremely precise handwriting only a sociopath could possess.

Goddamn it. Now she was going to like flowers. Son of a bitch.

"Let me see!" Glory took the note from her and frowned at it. "Huh? What the hell is that? It's creepy."

Cyn took the note back. "None of your business." She took the card and the flowers back to her office, ignoring the idiots behind her. No way would she admit to them that she knew what the fuck a Care Bear was, let alone the name of one. She set the flowers where she could see them but wouldn't accidentally knock them over.

The card, she tucked into her secret drawer, along with a photo of her mother and the first set of keys to Living Art.

After all, no one had to know she'd kept it, right?

"Well?"

"Well what?"

Julian suppressed his growl. "Did you like them?" He was weary to the bone, but he refused to give up a date night despite the emergency that had forced him to use his powers. The man would have died right in Jamie's office if Julian hadn't

57

stepped in. Jamie was both appalled and grateful, but the patient had no clue how close to death he'd been.

Two more minutes. Just two more minutes and the aneurysm would have burst, and the resulting stroke would have killed him instantly. Jamie ordered the patient in for a round of tests and Julian to the break room until his hair and eyes returned to normal. Thank God it had been a shifter patient; a human would have run screaming from the room or declared the second coming.

"Like what?"

He pulled over. He was too tired to play the game tonight, damn it. "I'm sorry. Could you drive?"

"Jules?" Cyn put her hand on his forehead. "Are you sick?"

He stared at her.

"Bears catch colds like everyone else, right?"

He blinked. She had to be joking.

"Fine. Keys." She held out her hand and he gave them to her, sighing gratefully when she climbed out of the passenger side. He managed to pull himself out of the driver's seat and took her spot, but his knees were wobbly.

Damn. He was a *lot* more tired than he'd originally thought.

"Jeez, you look like shit. Let's get you home, okay?"

He closed his eyes and nodded, leaving everything in her more than capable hands. Within seconds she was gently shaking his shoulder. "We're here." Julian opened his eyes. He must have nodded off. She'd taken him back to his place, thank the ancestors. He wasn't up to dealing with Glory's perkiness right now. Cyn got out of the car and held up her hand when he tried to follow. She opened his door and helped him get out. "In case you were wondering, we're going to order in pizza and watch chick flicks." She held up a bag and shook it, the videos she wanted to watch rattling around inside.

He couldn't help but smile. "If you have a real chick flick in there I'll let you tattoo anything you want on my ass."

"Define real." She opened her front door and tugged him in, plopping him on the sofa before turning on the lights and shutting the door.

"My idea of real, not yours. *The Devil Wears Prada* does not count."

"Damn. There goes my vision of My Little Ponies dancing down your rainbow colored butt."

He kicked off his shoes and lay down, his head beginning to pound. "Could you bring me some aspirin?" Back home he would have requested another Kermode help him, but he wasn't home, and while he could call Alex or Ryan for help, he was strangely loathe to do so. He'd rather take aspirin and spend the evening alone with his mate than have his well-meaning friends come "help" him.

God forbid they called and told their family he wasn't feeling well. He shuddered at the thought of his house filled to the rafters with yappy Foxes and growling Grizzlies. He'd dealt with that while recovering from saving Chloe, and the noise levels alone had his landlord threatening him with eviction. Any night where he'd had time to prepare for the onslaught would be fine, but he just wasn't up to it right now. "So what is your idea of a chick flick?" This he had to see. He doubted it would be either sappy or sentimental. Maybe *First Wives' Club?* His mother loved that film. Hell, even his father chuckled at the window washer scene.

She brought him his medicine and smirked. "You'll see." She picked up the phone and called for two pizzas, one Hawaiian, one pepperoni and mushroom.

He must have dozed off again because the smell of tomato sauce woke him. He hadn't even heard the doorbell ring. His stomach growled. "Damn, that smells good."

Cyn put the pizzas on the coffee table and brought them some sodas. "Ready for the horror?"

He grinned. He was beginning to feel better. "Sure."

Two slices later he was staring at the screen, wondering what the hell he'd gotten himself into. "Your idea of a chick flick is *She-Devil?*"

"That pink palace princess deserves everything she gets."

Cyn's grin was chock full of childish, evil glee. She munched her third slice of pizza, her gaze glued to the screen as Roseanne Barr blew up her own house with a happy sigh.

He smiled and settled back down, pleasantly full of good pizza. He watched his mate enjoy her movie and hid his grin.

His mother was going to adore Cyn.

Chapter Six

Julian nodded off again long before the movie ended. Cyn stared at him, worried at the thin strands of white still silvering his hair. She hadn't seen the silver sparks in his eyes when he'd first picked her up. It had been too dark outside the shop and in the car. Now that they were in Julian's home those sparks were obvious, and worrying. They weren't fading the way they were supposed to, and he was almost as weak as he'd been after saving Chloe.

What the fuck had he done to himself?

She covered him with a blanket and left him, determined to let him rest. She left the film on loop so the lack of noise didn't disturb him. She just turned it down before heading into the kitchen with the pizza boxes. She put the leftover pizza in the fridge and pondered what to do next. Should she leave him on the couch? Call Alex and Tabby and the rest of that insane gang of shifters? They might have a better clue what was wrong with him.

She didn't like not knowing how to help him. Not one little stinking bit.

Hell. She was beginning to mutter in Spanish under her breath. Maybe it was time to call for some back-up. Cyn picked up the phone. If Julian was sick or needed help, then she needed Alex.

"Hello? Cyn? What's wrong?"

Cyn grimaced at the breathless tone of Tabby's voice. "Did I interrupt something?"

"Yes."

"Oops. Sorry. Julian's hair is white and he's passed out on his sofa."

Tabby sighed. "Why don't you sound sorry?"

"Because I'm not. Put Alex on the phone for me. Good girl. *Good* girl."

"Damn it, I'm not a dog, y'all. And stop leaving that bag of kibble in front of my door!"

Cyn heard deep, muffled laughter, and then Alex was on the phone. "What's wrong with him?"

Damn, Bears had good hearing. She'd have to remember that. "Not sure. He picked me up at my shop, but halfway to his place he pulled over and asked me to drive. Honestly, once we were inside I was shocked. His hair is half white and his eyes are washed out."

"Shit. I'll be there in ten minutes." The phone clicked shut. Cyn headed back into Julian's living room to wait for Alex and Tabby, because where one went the other was rarely far behind.

She sat on the edge of the sofa and studied the man who claimed he was her mate. The white streaks didn't bother her at all; in fact, they gave him an otherworldly look that was stunning. His Native American heritage was obvious in his dusky skin color, deep brown eyes and high cheekbones. His full lips invited kisses; his strong jaw showcased his stubborn side. The thin laugh lines at the corners of his eyes made her smile. His waist length hair was loose, lying around him in an inviting pool she wanted to sink her fingers into. He had the lean build she'd always preferred in her men, but with enough muscle underneath those scrubs to make her feel like she'd won the lottery. He had to be one of the handsomest men she'd ever seen, bar none, and he said he was all hers.

She still wasn't sure she believed it, but she certainly wasn't going to turn his fine ass away.

She sat and watched him until a soft knock on the door got her up off the sofa. She let Alex and Tabby in, directing Alex to where Julian lay.

"Oh crap. He looks like three-day-old dog poo. What did he do this time?" Tabby kept her voice low, but that southern drawl was more pronounced than usual. Tabby was worried, and that couldn't be good.

Alex rested his hand on Julian's forehead, his brow furrowing. Whatever the hell he was doing it didn't look comfortable.

"Well?" Cyn tapped her foot, impatience riding her hard. What was wrong with Jules?

Alex sat back with a sigh. He swayed and nearly fell of the sofa. "If I were to guess, I'd say he saved someone's life today."

Cyn ground her teeth. "Oh. Really."

Alex's hazel eyes had gone deep, dark brown. "He can't help it, Cyn. I think one of the reasons Kermode hold themselves apart from the rest of us is because Bear's gift is, for them, a curse as well."

She smiled, and it wasn't pretty. "So. How close to death was he this time?"

Alex's brows rose. "He's exhausted, but he'll be fine. I gave him what I could, but only rest will cure what ails him now."

Julian's cell phone rang. Cyn, not caring she was snooping, picked it up and frowned at the name displayed. "Who the fuck is Tai?"

Both Alex and Tabby shrugged, but before they could speak Cyn answered his phone. "Hello?"

There was a pause, then a male voice spoke. "Is Julian DuCharme there?"

"He's sleeping at the moment. Could I take a message?"

"Who is this?"

The arrogant command in the man's voice got Cyn's back up. *None of your business,* cabrón. "A better question would be who are you?"

"Fine. Who are you?"

Lovely. Another smart-ass. This one had an undertone of condescension she had no intention of bowing to. "Cyn." She left it hanging and waited for his answer.

There was a deep, frustrated sigh. "Could you tell Julian that I called?"

Another command. She had the feeling she was going to *love* this guy. "Why?"

"What do you mean, why?" He sounded baffled, and a little annoyed.

"You're not his boss, you're not his significant oth...wait, are you?"

The man actually growled before abruptly cutting it off.

"Because that would mean he's cheating on your ass."

"He's not my—"

"He does have a nice one, doesn't he? Ass, I mean."

"His life is in danger."

Cyn paused, her intention of playing with Julian's rude caller momentarily suspended. "Is that a threat?"

Tabby, a Wolf and a predator, took a step back at the cold chill in Cyn's voice.

"Tell him this: Two becomes one, one becomes three. Bear knows the way, but Fox holds the key. Tell him, mate of Julian, that every fucking Kermode has had this same dream. All except me."

She took a deep breath. A shiver ran through her. "I'm not his mate." How the hell did this stranger know she was Julian's?

"The dream I had showed Julian lying on the ground, covered in blood."

She didn't even react when the asshole hung up the phone. Alex had to pry it out of her cold hand. "We heard."

Tabby took a deep breath, her hand going over her still flat stomach. "I'll rally the troops."

Alex shot Cyn a worried look before picking Julian up like he weighed less than nothing. "I'll carry Julian to bed. Man has to be getting a crick in his neck."

Cyn could barely see her friends moving around her. She was too busy bristling over the threat to Julian. She might not want to admit what she felt for the annoying, quirky, hot-as-fuck Bear, even to herself, but there was one thing she hadn't failed to grasp.

Tai's vision was never going to come to pass. Not if Cynthia Reyes could stop it.

Julian stirred. Something was different, out of place. What the hell had woken him—?

A loud snore interrupted his thoughts. He opened his eyes and stared down at the face he'd grown to love since he'd moved to Halle three months ago. Despite the hectic scramble to get his nursing certificate and keep his visa he'd managed to make friends with all the girls at LA, but none of them meant more to him that Cyn did. The first moment he'd seen her, her dark hair was streaked a delicate pink. Her laughter was contagious to a man who was feeling desperately homesick. Her dark, sparkling eyes had captivated him. He'd been smitten before he'd ever caught her scent, but when he had that was all she wrote.

She was the one.

He'd been wandering through Halle, happy to have made it, worried that he hadn't been in time. He hadn't understood why Bear wanted him to leave home and come to this small college town in the middle of Pennsylvania, but the hassle of getting into America without a work visa had taken months to clear away. In the end it had taken Tai's political clout to get him here.

He'd almost ignored the tattoo parlor, but the girls had propped the door open to the early summer breeze. He'd been enchanted by the easy laughter, the sweet smiles of the two girls he'd seen. Then Cyn had stepped out from behind the curtain blocking the work area from the front of the shop, laughing and joking with the sisters of her heart, and his world had tilted on its axis.

He'd found his mate.

Convincing her he was hers, on the other hand, was turning out to be a major undertaking. Good thing he was stubborn when it came to the things he really wanted.

He hated to admit it, but he was curious why she was sleeping in his bed. They hadn't reached the part of their relationship where Cyn would be comfortable sleeping with him.

Or had they? He sniffed the air, hoping against hope that he hadn't somehow mated her and, spirits forbid, *forgotten it*. He breathed a sigh of relief when he realized he hadn't, not yet, anyway.

Another indelicate snore made him smile. She was so tough when awake, so vibrant and alive, it was odd to see her like this. She was practically sprawled on top of him, one leg thrown over his, one arm pinning him down, her head tucked just under his chin. She felt so good, so right, he was reluctant to move her.

But god *damn* did he have to piss.

He moved cautiously, gradually working his way out from under her and headed for the bathroom, breathing a sigh of relief as he finally let nature take its course. The headache was gone, and when he took a look at himself in the mirror he was almost back to normal. A few white strands remained, a few gray specks in his eyes. *Nothing to see here. Please move along.*

"Jules?"

He headed back into the bedroom at the sleepy sound of her voice. It had taken on a husky quality that sent blood racing straight to his cock. "I'm here."

She was sitting up, pushing her mass of multicolored hair out of her face. "Where'd you go?"

"Bathroom." He hit the foot of the bed and, instead of getting in on his side, began crawling up it until he was hovering over her. "Hi."

She glared up at him. "You're in big trouble."

He whimpered. Fuck. He had her in his bed and he wasn't going to be allowed to play? That was like chaining a recovering chocoholic in front of a Godiva store that was giving out free samples. "Why?"

Cyn bopped him upside the head. "You could have *died*, asshole."

He sat back on his heels, his erection completely forgotten. This was something that couldn't wait, something every Kermode had to do before mating with someone from the outside. "This is who I am, what I am. Bear made me this way for a reason."

"Does that mean you have to risk your life?"

"Yes." He sighed and stroked his hand across her knee. "He was two minutes from death. An aneurysm. What would you have me do, let a man die right in front of me when I can save him?"

She blew out a breath and refused to meet his eyes.

"I'm a nurse *because* of what I am. The urge to heal is strong within all Bears, but more so for the Kermode."

"Alex said that was the reason the Kermode hold themselves apart."

"He's partially right. There's more to it than that. The First Nations say that Kermode were made white by Raven to remind us all of the Ice Age, but it's not true. Kermode were made white because..." He grimaced. "The truth is, not all Kermode are white. Only one in ten is, and they're the ones with the special gift. But those of us who are born Spirit Bears are slowly dying out." And the majority of human mates turned never became Spirit Bears. He doubted Cyn would be any different.

"Genetic problems?"

"Partly. We have our own problems as well, problems that up until now we've tried to deal with on our own."

"Tell me."

He hid a grin. He couldn't wait until Tai and Cyn spoke for the first time. He had the feeling they'd seriously butt heads. "I can't." He held up his hand, stalling her objection. "I'm not allowed to. Bears might not have Alphas and Packs, but we have our own way of doing things. Tai Boucher is the closest thing we have to an Alpha, and until he tells me it's all right to tell you, or until you accept the mating and become one of us, I can't." He shot her a cheeky grin. "It's a Spirit Bear thing. You wouldn't understand."

"Your leader's name is Tai?"

Hell. He couldn't remember the last time he'd heard that much guilt in someone's voice. "Yes. Why?"

She rolled her eyes. "Then trust me when I say he'll never give you permission."

His stomach rolled. "Crap. Did Tai call while I was sleeping?"

She nodded. Her expression now matched her voice.

"What did you do?"

"Nothing!"

"Cyn."

"I *may* have taken exception to his tone of voice. I might even have retaliated a little. Just a tiny bit."

He rubbed his forehead. Wow, look at that. A headache really *could* come roaring back to life. "What did he want?"

"He said to tell you that every Kermode has had the same dream, something about a key and a Bear, I forget exactly what he said." She waved it off even as a shiver worked its way down his spine. This was bad. "He also—" She bit her lip and frowned ferociously.

"Also what?"

She looked him dead in the face and lied her pretty ass off. He'd made it a habit to study all things Cyn, and her left eyebrow always twitched just the tiniest bit before she fibbed. "Said to tell you hi."

He traded stare for stare with her, but she didn't back down, didn't give him what he wanted: the truth. "Is that all he said?"

"Would you like some cookies?"

What the fuck? "I doubt he said that."

"No, I'm hungry." She pushed him away and clambered out of bed. "I want cookies."

"I want answers." He followed her to the kitchen where she helped herself to a large glass of milk. "What did Tai say, Cyn?"

"Oreos? You don't have any chocolate chip?" She put the bag on the counter and ripped into it. "You need to do a grocery run."

"I need to paddle your ass if you don't tell me what he said. And Oreos are manna of the gods, you evil heathen. Especially if they're double-stuff."

She glared at him and shoved an entire Oreo in her mouth.

"Oh, that's attractive."

She grinned at him, black goo staining her teeth.

"Not even you are cute enough to pull that look off." He handed her the milk and watched her devour six cookies at once. "Why aren't you the size of a whale?"

"Metabolism." She put the cookies back and finished her milk. "Well, it's been fun, but I'm outta here." She waved and started toward the front door. "See you later."

She wasn't. She couldn't be. Julian chased her to the front door, but he was too late. She'd already climbed into *his* car, locking the doors behind her. She gave him an evil little wave and left him stranded on his front porch in the early dawn light.

Julian turned around and stalked back into his living room. He picked up his cell and dialed Tai. Fuck the time difference. He needed answers, and he needed them now. He left a message for Tai to call him back pronto, then headed off to shower.

An hour later he called Alex, because the other thing he really needed was a ride to work. Damn that sneaky Oreo-stealing, car-thieving female.

But he still couldn't stop himself from sniffing his shirt right where her head had rested through the night, nor the smile that followed.

Chapter Seven

Cyn pulled into the parking lot at the back of LA Tattoos and picked up the bag of donuts and coffee. She was starving, despite her cookie raid that morning. She ran her fingers over Julian's steering wheel, smiling for no reason she could figure out, and climbed out of the car.

A shadow out of the corner of her eye was her only warning. Cyn twisted, the sound of shattering glass shocking her into freezing for a second too long. A painful blow to the side of her face left her sprawled on the gravel, piping hot coffee burning her hand.

She sat up, ready to fight for her life, when a low growl sounded from behind her. Something gray and silver with an odd blob of green at the top of its head landed in front of her. Tabby had sailed over Julian's sedan in Wolf form and hit the gravel in front of Cyn, snapping at the shadows. Her fur practically stood on end as she lunged at something Cyn couldn't even see.

That was when Cyn realized it wasn't a simple mugging. So she did what any sensible, modern woman would do. She grabbed her keys. "*Adiós*, asshole." She pressed the button on her keychain, setting off a high-pitched alarm that had Tabby whining and burying her head in her paws. Cyn felt her own eyes cross, but if it affected her assailant the way it was affecting Tabby she was glad to sacrifice a little hearing for a day or two.

She dragged herself to her feet and grabbed hold of her other self-defense item on her key chain, a baton with a slight point at the end. She waved it toward the shadows, her finger still on the button of the alarm. "C'mon! Bring it, you fucking coward!"

Something indistinct dashed from the shadows and out into the street, too fast for Cyn to follow with her eyes.

"For the love of all that is holy, please stop."

Cyn stared down at her naked, weeping friend. Tabby was human, covering her ears with shaking hands. "Get dressed. I think we're about to have company." She stood by the car door and tried not to tremble like a little girl while Tabby obeyed her orders.

"Cyn?"

Cyn grabbed the third thing on her key chain that wasn't a key, a tiny flashlight, and aimed it at the street. "Mrs. H?" Crap, it hurt her jaw to talk. Son of a bitch had clocked her but good, and now that the danger had passed the pain was starting to make itself known.

Evelyn Hagen, one of LA's older clients, put her hand to her chest and started toward her. "I heard the alarm and practically ran to get here. Are you all right? What happened to your car?"

Cyn turned and stared at Julian's driver's side window. Shit. He was going to be pissed about that. "I got mugged."

"I got here just in time." Tabby stepped out from behind the car and ran her fingers through her hair. She looked pale, fragile, like she was the one who'd gotten attacked.

"Are you two all right?"

Cyn nodded, doing her best to ignore the throbbing pain growing in her skull. "As right as we can be."

Mrs. H. relaxed a little, the keychain baton in her own hand sliding into her back pocket. "Cool. I never really wanted to test out my karate skills." She winked and followed them to the back door of LA. "You want me to call the cops?"

Cyn and Tabby exchanged a look. "Could you get them to send out Gabe Anderson?"

"The sheriff? Why?"

"Just tell him Tabby and I were attacked again. He'll understand."

Mrs. H. nodded, but her expression was anything but reassured. "I'll do it. You need to put in security cameras back there."

"We tried, but the landlord wouldn't let us. Said it would damage the brick façade of the building." Tabby shrugged.

Mrs. H. grunted. "Who's your landlord?"

Tabby rattled off the name while Cyn fisted her hands at her sides. She didn't give a crap about that fat asshole. Her jaw was getting worse, and she thought one of her teeth might be loose. "Tabs? Call Bunny."

Tabby waved off Mrs. H. after reassuring her they were both fine, then pulled out her cell phone. "Alex? Cyn and I were just attacked again."

The roar forced Tabby to pull the phone from her ear. "I'm *fine*. Cyn was the one who got beat up." Tabby's brows rose and she glanced at Cyn. "Yeah, I'll tell her. No, Glory's not here; she's got afternoon to evening tonight."

Cyn unlocked LA's back door and let them into the shop. Fuck. Her head was pounding, she was nauseated and her jaw was feeling even worse. Was she going to have to go to the hospital? She didn't *think* her jaw was broken, but she wasn't a doctor. It was entirely possible the son of a bitch had broken something in her face. She headed for the front of the store and sat gingerly on one of the chairs. She tilted her head back, listening to Tabby's soft voice as she tried to calm her frantic mate.

A few moments later Tabby was unlocking the front door. Alex burst through, his eyes wild. If he had any hair on his head it would have been standing on end. He scooped Tabby up as soon as he saw her, cradling her in his arms like she was a child, setting himself down on one of the guest chairs and checking every inch of her with his hands and eyes.

Cyn didn't really care if they stripped naked and danced the hula. She just wished the pain in her head would fucking *stop*. She closed her eyes and ignored the pair, focusing instead on disregarding the pain.

A warm, gentle hand caressed her cheek. "You get into more trouble, I swear."

She opened her eyes to find Julian hovering over her, his eyes silver, his hair pure white. The pain in her jaw immediately eased away to nothing and her nausea receded. She was still woozy and shaking, but at least she no longer wanted to chop her own face off. The fierce frown on his face worried her. "I broke your car."

"Shh." He stroked his finger along her jawline and she felt, actually *felt* the loose tooth firm up in its socket.

"Is she all right?" Alex's voice was rumbly, a sure sign his Bear was close to the surface.

"Her jaw was broken, some teeth loose. I fixed it."

She worked her jaw back and forth, never more grateful for the lack of pain. "Thanks."

His brow quirked. "You're welcome." Then he crossed his arms over his chest and ruined it. "Why didn't you call me immediately?" His gaze focused on her burned hand and immediately it felt better, the burn fading away as she watched.

She stood and faced him, just like she had her attacker in the parking lot. "My jaw was broken. Didn't feel like talking. Besides, you should be resting. You did enough yesterday."

Julian took way too much on himself. Someone had to make sure he didn't get hurt using his powers, and it wasn't going to be him. He'd already proven that.

Cyn heard his teeth grind together. "I. Would. Have. Come."

"How? Super Bear would have thrown on his cape and tights and flown?"

Tabby threw up her hand. "I'd pay to see that."

Julian ignored Tabby, his gaze never leaving Cyn's face. "I have my ways."

"I have your car."

He took a long breath. "Don't push me right now. You were *attacked*, your jaw broken." He turned to Tabby. "Was it a shifter?"

"Yeah, but one I've never smelled before. It was fast, way too fast for me to track or I might have gone after it."

Alex growled. "You think it was the same people Gary worked for?" When Tabby squirmed in his lap he tightened his grip. "You're not going anywhere, baby."

Tabby rolled her eyes but stayed put. "I keep telling you I'm not a dog. Sit and stay doesn't work on me. Besides, it wasn't me they wanted this time."

"They?"

Tabby nodded at Julian's barked question. "There was more than one. I'm certain of it."

"And you were going to go after them? Alone?" Alex's hazel eyes turned dark brown. Six-inch claws sprang from his fingertips.

"Down, sugar." Tabby patted Alex's chest, but it did little to calm the Grizzly.

"You think that this time they wanted me?" Cyn shared a confused look with Tabby.

Tabby shrugged. "I have no idea."

Alex pulled out his cell phone. "Dad. We have a situation."

Cyn bit her lip as she stared at Tabby. She was getting sick and tired of this bullshit. If she were a shifter she could have changed and defended herself better rather than relying on her pregnant friend. Maybe if Tabby bit her she could—

"Don't even think about it." Julian grabbed her jaw, pulled her face around to his and kissed her so deep and so hard she was surprised her lip didn't bleed. His silver eyes sparkled down at her. "You're mine. No one else gets to change you."

Cyn swallowed. She shouldn't feel relieved, damn it. She was an independent woman who could take care of herself.

Of course, she'd be able to do it a lot better once she was fuzzy.

His lips drew up in a sly smile. The kiss he gave her this time was softer, more sensual, a hell of a lot more bone-melting. Cyn clutched his shoulders, his hair brushing against the skin of her hands. She moaned into his mouth and he pulled her closer to him, pressing his hands into the small of her back until they were practically inside one another.

"I think I might be too young to see this," Tabby muttered.

"I think *I* might be too young," Alex chuckled. "Get a room, people."

Cyn flipped them the bird even as she refused to allow Julian to end the kiss, grabbing the back of his head when he tried to pull away.

She had no idea you could smirk while kissing someone else, but damn it, the son of a bitch managed it.

She was breathless when she finally let him go. Julian nuzzled her cheek before releasing her and settling her back on the chair. "Gabe's here."

"How—"

The bell jingled, and Halle's sheriff sauntered into the shop, took one look at the four of them and put his hands on his hips. "Can't leave you people alone for a second, can I?"

"Cyn was attacked by shifters." Julian wasn't pulling any punches. He placed himself slightly in front of Cyn, almost as if he was ready to defend her against Gabe, of all people.

Gabe shook his head. "Any idea why, or who?"

"Or what." Tabby got up off Alex's lap and wandered over to the counter, picking up a pen to tap on the glass. "I got a whiff, but I didn't recognize the type of shifter."

"So not Wolf, Bear or Puma." The men exchanged worried glances. "The college?"

Cyn winced. "What other types of shifters are there?"

"Lots and lots." Julian sighed and sat next to her, still in the seat closer to Gabe, but it was an improvement. *Not overprotective my well-padded ass.* "There are Lions, Tigers, Bears, Pumas, Wolves, Foxes, Coyotes, you name a predator and odds are good they've got shifters."

"You mean there might really be Alligators in the sewers?"

Every shifter in the room stared at her like she was nuts. Alex actually looked insulted. "Limit that pool to mammals, please."

"Like werebats? Or wererats? Oh! What about—"

"*No.*" Julian sounded stern, but he couldn't completely hide his amusement from her. "There are no werebats, wererats, weremoles, werevoles or werehamsters."

"And thank God for that." Alex shuddered in disgust. "Seriously. Werehamsters?"

"What about weredolphins?"

"N— actually, now that you mention it, I'm not certain. I've never met one. Have you?"

The others shook their heads. "They're a legend," Tabby added.

"Sort of like wereorcas. If they did exist they're more than likely extinct now. None sit on the council, I know that much." Alex replied. "None of this has anything to do with you having your face smashed. Did you get a look at your attacker?"

Julian growled under his breath. "Good question."

"Nope. Shadows, shattered glass, pain. Tabby with a lime green Mohawk in Wolf form. That's about it." She shrugged; there wasn't much more she could add. She didn't have the nose Tabby did. "There was a blur as one of them ran away. I could barely see it, though."

Gabe stroked his jaw. "Cheetah, maybe? I hear they can be pretty damn fast."

"I did get a scent of cat shifter in that alley, and it wasn't of the local variety." Tabby exchanged a worried glance with Alex.

"Could be." Alex was at Tabby's side again, his arms around her protectively. He cradled her close, his huge hands resting naturally over her belly. "We need to figure out what the hell is going on."

"Before someone gets seriously hurt." Gabe took out his pad and pen.

"Someone *was* seriously hurt. Cyn's jaw was broken." Julian's anger didn't affect the gentle way he stroked her shoulder.

Gabe peered at her face in concern. "Shit. Are you all right?"

"Yeah." Cyn patted Julian's knee. "Super Bear fixed me up."

Julian stared at where her hand rested on his knee. "Why yes, of course you may."

Before she could ask what he meant Julian had her in his lap, and looking mighty smug about it too. "I didn't ask to sit in your lap."

"Yes you did. You patted my knee and said let me sit in your lap."

She stared at him while behind her the hyena twins began to laugh. "You are so full of it. You know that, right?"

He grinned. "Yup."

"Well. That's good. So long as you're aware of it."

Gabe choked out a laugh and closed his notebook. "Okay. I'm going to go sniff around the parking lot, see what I can find. Ladies, please. For the love of all that is holy, *be careful.* Someone is out to get you, and until I catch them you're vulnerable." Gabe ignored Alex's rumbling, warning growl and pointed toward the front door. "Park on the street if you can, under bright lights. Gentlemen, keep an eye on them—and yes, that's an order from Halle's Second."

Julian stiffened. "Is it an order from one of the Northeastern Hunters?"

Gabe nodded firmly. "Yes. It is."

Cyn gasped as Julian's fangs descended. Her sweet, funny teddy bear morphed into a lethal predator, right in front of her eyes.

Since when were fangs *hot?*

If those sons of bitches came near his mate again Julian would rip their arms off and heal the holes shut. After all, it would be hard for even a Cheetah to run down a human woman if it only had two legs.

"Oh my God! What happened here?"

Glory stepped into LA Tattoos, her eyes darting between all of them. Her gaze kept returning to Julian's mostly white hair and obvious fangs, her skin paling as the implications hit her. "Who's hurt?"

"No one, not anymore." Cyn rubbed her jaw, and Julian bet she could still feel the painful blows like an echo. She took a deep breath and filled Glory in on what had happened.

"Who called Glory?" Julian muttered.

"I did." Ryan stepped into the shop behind Glory, his expression mutinous. "She deserved to know what happened." Julian agreed with him. If they went after the human females, then Glory needed to be ready to protect herself as best she could.

Glory looked ready to come out of her skin. "What the fuck! How did this happen? Shouldn't one of you have been here? It's not like Ryan isn't here trying to sniff my butt twenty-four-seven."

"I'm not here twenty-four-seven," Ryan replied. His tone was mild but his gaze was hot with anger and fear. "You're not here that much."

Julian bit back a groan. Did the man ever want to claim his mate? Maybe he was a closet masochist, because he sure liked taking a beating from Glory.

"Please tell me you're not sitting in the bushes at night outside my apartment." She looked horrified, and Cyn didn't look much better. Having a possessive Grizzly hanging around outside your home was enough to put anyone off. Hell, he wasn't certain he liked the idea either.

Ryan smiled grimly. "I have night watch."

Julian rolled his eyes even as Alex nodded. "Tabby would kill me if anything happened to you two. I don't care how cute you are or how much you pout, you've got security round the clock."

"I agree." Julian ignored the glare Cyn shot him. There was no way he was going to allow his mate to be in danger again. Didn't she understand how precious and rare she was? "Who picks them up and drops them off?"

"I will." Alex shrugged. "One of the perks of being your own boss. I can come and go a lot easier than you nine to fivers can."

"And one of the perks of having your cousin be your boss is he understands when I take time off to protect our mates." Ryan tried to take Glory's hand, but she stepped away from him. He solved the problem by picking her up and holding her against his hip like a cranky two-year-old.

Yup. Glory was going to kill him. The look on her face did not bode well for the Grizzly's health. The way she eyed her piercing gun gave him a clue as to how she'd do it.

Glory, in the tattoo parlor, with the gun.

"We just want you three to be safe while we figure out what the fuck is going on. You can't protect yourselves the way we can, not from shifter attacks."

"Although if it were humans bothering you like this we'd still rip their heads off and bowl with them." Ryan swatted Glory's hip absently when she struggled to get down. "Stay still, sweetheart. I don't want to drop you."

"Drop me. Feel free, you Neanderthal."

Ryan and Glory exchanged a heated glance. Ryan shrugged. "It's your ass."

She landed with a shriek and a thud. "Ow." She rolled to her hip and rubbed her ass, wincing.

"Told ya."

"Children, play nice. Or do I have to separate you?" Julian wagged his finger at Ryan. "Stop playing with your mate, Ryan."

"But I like playing with her, Julian. She's so shiny and squeaks when you squeeze her."

Glory squeaked in outrage.

Julian turned to Glory. "Please, for the love of the ancestors, be the adult here and stop torturing him."

She crossed her arms over her chest and humphed, turning away from both Julian and Ryan. What she had against the mating he had no idea, but sooner or later the Grizzly was going to snap and she'd find herself over his knee, bitten and spanked.

He eyed her, wondering if maybe that wasn't exactly what the little brat wanted.

"Jules?"

He turned his attention back to where it rightfully belonged, on his own mate. "Hmm?"

"Go home."

Crap. She had her cell phone in her hand. "Did you just call me out of work?"

"Uh-huh. Jamie says get some rest today, he'll see you tomorrow."

"Cyn, I need to work." His ability to remain in the United States rested on his work visa, at least until he could convince Cyn to marry him. If he didn't work, he could be deported.

She cupped his face in her warm, strong hands. Her expression was stern, but he could see the concern she felt. Her fingers stroked the white strands of his hair, reminding him of why he was so tired. "Go. Home."

He rested his forehead against hers and brushed the tip of his nose against hers. His mother had always called the gesture Eskimo kisses. "Only if you promise to call me if something happens again."

"Jules—"

"Yes or no, Cyn." If she gave him the promise she'd keep it. It was getting the promise that was the hard part.

He could actually hear her teeth grinding together. "Fine. I promise."

"Good." He stood, pulling Cyn to her feet with him, and kissed her good-bye. He was determined to bring at least the taste of her back to his home. "I miss you already."

She scowled, but she blushed too. She'd probably beat him to within an inch of his life if he ever told her how adorable she was. "Go!"

"Going." He waved to Alex. "Take me home, you stud you." He batted his lashes at Alex, grinning when Alex laughed.

"Sorry, you're not my type. Your hair isn't green enough. Ryan, I'll be back in a few." Alex kissed Tabby good-bye and gestured toward the front door. "After you, princess."

Julian flipped his hair over his shoulder and sauntered toward the door. "My hero."

He grinned as Cyn giggled, then tried to hide it behind her hand. It was becoming his mission in life to make her laugh.

So far, so good.

Chapter Eight

"So."

Julian smirked into his coffee cup. "So?"

The cousins exchanged an amused glance. Gabe had caught up with them outside LA and declared he would watch the shop while the three of them grabbed a quick breakfast. It had been either that or watch while Glory eviscerated her mate with a tattoo needle. As entertaining as the second would've been, they'd all agreed pancakes were the better option.

Julian shrugged. "She's mine." Did he really need to say anything else?

Ryan snorted. "Tell me you didn't actually say that to Cyn."

Julian shrugged. Hell no, he wasn't that stupid, but there was no way he was saying that in front of two Grizzlies. A man had some pride after all.

"And you lived to tell the tale?" Ryan shook his head. "Damn. Maybe I should just bare fang on Glory and see what happens."

Julian almost choked on his coffee. "Your gonads would wind up dangling from one of her charm bracelets."

"Ouch." Alex grabbed the cantaloupe, smacking Ryan's hands away. "You get the green melon thingies."

"I like the yellow melon thingies better."

The cousins glared at each other.

"If you two start bitch slapping each other over cantaloupe I'm not going to tell you what I learned from Chloe."

They immediately focused on him. Alex immediately scowled, the mere mention of his cousin causing the big Grizzly's protective instincts to go into overdrive. "Tell us what?"

Ryan's expression turned grim. "Someone's going to attack Glory, aren't they?"

Julian shook his head. "If I knew why they'd gone after Cyn, I'd be able to say whether or not Glory is in danger as well."

"Then we assume all three of them are in danger and go with that." Alex picked at the fruit. "I won't lose either of them; it would kill Tabby. She's already telling the baby stories about Aunt Glory and Aunt Cyn. Some of them are even rated PG."

"Agreed." Ryan sat back with a grunt. He ignored the huge stack of waffles in front of him turning limp in the sea of syrup he'd poured over them. "I need to claim my mate."

"Yeah, you do." Alex pointed at Julian. "So do you. And you need to tell us what you learned."

Julian sighed. He had no idea how the two of them would react to Bear's message. "Two becomes one, one becomes three. Bear knows the way, but Fox holds the key."

They sat there and stared at him expectantly.

Julian shrugged and drank his coffee. He didn't have to wait long before Ryan lost patience. "That's it? That's why you had us get up at the ass-crack of dawn?"

He glared at Ryan, his eyes flashing silver. "You mean other than the attack on my mate?"

"Well, yeah, but... It's eight a.m.!"

"Let me guess, long night sitting outside Glory's window?"

"Exactly." Ryan looked horrified. "You could have emailed me that."

"But then I wouldn't see your lovely face so bright and early." Julian batted his lashes at Ryan, grinning when the

Grizzly grumbled and finally attacked his waffles. "Seriously, when Bear delivers a message like that, it means he wants us to pay attention. You have syrup on your cheek, by the way."

"How did I get stuck sitting next to you?" Ryan scrubbed the syrup away, but Julian could tell his heart really wasn't in it. The threat to his mate was scrambling his good humor.

Alex's focus remained on Julian. "What do you think it means? The message was meant for you, right?"

"I'm not sure." Julian tapped his finger on the rim of his coffee cup. "But Chloe got the same message from Fox."

"She did? She didn't mention it to me." Ryan put his napkin down and picked his fork back up.

"Maybe because someone's been a Crappy Chris lately."

This time Ryan snorted, but didn't respond, due to his mouth being full of waffles. But his death glare was pretty good.

"Don't you mean Grumpy Gus?" Alex's brows rose as he stared at the two of them in confusion.

"If I did, I would've said that." Alex rolled his eyes, but let it go. "Chloe made it a point to mention that Fox was specific in that two *becomes* one, not two become one."

Alex froze. "Two becomes one, with an s?"

"Yes." Julian was worried. Alex's eyes had turned dark brown. "Why?"

"When two becomes one, what does that mean?"

Ryan cursed softly. "Someone loses a mate."

Julian shook his head. "The loss of a mate would mean the death of the remaining mate, remember?"

Alex grimaced. "Unless the shifter either has more than one mate, or it wasn't a true mating."

"There aren't that many shifters who have more than one mate." Ryan shoved what looked like half a Belgian waffle in his mouth.

"Wolves, Lions and Coyotes can have more than one mate. Other than that, I can't think of any." Julian waved their waitress over. He needed more caffeine before he dealt with everything going on. He'd have to call and leave Tai a message again. The Kermode hadn't called him back yet. Julian was beginning to worry. Could Cyn have really ticked Tai off that much?

"You say Chloe got the message too?" Alex grinned, and it wasn't a nice one. "Perhaps that means she's the one who will get two mates?"

Julian shook his head. "No. I'm pretty sure Chloe isn't the one. Neither am I." And thank Bear for that. Julian had no need for a second mate. His Cyn was more than enough for him. Besides, once she was marked and changed her mating instinct would kick in and she'd eat anyone who came between them.

"Then who?" Ryan's voice was beginning to rumble, his Grizzly close to surfacing.

"Two becomes one. It might not have anything to do with mates. We could be completely off base." Alex ate the last bit of cantaloupe, rolling his eyes when his cousin snarled. "It could mean anything, really. When two becomes one, it means they join, right? So that means that when two becomes one, they separate. So what separates?"

"Eggs. Old mayonnaise. The Schwarzeneggers." Ryan blinked as they stared at him. "What?"

"But then one becomes three." Julian poured sugar into his coffee, ignoring the grimaces of distaste on their faces. So he liked it on the sweet side. Did Ryan really have to gag like that?

"Could it be chemistry? Or atoms, or something like that?" Ryan picked up his own mug of pure black coffee and took a sip, sighing in satisfaction.

"It could." But Julian didn't think so. Something told him this had to do with shifters somehow. He just couldn't see the connection yet. "By the way, Gabe wants us to think about the possibility that whoever is after Cyn could be associated with the people who were originally after Tabby."

"Well, isn't that just fucking great? I'd hoped I was wrong about that." Alex shoved his empty plates away with a rough sigh. "Who the hell stood over my cradle and cursed me to live in interesting times?"

Ryan's expression was distracted, as if he hadn't heard a word they'd said. "So what else separates then rejoins, other than people and chemicals?" Ryan shoved the last of the waffles into his mouth. He'd decimated a stack that would choke a horse in four bites. Julian wasn't sure if he should be impressed or horrified.

"Seriously, Ryan, you have mating on the brain." Alex grabbed his own plate and attacked the scrambled eggs. "Just bite her already. It worked for me, didn't it?"

Ryan's eyes darted to something just over Alex's shoulder. "You think so?" Julian smothered his laughter as he saw what, or rather who, Ryan was staring at, a bag filled with take-out boxes in her hand.

"Oh, yeah." Alex sat back with a self-satisfied smirk on his face. "I haven't heard a single complaint yet. Tabby recognizes who's the boss."

"Really?" A soft, feminine voice with a deep southern drawl caused Alex's face to freeze. "You think you're the boss of me, sugar?"

"Shit." Alex dropped his fork, paling at the sound of boot heels tapping on linoleum.

"Busted," Ryan snickered, stealing Alex's last bit of bacon as the big Grizzly turned to face his mate.

"Hey, baby." Alex was out of his seat so fast Julian could've blinked and missed it.

"Don't 'hey baby' me, Alex."

"Aw, come on, don't be that way." Alex reached for Tabby, but she danced out of the way. "I didn't mean it like that."

"I think you meant it exactly the way you said it." Tabby batted at Alex's hands. "Don't think you're going to get out of this by being cute."

Alex pouted. Even Julian had to agree that Alex was damn cute when he pouted. He really did look like a giant teddy bear. "Aw, come on."

Tabby turned on her heel and started to walk out of the restaurant. "Hmph."

"Tabby!" Alex ran after his mate, leaving his cousin and Julian to pay the bill.

"That was almost worth how much this is going to cost me." Julian waved the waitress over as Ryan doubled over and laughed his ass off. "Check, please!"

"Thinks he's the boss of me, huh?" Tabby was damn near growling, her eyes flickering back and forth between their normal deep brown and her Wolf's gold. "Just kidding, my ass."

Glory tilted her head. She looked completely innocent, so Cyn knew something outrageous was about to pop out of her mouth. "But I thought non-Alpha Wolves liked being submissive and stuff like that."

Tabby snarled, and—

—were those *fangs*? Someone was cranky today.

Cyn rolled her eyes and pointed to a chair. "Down, girl. Sit. Stay."

"Yeah, no eating the coworkers," Glory snickered. "It's bad for business."

"Glory? Shut the hell up." Seriously. What was she going to do with these two? They had been rubbing each other the wrong way all day. Cyn was ready to boot both their asses out the door.

"You know what we need?" Glory spun in her chair, her head tilted back as she stared up at the ceiling.

"New shoes?" Tabby's expression lightened at the thought of going shopping.

"Only if they're dancing shoes." Glory's expression was positively wicked as she stared at Cyn and Tabby. "When was the last time we drove into Harrisburg for a night out on the town?"

"Do we dare?" Tabby nibbled her thumbnail, a sure sign she was tempted to do something she probably shouldn't. "With everything that's going on it might not be the safest thing to do."

"We could always ask the boys to join us." Cyn wouldn't mind dancing the night away in Julian's arms. Just the way the boy *walked* made her drool. Being on the dance floor was a whole other experience, one that should probably be illegal in several states.

Glory was already shaking her head. "Oh *hell* no. There is no way Ryan is horning in on my girls' night out."

Cyn had an idea. She began rubbing her finger on the glass counter. Something had to be done about Ryan and Glory before they drove her completely insane. "It's the perfect opportunity to make him crazy."

"He already is crazy." Glory was mumbling, but that evil pixie sparkle was starting to appear in her eyes. She probably had a clue where Cyn was going with this, or at least *thought* she did.

Tabby coughed, hiding a grin behind her fist. "It could be fun. Think about it. You in a short skirt and a teeny top, out on the dance floor, surrounded by men. Dancing with everyone but him." Thank God Tabby had caught on quickly. She, too, was getting tired of the way Glory was dancing around her attraction to Ryan. She never gave anyone this level of shit unless she was interested. "I don't think he's ever seen you in a club, has he? Every time he's been around you you've been in your mystic geek gear."

Glory frowned and picked at the beads on her skirt. Her head was down, but Cyn could just make out the evil little smirk on her face. "You're right. I don't think he has."

"And nobody says we have to tell him where we're going."

Tabby shared a grin with Cyn. "Just because we tell Julian and Alex..." She left it like that, knowing full well neither Julian nor Alex would leave Ryan in the dark about this little expedition.

"Nocturne?" Cyn named their favorite hangout in Harrisburg. It had been months since they'd been there.

Glory looked up through her bangs, her expression at once both innocent and sinister. Glory was the only one Cyn had ever met who could pull that look off and have it be totally believable. "Doesn't Cyn's ex-boyfriend bartend there now? The really hot one with the ripped abs and the to-die-for blue eyes?"

Cyn waved her hand dismissively. Her ex-boyfriend wasn't an issue. He wouldn't bother trying to start anything with her. And if Glory tried to start something with him Ryan would take care of it. "Old news. I'll be bringing the latest headline along, so it shouldn't be a problem."

Tabby was practically gnawing her finger through. "You think we should check with Gabe, make sure this is safe?"

"Good idea. Why don't you give him a call and tell him what we're thinking of doing." The bell over the door jangled, and Cyn turned with a smile to greet the customer. "Welcome to Living Art Tattoos. What can we help you with?"

Ryan and Alex escorted Chloe and Heather into the shop, and Cyn grinned. From the chastised look on Alex's face, it was going to be an interesting visit.

She smiled at the ladies, hiding her wince at Chloe's shorn hair. When it grew in it would be like a really cute pixie cut, but until it did the thin trace of her scars would be obvious. "What can I do for you ladies?"

Heather and Chloe exchanged a glance and both began talking at once. Cyn leaned back and enjoyed the vivacious chatter of the cousins as both girls became excited over the thought of matching, two-tailed kitsune tattoos.

At least her life was never boring.

Julian stared at the phone as if it was going to reach out and bite him in the ass. "You want to do what where now?"

"Dancing." The *duh* tone of Cyn's voice was obvious. "It's that thing you do when you move your body to music and pray you don't look like a total spaz like that woman on the *Seinfeld* reruns."

He sighed heavily and brought the phone back to his ear. "Sweetheart, did you clear this with Gabe?"

"I had the *Stupid* tattoo removed from my forehead a long time ago, Jules. He says we should be all right as long as we bring you guys with us and keep him informed if anything happens."

He thought over his schedule for the following day and realized he didn't have to be in work until the afternoon. "Sounds fun then. I'm in."

"Excellent."

"I don't suppose you could wear the Sailor Mars outfit just for me?"

"I'm planning on wearing something even better."

His heart nearly stopped even as his cock sprang to attention. "There's something *better?*" Man, his voice hadn't cracked like that since he was thirteen.

"Think leather. *Tight* leather." She chuckled, low and rough and so very Cyn. "Don't whimper like that, you'll get to see it tonight."

Damn. She'd heard. "But tonight is so very far away."

"Don't pout, Care Bear. Maybe tonight I'll rub your tummy symbol."

If he were a canine he'd have been panting. "I'm going to hold you to that."

"You might get to hold something else if you're *really* good."

Did he just whimper again? He was *dying* to get to second and third base. He figured he really would die if he ever slid home. "Did you tell Alex and Ryan where we're going?"

"Nope. Tabby might tell Alex, but we're leaving it up to you to tell Ryan. You've never seen Glory in club clothes, have you?"

He groaned. "I'm not going to like this, am I?" If Glory was going to flirt with danger, she was going to get her cute little ass bit. If Ryan caught another man's scent on her, he'd go ballistic. They'd be lucky if he didn't kill the man.

It was never a good idea to taunt a Grizzly.

Then again, he might have a way to keep Ryan occupied. "What do you think about bringing Chloe with us? Poor girl hasn't been out of her apartment for weeks except for doctor trips and physical therapy."

"Can she handle that level of noise and light?"

Julian was touched by the level of concern in Cyn's voice. "I can ask her. If she can go it might just cheer her up and keep Ryan distracted at the same time."

"Much as I might like having her there, the whole point of inviting you guys along is to protect us. If Chloe is there, Ryan will be too busy taking care of his sister."

Julian laughed. "I don't think you understand exactly how strong the mate bond is. If he thinks for even one second that someone else is trying to steal his mate that person will be twisted into a pretzel so fast not even Bear himself could stop it. He's already on red alert thanks to the attack on you. Trust me, he's going to notice every move she makes."

"And if he doesn't?"

"Then we've entered some sort of freaky alternate reality where shifters don't exist, 'cause that's the only way that's going to happen."

"If you say so." He could practically see her shrugging, dismissing Glory and Ryan's budding mating. "Will you be noticing every move I make?"

Damn. He really needed to stop whimpering. It was so…unmanly.

Chapter Nine

A woman's figure caught Julian's eye before he'd taken two steps into Nocturne. He found himself fascinated by her movements. The skin-tight black leather pants showed off a well-rounded derriere. The tight pink tank top she wore showcased slim, strong shoulders and lean, lightly muscled arms. On one wrist was a thick leather band, a huge gleaming turquoise decorating the center. Perched on her head was a black fedora with a silver band. The fedora was just the accessory she needed to showcase her multihued hair.

She danced like a woman who knew who she was and challenged every man on the dance floor to dare to take her on. One tried, and was dismissed with the wave of one slender hand and a derisive toss of her head. It was a miracle that hat didn't fly off and hit the guy, not that Julian would've minded. No one should be sliding up to his woman like that, eager to touch her. He was the only one who got that privilege, thank you. Her hair swung gently as she moved to the beat, her body twisting and writhing in a primitive rhythm that had every nerve in Julian's body standing at attention. He found himself unable to tear his eyes away from the sight of his mate as she danced with her friends.

"Holy shit. Is that—?" The shock in Alex's voice had him turning to look at the Grizzly. Alex's mouth was hanging open, his expression full of unholy glee.

"Oh *fuck* no. No, she didn't." Even over the pounding music Julian could hear that Ryan was growling. His hands fisted and his blue eyes darkened to near black.

Julian turned back to the dance floor to see what the two of them were staring at. His own jaw dropped at the sight that met his eyes. "Holy crap, is that Glory?"

And he'd thought the Sailor Mars skirt was short. She'd be more covered up wearing a bikini bottom. He might be nearly mated, but even he could admit she had a damn fine ass. He tilted his head as he stared at far more of Glory than he'd ever thought to see. That pale blue mane of hers was playing an interesting game of peek-a-boo between her butt and the men dancing around her. She'd somehow straightened the curly mass, causing it to fall nearly to her knees. Thigh high boots gave the outfit the illusion of decency. "I thought people weren't allowed to go out dancing in just their underwear."

Ryan's low growl showed the man was not amused.

"She's wearing a corset." Alex's gaze drifted over to his own mate, dressed in her own pair of skintight jeans and one of the lacy tops Tabby tended to favor.

"I noticed." If the Grizzly clenched his jaw any harder his teeth would snap.

Alex tilted his head, a slow smile drifting across his face. "Do you think she'll tell me where she got that? I'd like to get one for Tabby."

Julian eyed the corset. It was one of those strapless thingies that turned Glory's molehills into mountains. He could just imagine what it would do to Cyn's glorious breasts. "Ditto."

From the way Ryan's chest was heaving Julian figured he was two seconds away from storming the dance floor.

But then he forgot all about Ryan as Cyn caught sight of him. She crooked her finger at him with a wicked grin, daring him to join her. Julian knew his eyes had gone silver, but he didn't care. He stepped out onto the dance floor and grabbed his mate, pulling her close. He could practically smell the disappointment in the men around him as he showed that Cyn belonged to him. "Having fun?"

"Always." She glanced behind him. "Where's Chloe?"

"She decided not to come. She still tires easily."

She shimmied and he damn near moaned. Cyn looped her arms around his neck and tugged on his braid. "I should have asked you to wear your hair down."

He rolled his eyes. She had the strange obsession with his hair. "Should I have put it in curlers first?"

"Sure. I was also thinking of scheduling us for matching facials and mani-pedis."

There was only one response to that. "The one with the cucumbers over the eyes? Sign me up! I hear they do wonders for your pores."

Cyn shook her head. "I am so tattooing a purple fairy on your ass."

"I'd rather have your name." It was an ongoing argument between them, because for some strange reason she thought he was joking. He'd been trying to get her to tattoo *Property of Cyn* on his ass for weeks now, but she blocked him at every turn. Perhaps it was time he had a chat with Tabby. She might do it for him. He'd just have to make sure she didn't laugh her way through the whole tattoo. He'd hate it if it looked like it was done by a five-year-old.

They settled into an easy rhythm, moving and swaying together as if they danced with each other a thousand times before. It wasn't long before her head was resting against his chest, her hat perched on his head. Her fingers stroked through his loosened hair, combing it for him. She'd shoved the rubber band into his back pocket, copping a feel before stroking his hair once more. He let his own fingers do the walking down her back. When his hands landed on her ass he squeezed. Damn, he liked these pants. He'd have to see if he could get her to wear them on their next date night.

She tilted her head back and looked at him through her lashes. It didn't take him long to find out what she was up to. She began to nibble on the exposed skin of his throat, licking and tasting him. He shivered and tilted his head when she found an especially sensitive spot.

"Somebody likes that," she whispered, her warm breath tickling the moist spots she'd left behind.

"Oh, yeah, somebody definitely does."

He felt a tug on his hair and allowed his head to be pulled back. He was rewarded for his obedience by more warm, wet kisses. He closed his eyes, savoring the touch of his mate and the fact that she wanted him. It was hot as hell to have her taking the lead. Normally he was the one who instigated any touches or kisses. To have Cyn take the initiative made him weak in the knees. He was so hard he could probably drill holes in granite.

"Shit." She caressed the back of his head gently, and his hair swung free once more. "Imminent Grizzly attack at two o'clock."

Julian opened his eyes to find Ryan pulling a cave bear routine. He was close to shifting, he was so agitated. Glory was doing her best to ignore him, dancing with her back to him, surrounded by men who kept reaching out to touch what they shouldn't be.

Glory had no idea what she was unleashing, and if Julian didn't do something fast someone was going to die.

He allowed his other power to flow through him, the power he rarely tapped. He stepped out of Cyn's arms toward Ryan. "Calm down." He tapped in to that part of Ryan where his rage lived, soothing the beast before he could savage the humans. Ryan's back straightened, his hands unclenched and his dark brown eyes turned blue again. Julian wasn't certain how long he'd be able to hold the Grizzly, so he did the only thing he could think of. He had to get Ryan out of here. "Follow me."

He backed slowly out of the dancing crowd, his gaze never leaving Ryan's. Occasionally he would restate the command to follow, keeping the Grizzly under his control until they were out of the building and in the parking lot. He pointed to the seat of Ryan's motorcycle. "Sit."

Ryan sat, and Julian allowed his power to go back to sleep.

"What the fuck was that?" Ryan's expression was part awed, part terrified.

"The other reason Kermode stay separate from all of you." Julian joined Ryan on the seat and stared at the club, kicking one heel against the asphalt.

"Holy shit. You're Alphas. *All* of you."

Julian winced. He hated it when somebody used that title. It wasn't accurate, not in the way they meant it. "Not...exactly."

"So what are you then?" Cyn was standing before them, her arms crossed over her chest, her foot tapping to the beat they could all clearly hear. She didn't look nervous or scared, just curious. This was good, because hopefully she'd be just like him.

Julian took a deep breath. "Spirit Bears are Shamans, *not* Alphas. We have no desire to rule others, only to help them and guide them when needed." He laughed, but even he could hear the lack of humor in it. "What would I do with the whole pack of Bears?"

"Rule the world?" Ryan's tone was thoughtful. Perhaps he did have a clue what Spirit Bears could truly do if they ever set their minds to it.

One of Cyn's dark brows quirked upwards. "Steal the world's honey supply?"

Great. He'd gone from being a Care Bear to Winnie The Pooh.

Ryan darted a quick glance at him. His shoulders relaxed for the first time since they'd entered the club. "Turn salmon into an endangered species?"

"Demand toilet paper in every forest in the land?"

"Ooh, that's a good one. Because Bears do shit in the woods."

"I bet those pinecones are scratchy as hell." Cyn's expression was solemn, but Julian could see the grin trying to break free.

"You have no idea. And God forbid if you haven't figured out what poison oak looks like yet." Ryan shuddered melodramatically.

"I sense a story there."

"Not one I'm willing to tell."

Julian rolled his eyes. "Children, behave please."

Cyn batted her lashes at him. "Yes, Daddy."

"Say that again when we're alone." He heard Ryan's sigh even over Cyn's quickly muffled giggle. "Stay here and guard Cyn. I'll go fetch Glory."

Cyn's brow rose. "How are you going to get her to leave? She was having a pretty good time, and Glory loves to close the club down."

From the way Ryan's shoulders tensed once more the club would be permanently closed if they didn't get Glory out of there soon. "Don't worry about it. I've got this one covered." He patted Ryan's shoulder sympathetically. Honestly, if his mate had pulled half the stuff Glory had he wouldn't be handling it nearly as well.

He stepped once more into the club and scanned the sea of dancers looking for pale blue hair. He spotted Glory quickly and cursed under his breath. She was at the bar and flirting outrageously with the bartender. She brushed his hand and shot him a coy look, a look that clearly stated she was ready, willing and available.

She might be ready and willing, but she certainly wasn't available no matter what she thought. Julian plastered on his most innocent smile and sauntered to the bar. "Glory! I've been looking all over for you."

He could see Glory's teeth clenching as she shot him a dirty look. "Go away, Julian."

The bartender scowled. "Is this man bothering you?"

Only the genuine concern Julian could sense pouring from the man kept him from fetching Ryan. "She's a friend of my girlfriend, Cyn. We were worried about her."

The man's smile dimmed. "Cyn is here? And you're dating her?"

Now it was Julian's turn to clench his teeth. Who the hell was this guy? "I most definitely am."

Pain flashed across the bartender's features, but was quickly masked by resignation. "Oh. Well, I hope things go better for you than they did for me."

"Thanks. I'm planning on making it permanent." While Julian felt some sympathy for him, there was no way in hell he wouldn't stake his claim to Cyn. But right now he had other things to worry about. He placed his hand on Glory's shoulder, and smiled. "Time to go!"

"Ugh. I don't think so." She tried to brush his hand away but he wasn't budging. "Rude much?"

"Aren't you feeling tired? Maybe even a little dizzy?"

She wobbled on the stool, her eyes going wide with horror and suspicion. "You son of a—"

"Like I said, time to go. You'll be fine once we get a few carbs in you." He tsked and shared a look with the bartender. "She was so excited to come out tonight she forgot to eat."

He could tell the bartender wasn't buying it, but when Julian waved to Tabby and got a wave back the bartender backed down. Julian helped Glory down from the stool, wrapping one arm around her waist when it was obvious she couldn't stand on her own. When they were far enough away from the friendly bartender she growled at him. "When I get changed into a Puma I'm going to eat your face off."

Was she still going on about that? Ryan would never allow anyone, not even Emma, to change his mate, no matter how many times the Puma Curana offered. "Aw, you're so cute. Sort of like a rabid weevil. With anthrax."

She tried to stomp on his foot but missed horribly, nearly sending them both to the pavement. "I *hate* Bears."

"Is that any way to speak to your future pseudo-brother-in-law?" She growled again and Julian laughed. By the time they reached Ryan she was beating him with tiny, ineffectual fists. He deposited her on Ryan's lap. "Yours, I believe."

"Whether she likes it or not." Ryan's eyes had begun to take on chocolaty tones again, sort of like a half-melted blue M&M.

"Not!" Glory struggled to get out of Ryan's arms, but he wasn't letting go of his prize any time soon.

Julian watched her wriggle, and nearly burst into laughter. Now he remembered who she reminded him of. "By the ancestors, I get it now."

Cyn wrapped an arm around his waist and Julian pulled her close, cuddling her up against his side. "Get what?"

"The blue hair."

"What about it?"

They both watched as Glory slumped over Ryan's arms and panted for a few seconds before renewing her struggles.

"She's Super Grover."

Glory snarled at them both as he and Cyn collapsed together in a cackling heap of oh-shit-you're-right.

How in the hell had she wound up here?

Marie Howard held out the wicker basket. "Breadstick?"

She stared from the basket to the woman and back again. "Why the hell not?" She picked up one of the garlicky, buttery pieces of heaven and bit in. Noah's had the *best* food, but it wasn't exactly what she'd expected to eat for lunch today. Cyn's salami and provolone sandwich was currently sitting in the fridge back at Living Art Tattoos, "stinking up the place" as Tabby put it. When the invitation for lunch had arrived from Marie she'd been startled, but intrigued.

If Marie had told Cyn she was taking her to Noah's she would at least have grabbed her fedora. As it was, she felt woefully underdressed. A black tank top and jeans weren't exactly the classiest thing to wear to a place like this.

"Are you all right? I heard about what happened at your shop. Jamie was worried about you."

Cyn smiled. Jamie and Julian were becoming good friends. Making nice with Marie made sense, even if they had nothing in common. They were going to wind up spending at least some time together, thanks to their men. This was a good place to start learning about one another. "I'm good. Super Bear fixed me up just fine."

"That's good to know." Marie twisted the breadstick, jumping as it fell apart. She dusted off her fingers, her gaze glued to her plate. Cyn had never seen anyone so nervous in her life. "So."

She stared at Marie, waiting. It was obvious she was up to something, but Cyn had no clue what it could be. Marie was toying with half her breadstick, ripping it to tiny crumbs. "So?"

Marie loomed up with a grimace. She took a deep breath. "So. You and Emma are friends, right?"

Oh. Huh. This was not quite what Cyn had expected. She'd thought that it was a get to know my mate's friend's mate lunch, not...whatever the hell this was. "Maybe? I'm not sure." The Puma Curana was a hard one to figure out, at least for Cyn. She had a way of bowling everyone in her path over, and for some reason the people she ordered around actually felt *grateful* for it. Cyn just didn't get it, or her, but she had to admit it was fun whenever Emma came by LA. The bikers especially adored the Little General. "I like her, except when I don't, if that makes any sense."

Marie laughed. "I think it does. She's a force of nature." She blushed. "Look, can I trust you?"

Cyn nodded. She didn't know if what Marie wanted to talk about was good or bad, but if it affected Marie, then it affected Jamie. If it affected Jamie, then it had the potential to affect Julian, and Cyn wouldn't have that.

"Oh. Good." Marie blew out her breath, but Cyn could tell she still wasn't entirely comfortable. "This is Pride business, okay? You can't let anyone know I talked to you about it."

Cyn mimed zipping her lips shut.

Marie grinned. "Thanks. Emma and I, we..." She gulped again. "We had a falling out early on in her reign. Now we're cordial, but not nearly as close as we used to be."

"It has something to do with Belinda Campbell, right?" Marie winced at the name of the Poconos Pack Luna, and Cyn nodded. "I thought that might be it. Even I've heard of how Belle left Halle in a cloud of suspicion. What the hell happened?"

Marie sighed and took a sip of her soda. "Belinda was so close to Livia, I thought for sure she was in on the plot. I mean, she was Livia's best friend. How could she not know?"

Cyn tilted her head, confused. "Plot?"

Before Marie could answer the waiter came by to take their order. Cyn ordered her favorite, the lasagna, while Marie went for the pasta e fagioli and a salad. Once the waiter was gone Marie answered her question. "When Max claimed Emma as his Curana, Livia was furious. She thought she should be the Curana, always did. She was just waiting for Max to return home from college before she mated him."

"I thought mates were destined by fate." Cyn ate another breadstick, fascinated by this insight into the local shifters. After all, she'd be joining them soon.

"Usually, yes. But if you don't meet your mate by the time you're thirty, it's safe to assume you never will. Most people will choose to mate with someone they fall in love with rather than wait any longer. It's not a true mating, but I've known people who lived very happy lives with their chosen spouse."

"What happens if the mate actually shows up?"

Marie shivered. "I have no idea, but it can't be good." She smiled at the nice young man who brought her salad. "Anyway, Livia wanted Max, Max wanted Emma, and Max took Emma."

Cyn laughed. "Max *took* Emma?"

"Alphas can be pretty strong-willed."

"That explains why she calls him Captain Caveman." Cyn waggled her eyebrows, happy when Marie laughed.

"Anyway, Max wasn't going to give Emma the chance to say no. He marked her before he told her what he was, and from all accounts she took it pretty well." Marie finished her salad and pushed the empty plate aside. "When Livia found out who the new Curana was, she went nuts and attacked Emma's best friend Becky, hoping to get the Curana's ring off Emma's finger."

"What ring? And why Becky?" This Pride shit was confusing as hell. Thank God Julian was a Bear. Since Bears lived in family groups rather than Packs or Prides, Cyn wouldn't have to deal with this kind of crap very often.

Then again, I haven't met his parents yet. Maybe I should reserve judgment until I do. For all she knew the DuCharmes were just as insane as the Bunsuns.

"Puma Alphas wear rings signifying their status. Since there are only two cat species who form Prides, the ancient Pumas decided to follow the example of their Lion brothers and sisters, who also wear rings, rather than the Wolves and Coyotes, who don't."

"Why is that, anyway? That's been bugging the shit out of me." Cougars were solitary cats in the wild, so why did the shifter Pumas form a Pride?

Marie grinned. "I love telling this story. Let's see. It's said that, long ago, the spirits chose humans to meld with, creating the first shifters. The Lions were first, making the Leo the ruler of us all. He formed the first Pride, his Lion instincts driving him."

"In other words, his cat wanted its harem."

Marie coughed. "*So* not going there." Cyn chuckled, and Marie continued. "Anyway, the Wolves and Coyotes also formed Packs, the Bears and Foxes had their family groups, but most of the cats, they were solitary creatures who preferred to live alone. The Wolf Alpha received the ability to talk to anyone in his Pack. The Leo, he could command anyone, and I mean *anyone*, because he was the shifter King. All Lion Alphas have that ability to some extent, but none stronger than the Leo.

Foxes could hide better than anyone, Bears could heal, Coyotes got the gift of sensing lies, et cetera. Anyway, when it came time for the first Pumas to ask for their gift, they took a look around, pointed at the Lions, and said basically 'We want that.'"

"What they meant was the ability to command others, right?"

Marie shook her head. "Nope. They wanted the safety of numbers that a Pride gave the Lions. So, even though it's not in the puma's nature to bond in that way, all Puma Prides have the same structure as a Lion one. When the more solitary shifters were hunted for rights to their land by other shifters, only the Pumas and the Lions were able to hold on to their territory. The Tigers were hunted to near extinction; only the intervention of the Leo prevented it."

Cyn whistled. "That's...damn."

"Yeah. I don't think any Puma has truly regretted the bargain the first made with the spirits. We *like* our Prides, thank you very much." Marie shrugged. "So Emma is the Curana, ring or no, but not everyone understands that the ring is just a symbol. If it fell down the drain tomorrow Emma would *still* be Curana. Nothing would change that."

"Let me guess. Livia didn't believe that."

"Not one little bit. She also knew Emma would do almost anything to protect Becky except give up Max." Marie shook her head. "Livia never understood what being the Curana truly meant. You can't be the Curana without being the mate of the Alpha. A female Puma who leads a Pride is called an Alpha, *not* Curana. So when Livia attacked Becky and pretty much ordered Emma to surrender the ring and her position as Curana, it wasn't Emma's title Livia was threatening, it was her bond with Max."

"And you don't threaten a mate bond." Cyn understood. Just watching the way Alex was with Tabby, the way Ryan watched Glory, had taught her that much.

"Nope. Not without severe repercussions. Livia believed that if Emma handed over the ring the Pride would view her as being weak. She thought the Pride would force Max to name her Curana in Emma's stead, making her Max's mate and Emma Max's piece on the side. Add in the fact that Livia had hurt Becky, and Emma was *pissed*. We were in the ballroom and they were in the garden, and we could still feel just how ticked off Emma was. She used her powers to force Livia to obey her, proving once and for all that she was the Curana, ring or no ring."

"I bet that went over really well."

"Rumor has it that Livia was fit to be tied, but it no longer mattered what she felt. Max Outcast her, and each of us could feel that bond sever, no matter how far away we were." Marie grimaced. "Here's where it gets a little tricky. See, everyone believed Belinda knew what was going on, since she'd been in the house trying to pick up Simon." Marie shook her head, her expression grim.

Cyn frowned, still somewhat confused. Belinda "Belle" Lowell, once Campbell, was the Luna of the Poconos Pack. What the hell did she have to do with all of this? "Wait. You think because they were friends Belle was in on Livia's plans to attack Becky?"

"They weren't just friends, they were *best* friends."

"But didn't I hear that *you* were friends with Livia? Wouldn't that make you suspect too?"

"We were friends, but not best friends. I mean, what *don't* Tabby and Glory know about you?"

Cyn thought about that for a moment. "Not much, but if I were about to go postal on the Mayor I might not tell them about it first. They'd probably guess if I was upset or angry, but not that I was about to do something so monumentally stupid."

"Why not?"

Cyn shrugged. "Because I wouldn't want them in trouble with me."

Marie gaped. "You're joking. Right?"

"Nope." She was serious. If she ever went off the rails like that she wouldn't want to drag Glory and Tabby down with her. They'd suffered enough in their lives.

Besides, they were her family.

"Huh." Marie shrugged. "I don't think Livia was ever that altruistic."

"Perhaps." Cyn tapped her fork against her plate. "It's also possible she thought Belle would rat her out. Let's face it, from what I've heard Belle has more than proven her loyalty to the Pride. It could be that Livia pointed her toward Simon without once mentioning why she was supposed to be distracting him." Cyn tore into another breadstick. Damn, they were *good.* Almost as good as the lasagna. "Wasn't Belle in love with Simon? I'm pretty sure she could have been persuaded to keep him occupied." Even Cyn had heard of Belinda and Simon; she'd been in the same high school, just a year or two behind Belle.

"She *was* in love with him. Desperately." Marie stroked her forehead. "Maybe you're right. But I wasn't the only one who thought Belle had betrayed our alphas. Most of the Pride agreed with me."

"What did they do?" God, the lasagna here was *incredible.* She'd have to drag Super Bear's butt here sometime soon. The best part was there were no Bears or Foxes in sight.

"Everyone practically shunned Belinda." Cyn noticed that Marie never once called the Luna Belle the way everyone else did. It was as if she refused to admit that Belle wasn't the woman she'd always thought her to be. "But she helped Becky when she got sick, then sacrificed herself to save Sheri, and attitudes started to change. Emma and Becky both agreed that Belinda hadn't done anything wrong. Even Max and Simon believed her."

"But you don't."

Marie shook her head. "I'm sorry, I don't. She had to see something was going on that night. It's like those women who marry serial killers. How can they not know that their husbands are crazy?"

"Sometimes you see what you want to see, instead of what's right in front of you." Cyn had lived with someone just like that. Her mother had adored everything about her father, even the things that weren't good for her. Oh, her father had never been abusive, but he'd controlled every aspect of their lives. Her mother had fallen apart after his death, and was still picking up the pieces.

Marie shrugged. "True."

"So what does this have to do with my friendship with Emma?"

"I'm hoping you could put in a good word for me." Marie winced. "It's a lot to ask, but this isn't just about me anymore. There are a number of Pumas who feel the same way I do about Belinda, but none of us want the Curana's anger directed at us. We just want to heal the breech in the Pride." She stared at Cyn, her gaze determined, and sad. "It's gone on too long."

Cyn had no clue what she could do to ease Marie's pain. The woman had obviously brought this on herself. "Have you apologized?"

"Should I apologize for something I believe to be true?"

"If Belle proved to her Alphas beyond a shadow of a doubt that she was innocent, shouldn't you grant her the courtesy of belief?"

Marie took a deep breath, then let it out in a rush. "I'll give it some thought."

"I hate to say it, but I think the healing needs to come from you, and all the ones who feel the way you do. I think you're the only ones who can end it."

Marie nodded slowly, but it was obvious she was unhappy about it. "I'll talk to them. Thanks, Cyn." She smiled softly. "I think we're going to be good friends." Marie suddenly grinned. "Now, on to more important things." She leaned forward, her gaze darting to Cyn's neck. "When is that hunka hunka going to mark you?" She waggled her brows with a lecherous grin.

Cyn snorted, amused. "Please. He hasn't been properly trained yet."

Marie laughed. "Call me if you need any pointers. Those men of ours need to be reminded who really rules the roost. Oh!" She started digging through her purse. "I have the cutest little safari hat you can borrow.

Cyn giggled as Marie shoved a cell phone in her hand. On it was a picture of Marie, safari hat perched on her head, her mate at her side. "Are those bear ears?"

"Yup. I totally made him dance too."

"You're nuts." But she was Cyn's kind of nuts. Marie was right; they were going to be good friends.

Satisfied that her Dr. Phil moment was over for the week, she polished off her lasagna and wondered what Julian would have to say about all of this.

She pushed thoughts of Julian aside for later. Right now, she had tiramisu to conquer.

Chapter Ten

"I'm glad you didn't have any trouble while you were out last night." Gabe Anderson snatched the tapping pencil out of Tabby's fingers. "I still think it was reckless, though."

"That's not what Glory told me you said." Cyn rolled her eyes and thought about how insane her friend was being. "I hate to say this, I mean I *really* hate to say this, but I think somebody should just bite her ass." Maybe then she'd get over the massive cranky fit she was having.

"You're just saying that because I've been singing Weird Al Yankovic all morning." Glory smirked at them as she worked on the belly button ring display.

Cyn turned and glared at her. "This is revenge for the Super Grover comment."

Glory's baby blues went wide with fake innocence. "Can I help it if I love 'Perform This Way'?"

Gabe cleared his throat, gaining their attention once more. "I'll be checking in regularly with you ladies, but just in case here's my cell number. Call me if anything seems to be even remotely off. Until we find out what these guys are after I'm not going to risk your safety." Gabe tossed the pencil back to Tabby and sauntered out of the shop.

Glory set the display back in the case and dusted off her hands. "Be right back. Feel free to talk about me while I'm gone."

"What the hell is up with her?" Tabby's accent had thickened into a deep Georgia drawl, an indication of exactly how upset she was. "She's acting like a total brat."

"It's that whole don't tie-me-down thing that's tripping her up."

"Maybe I should change her." Rat-a-tat-tat went Tabby's pencil. "Maybe then she'll understand why Ryan's close to losing it."

"Might not be a bad idea. If she feels that mate pull you guys talk about she'll stop fighting it so hard."

"At least you've stopped fighting it."

Cyn shrugged. She couldn't say she'd completely stopped fighting it, but it was more girl slap now than *Gears of War.* Julian was proving he was nothing like her father, and she was proving to herself she was nothing like her mother. Now if only she could get over the fear that he'd do a complete one-eighty once he bit her they'd be golden.

"Did I tell you, Micah called me again?" Tabby's tapping pencil picked up speed.

The new Alpha of Tabby's old Pack had been relentless in his attempts to try and speak with her. "Did you pick up the phone this time?"

"Hell, no. Alex still wants to go down there and find Dennis Boyd and rip him a new one. You think I'm really going to open up that can of whoop-ass on the Marietta Pack?"

Cyn shrugged. "What about your parents, have they called too?"

Tabby snorted. "Please. They tossed me away like last week's garbage. Even if they wanted to speak to me, I don't want to speak to them." She wrinkled her nose as if smelling the garbage she spoke of. "Besides, my pack and my family are here."

As long as Tabby was happy, Cyn didn't give a rat's ass if her friend never spoke to her biological family again. "In that case the next time he calls, tell him to fuck off."

"Genteelly, of course." She picked up the pencil and stared at it cross eyed.

"Uh-huh." What the hell was Tabby doing?

"Because I'm a lady." She sniffed along the pencil, starting when she poked her nose with the tip.

"More like a puppy. Don't eat that, you don't know where it's been."

Cyn ducked as Tabby threw the pencil at her head. She sniffed the air in short staccato bursts, then snorted much like a dog would. "What is that funky smell?"

The sound of a toilet flushing made Cyn giggle.

"Not that!" Tabby's nose scrunched up. "Although that's pretty ripe too."

Glory stepped out from behind the employees' only curtain and eyed Cyn, who was still giggling like a loon. "What the hell is wrong with her?"

"Do you smell something funky?"

Glory blushed and dug her toe into the worn linoleum. "Um, yeah, I'm sorry about that. See, I had cheese with lunch, and—"

"No! It doesn't smell...biological."

Cyn took a deep breath, but all she could smell was the shop itself. It was a combination of ink and paper and dust and glass cleaner, just like always. "I don't smell anything."

Tabby's nose wrinkled. "You can't smell that? It's like, kind of, ick." She was practically gagging. She pulled the edge of her shirt away from her neck and pulled it up to her nose, sniffing cautiously.

"Are you smelling coffee again?" Recently the smell of coffee made Tabby nauseous. Thank God she wasn't living in the apartment anymore. Glory would've had to kill her. Glory without her morning coffee was like the Terminator without John Connor—bat-shit insane and absolutely lethal.

Tabby wrinkled her nose in disgust. "No, it's not coffee. I don't think I've ever smelled anything quite like it before."

Cyn looked over at Glory who shook her head. "I can't smell a thing."

Cyn bit her lip, but it really wasn't that hard a decision to make. "I think this qualifies as anything weird. Call Gabe."

"On it." Glory pulled out her cell phone. She must have put the sheriff on speed dial, because within two seconds she was talking to him.

"I'm going to find where the hell that's coming from." Tabby stalked out from behind the counter and headed toward the back, into the employee–only area. "What is it?" She was muttering to herself as she followed the scent to the back door.

Cyn stuck to her like glue. No way was she letting Tabby go out there by herself. She grabbed hold of Tabby's arm. "Let's wait for Gabe."

Tabby's eyes had turned golden brown, her Wolf's eyes. "I have a *really* bad feeling about this."

She trusted Tabby's instincts. They'd sharpened since her friend had gotten pregnant. Cyn pulled Tabby back and away from the door. "Let's get out of here."

Glory was already out front, waiting for them. "I was just about to go in to pull you guys out. Gabe wants us to wait out here for him. He also wants to know what it smelled like."

"It was plastic and metal and...motor oil? Maybe? And something I can't even describe."

Gabe pulled up to the curb, lights flashing but sirens silent. He got out of his cruiser and sprinted toward the girls. "All right, Tabby, come with me." He pulled Tabby off to the side and whispered in her ear. Tabby in turn whispered back.

Gabe paled and pushed Tabby toward the street. "You three, get across the street *now*." He then sprinted for the back of the shop at breakneck speed.

Cyn didn't need to be told twice. She ran across the street and into the dry cleaners. "What the fuck is going on?"

Gabe came running back from around the corner of the building, his expression grim. He leaned into the cruiser, but Cyn couldn't see what he was doing.

Before too long he was jogging across the street. "Follow me."

Cyn, Tabby and Glory followed him to the corner. "Listen carefully." He was talking so softly Cyn could barely hear him. "I think there's a pipe bomb at your back door."

"A *what*?" Cold fury rushed through her. Whoever was after them had gone too far. A pipe bomb wouldn't just do property damage. The damn things were meant to kill people.

"I've already sent for the bomb squad. I want you girls to wait here until I tell you otherwise."

Cyn clenched her fists. "Tabby, did you scent Cheetah again?"

"No. It was...strange. Not human, I know that." She rubbed her nose. "It's really weird. I'd swear I smelled deer."

Cyn's brows rose in surprise. "There are deer shifters?"

"No. That's what's so strange about it. I could scent deer and charcoal and wool, but nothing else."

"Was that the scent that you couldn't describe?" Glory was playing with her hair, twisting the curls around her fingers over and over again. She was scared, and desperately trying not to show it.

"No. Maybe it was the explosive I smelled." Tabby groaned as a familiar motorcycle pulled up in front of them. "I didn't do anything."

The smile in Alex's face was easy-going, but his dark brown bear's eyes betrayed his uneasiness. "Tell me my mate wasn't threatened *again*."

Gabe sighed and pinched the bridge of his nose. "It's going to be a long day, isn't it?"

Alex spun on his heel and marched toward the tattoo shop. Tabby raced after him and latched onto his arm. "No, Alex!"

"Come back here so I can explain everything to you." Gabe grabbed hold of Alex's other arm. "Look over there. My deputies are starting to clear out the businesses around the tattoo shop. You *can't* go over there right now."

Alex growled but allowed himself to be led away. By the time they were done telling him everything that had happened Alex was sitting on the seat of his motorcycle, Tabby firmly on his lap. Dark five-inch claws had sprouted from his fingertips and drummed restlessly over her stomach. Tabby had her hands over his, trying to hide them as the sidewalk filled with humans. "This is getting ridiculous."

"I agree. But hopefully this time they royally screwed up." Gabe nodded toward the street. "Here comes the bomb squad. Maybe now we'll have some answers."

Cyn was shaking by the time the heavily padded men came back from around the shop. Between them was a black box, one she assumed held the pipe bomb.

"With any luck those idiots left fingerprints behind." Gabe's grin was feral; the Hunter in him had come to the fore. "I'll call you as soon as I have some news."

"Since when does Halle have a bomb squad?" Glory tugged hard enough on her curls to wince. "Now what?"

Cyn started across the street. "Now we go back to work." She ignored Glory's grumbling. How long would it be before whoever was after them decided to go to their homes? So far they only targeted the shop, but Cyn knew that couldn't last. At some point or another the bad guys would figure out that the three of them were too well guarded there.

It was time to try and lure them into the open. But how? She couldn't endanger Tabby or Glory, and if Julian found out she'd turned herself into bait he'd have a cow. Against a human attacker she had every confidence in herself, but she was facing shifters.

She paused, her hand on the knob, the door halfway open. The sound of the bell was still ringing in her ears.

Perhaps it was time she *really* went out for a bite.

"Bite me."

Julian stared at his mate and tried to hold back his frustrated groan. He should have guessed the moment she pulled him into the back room that she'd be demanding he change her. He'd seen how pale she was the moment he'd stepped through the door. When he'd gotten news of the pipe bomb he'd raced out of work like his ass was on fire. But instead of trembling and allowing Ryan to calm her like Glory or cuddling with her mate like Tabby, she'd demanded he mate her.

This was *not* the way he'd wanted to mark her. He'd planned on candlelight, decadent food and a full-on seduction. Instead he was in a dusty back room full of tattoo ink and needles, with nary a soft surface in sight so he could sink into her properly.

She snapped her fingers in his face. "Now, Julian. Let's get this over with. I have work to do."

She had to be shitting him. "Excuse me?"

"You heard me. Make with the fang." She pointed at her neck. "Do I need to mark the spot or something?"

He crossed his arms over his chest and prepared himself for a battle. "No."

She echoed his movement and almost distracted him. He couldn't help it if his eyes were drawn to the bounty her arms now hid. "What happened to wanting a taste?"

He hoped his expression told her exactly how he felt about her request, because if he opened his mouth right then he'd say something he'd regret. He had a pretty good idea why she was doing this, which was not a mark in her favor.

Cyn sighed wearily. "I'm not saying we're going to stop dating. I'm asking for safety." She waved her arms toward the curtains that hid them from the rest of the shop. "Tabby's pregnant and Glory is...Glory." Her eyes pled with him. "Please, Julian. Give me what I need to take care of them."

Fuck. She was pulling out the big guns. That stubborn determination to protect what was hers was part of her appeal, but it could get her seriously hurt if he didn't rein her in. "I can't." He held up his hand to stifle her immediate protest. "Look, there are things I haven't told you yet. Becoming like me is different from becoming a Wolf or a Puma, or even another Bear. It isn't just a bite."

"Let me guess. It's a Kermode thing and I wouldn't understand."

"Oh, you'll understand. Trust me. But if I'm going to bite you, it has to be done correctly." Not in a dusty back room. Not when she was this angry and afraid. If she thought she was hiding her fear from him, she was sadly mistaken. He could smell it pouring from her skin.

"Fine. What do we need to do?"

"I'll come to your place tonight. I give you my word I'll explain everything then." He stroked her cheek, unable to stop himself from touching her. He was tired of seeing her hurt; it had been bad enough when one of Gary's goons had clocked her, but seeing her broken jaw had driven home how much worse it could have been if Tabby hadn't been there. "Trust me."

"You say that a lot." But she pressed her cheek into his palm, reassuring him he was doing the right thing. Throwing her to Bear without some preparation would earn him a lot more grief than asking her to wait a few hours. "Fine. But I expect to be fuzzy by morning, got it?"

"It doesn't work quite that way. It will be a few days before your first shift."

She eyed him dubiously. "Will I sprout fur in the middle of the Save-A-Lot?"

"You could." He shrugged. "I was born this way, so I'm not sure. My parents knew it was coming and kept me isolated until after the change struck. I do remember it was sudden. Nothing like watching reruns of Gilligan's Island and popping fur in the middle of one of Ginger's scenes."

From the look on her face she wasn't touching that statement with a ten-foot pole. Darn it. "Then maybe I'll pay Emma a visit. Max changed her, so she might have a better idea of what to expect."

"Not a bad idea. While you're at it you can tell the Pride that there's going to be a new Bear in town."

Her brows rose. "Me?"

"Me. I'm applying for citizenship as soon as I'm allowed to." It would be two long years before he could apply for a green card, but it would be worth it.

The quickly hidden pleasure made the wait worthwhile. "You're staying?"

"Aren't you?"

That earned him a smile, and a proud lift of that stubborn chin. "Good." She took hold of his shoulders and turned him around. "If I'm not getting what I want then you need to get going."

He sighed dramatically, though inside he was ecstatic. She'd accepted his terms, and they'd both get what they wanted. "You only want me for my fangs."

"Yup. I harbor a secret vampire fetish. Didn't I tell you?"

"Vampires aren't real," he scoffed.

"Neither are shifters." With that she pushed him the rest of the way out of the back room. "Go rest!"

Rest. Right. Not happening, not if he was introducing his mate to Bear that night. Julian nodded to Alex and waited for the Grizzly to say his good-byes to Tabby. On the way out the door he whispered, "White or dark?"

"Hmm?"

"Chocolate."

Tabby grinned. "Dark. As dark as they make and still call it sweet."

"Cool."

"But Cyn prefers milk."

Was it just him or did all the women at Living Art Tattoos have the same evil grin?

He followed Alex out of the tattoo parlor and headed for the Harley Alex babied almost as much as he babied Tabby. "I'm marking her tonight."

121

Alex stumbled. "Oh."

"Yeah."

"Is she ready for that?"

Julian put the helmet on and shrugged. "Nope."

"In that case I have two words for you. Protective gear."

Julian had to concede the man had a point.

The bell jingled, announcing Cyn to the occupants of Wallflowers. She took a look around and tried to evaluate the place from a shopkeeper's perspective.

The ladies had certainly gotten the atmosphere right. Wallflowers specialized in anything that could hang on a wall. Hand crafted mirrors, masks, paintings, clocks; all sorts of things covered the walls, all with discreet price tags. An antique rug covered the distressed hardwood floors. A small Victorian sofa covered in soft cream brocade was placed in the center of the room, inviting people to sit and chat with the owners. A Queen Anne coffee table in rich cherry wood sat before it with a silver tea set. Two Victorian chairs in that same cream fabric faced the sofa, creating a cozy little conversation group that Emma and Becky used to hold court. Against one wall was a gas fireplace with an ornately carved mantelpiece.

Rumor had it the elaborate art piece over it had been crafted by Becky's mate, Simon, an artisan glassworker. Cyn salivated over it every time she saw it, the vibrant blues and greens contrasting nicely with the rose wallpaper. On that mantelpiece were silver-framed photos, all of them either black and white or sepia toned. A cherry and glass counter graced one wall. On it sat an old-fashioned-looking cash register. Cyn bet the credit card scanner was hidden underneath the counter.

Every time she came in here it was like she was being smacked upside the head with her femininity. She had the strangest urge to head home, put on a dress, and come back when she was presentable.

"Cyn! Oh my God, are you all right?" Becky dashed out from behind the counter, her eyes wide with worry, her long, frizzy hair practically standing on end. "We heard what happened."

"Yeah, I'm fine." She stroked her jaw without thinking. "Julian healed the damage and Gabe's looking into the attack."

"And then someone leaves a pipe bomb behind your store. What the hell is going on?"

"Wish I knew so I could find them and kick their asses." Cyn was done with this bullshit. Next person who threatened her people was going down hard.

Becky gestured to the sofa and the women sat. "Emma's not here right now, but I called her. She's seriously upset and wants to know if there's anything we can do for you."

Cyn blinked. That was more support than she'd thought she'd get. She wasn't one of the kitties, or even a shifter, but Becky and Emma were responding as if she were. "Thanks. Actually, I came here because...well, because Julian's going to mark me tonight."

She'd never met someone who could actually squee, but Becky did, loud enough to make Cyn's eyes cross. "Omigod, congratulations!" Becky tackle-hugged her, smothering Cyn in enough curly hair to make Lady Godiva proud.

"Thanks." Cyn tried not to spit out the curl that landed in her mouth. She didn't think that would be polite. "I need your advice. Can you explain to me what the change feels like for a human?"

Becky sat back. It took her hair a few seconds longer. "Ah. You want to know about the first change, or about the bite itself?"

"Either. Both." Cyn ran her fingers through her hair. "I'm not sure. Tabby shifted to protect me, and I can't have that." She got up and started to pace. "She's pregnant. I can't take the risk that she'll get hurt and lose the baby."

"Damn." Becky sat back. "You think this is another shifter attack, like what happened to Chloe."

"I'm positive it is. Tabby smelled cat, and not the local brand." Cyn stared at Becky and chewed her lip. "I need to be able to protect Tabby. Hell, I need to be able to protect Super Bear. He's been pushing himself again."

"Super Bear?" Becky snorted a laugh. "Okay, ask your questions and I'll answer as best I can."

"What's the change feel like?"

The Puma sat back on the sofa and crossed her thin legs. "Hmm. Let me think. I remember feeling kind of restless, like I was caged and couldn't get out. I marked Simon and didn't even realize it while we were—" She blushed bright red. "Um. But I think the first thing that changed were my eyes."

"Your eyes?"

"Yeah. Pumas don't see all the colors of the spectrum, so when I realized I couldn't see what color Simon's shirt was anymore I realized my eyes had changed."

"I wonder what colors bears see."

"Not sure. You'll have to ask Julian. Your eyes are already dark, so you might not even notice the change at first."

"But if they turn gray, like Julian's, someone will point it out, right?"

"I doubt Julian will leave you alone during your first change, and Dr. Howard might want to check you out as well. You'll be the first Bear shifter created in Halle and he'll be *dying* to get his claws into you."

Great. Just what Cyn needed. She'd be a giant, furry lab rat for an overly curious kitty. "What else?"

"Teeth and claws will come after your eyes change. But the change will be upon you when fur sprouts from your arms. You'd better be naked by then too, because this isn't some werewolf movie where your clothes magically disappear. You'll either rip right through them or hurt yourself trying to squirm free of them."

"Oh." Cyn sat on the sofa and grinned at the Beta. "So this was all just an excuse for Julian to get me naked."

"Funny, I said something similar just before my change." Becky held up her hand. "Hold on, phone's ringing."

What? Cyn hadn't heard—

The phone rang, and Becky answered. "Wallflowers, Becky speaking. How may I— Hey, Simon." A soft smile crossed Becky's face. "Sure, baby. I've eaten. Uh-huh. Glucose levels are good, I swear. Mm-hmm. Yes, I love you too. Bye."

"You're diabetic?"

"Hmm? Oh! No, I'm severely hypoglycemic. Be right back." Becky left the room and came back quickly with a glass of orange juice. "I had a nasty surprise right after Simon and I mated. I wound up in the hospital with low blood sugar after having hallucinations that an apple was trying to kill me."

And she thought Julian was weird. Maybe it was best to get Becky back to the topic that interested Cyn the most. "The bite. What does that feel like?"

Becky smiled. "The best god-damn orgasm of your life."

Now it was Cyn's turn to blush. "Oh."

"Yeah." Becky sipped from her juice, but her expression was wicked. "*Big* O."

The women exchanged a look before bursting into laughter.

Chapter Eleven

They pulled up outside Julian's house that evening in silence. Cyn was startled to find her hands were shaking. She was *so* not ready for this.

"It will be all right, Cyn."

His deep voice washed over her, attempted to soothe her, but there was no calming her. She was getting something she'd been begging for these last few weeks, and now that it was finally happening her damn nerves were getting the better of her. She lifted her chin, determined not to let Julian see how anxious she was. "Sure it will."

Julian shook his head and got out of the car. Cyn followed him at a slower pace up the walkway and through the front door. "Are we going to eat before we start? I'm starving."

"No." He hung his jacket up and took hers, placing it beside his own with an odd air of satisfaction. "You might puke it back up."

"Funny. None of the ladies mentioned puking as a side effect of the bite."

He grinned and led her into the living room. "That's because none of them were Kermode."

"Lovely." She took a seat on his sofa and glared at him. "So other ladies get mind blowing orgasms. I get to blow chunks."

The darkly sensual look he shot her should have melted her on the spot. "Oh, you'll get the orgasm. Trust me on that one." Julian settled next to her, far too close for her peace of mind. "But there are...side effects that occur when a Kermode attempts to change a human."

Her brows shot up. "Attempts?"

He sighed and tugged on his braid, a sure sign he wasn't as comfortable talking about this as he appeared to be on the surface. "I'm not allowed to go in to too much detail about what happens after the mating bite." He dropped his braid and took hold of her hand. "The absolute worst that could happen is you'll wake up unchanged and puking."

"The best?"

He kissed her palm. "You'll be like me."

She was still shaking. At least he wasn't trying to hide anything from her. "I thought the change was sort of a done deal once you sank fang into flesh."

"Not for Kermode."

"Because you're special."

"Yup. There are prices we pay to be what we are. Only a few learn what that means. Our mates are some of those few."

"Wait. Did I say we were mating tonight?"

That feral light was back in his eyes, the silver sparks widening until his irises were completely gray. A broad streak of white grew in his hair. "Yes."

The shaking got worse. She was *so* not ready for this. But what else could she do? "Fine. Let's get this over with."

"You're such a romantic." He stole a soft kiss. "Are you ready?"

Suddenly she couldn't sit still a second longer. She hopped up and began to pace like a caged tiger. "No. I'm not ready, damn it." She pulled her hair, hoping the pain would help her focus. "Shit. I'm tying my life force to yours for what, eternity? And we haven't even gotten past first base."

"I could remedy that before I bite you. Hell, I'm willing and able. Very able."

She whirled on him and pointed. "Favorite color."

"Lately? Pink. Used to be blue."

She flushed but refused to allow his response to throw her. He was staring at her hair again, his fingers twitching like he wanted to touch the pink, blonde and black strands. "Favorite food?"

"Blueberry muffins."

"Your—"

"Gemini, hockey, yellow gold, anything written by Joss Whedon, The Wheel of Time series and Jessica Alba." One eyebrow rose arrogantly. "Anything else?"

Her finger dropped. "You *like* the Wheel of Time books?"

"You don't?"

She shuddered.

"Oh. Well, let's just forget the whole thing then." He propped his hands on his hips. "And here I thought Jessica would be the deal-breaker."

"You're a Gemini. That alone is enough to make me think twice. You people are schizo."

"Says the fiery, temperamental Aries. At least you'll keep me on my toes, right?"

"Which set, oh Gemini? Good twin's or evil twin's?"

"Both." Julian was stalking her around the room, his eyes intent, silver-flecked. She didn't even realize she'd begun backing away from him until she banged into his coffee table. "I can smell you. Your need calls to me. I bet you're ripe for me, all plump and juicy."

Cyn stopped retreating. "You make me sound like a Ball Park Frank."

Some of the feral need on Julian's face dissipated, his quirky sense of humor coming to the fore. "Not quite the imagery I was going for. I'm not that in to wieners."

"So you *are* into wieners, then?"

"NO! Gah. No." Julian shuddered. "Not... Shit. Can I just bite you now?"

She took a deep breath and a flying leap of faith. "Thought you'd never ask."

Julian didn't pounce the way she thought he would, taking her down like a wounded deer. Instead, he reached out and cradled her neck in his hand. "This might sting a bit. If it does, I'm sorry."

She smiled and hoped it wasn't showing just how shaky she was. "Just do it already."

His eyes turned pure silver, filled with desire. He bent down and nibbled her neck, sending shivers down her spine. "You smell so good."

Cyn shuddered as his lips brushed against her skin. She wrapped her arms around his waist and tilted her head, giving him better access. Julian touched her in ways no other man ever had. She was still trying to figure out what magic he wielded to make her feel like this, like she couldn't decide whether to ravish him or run.

Then his teeth scrapped against her skin and the decision was made. That just felt too damn good to run away from.

"Mine," he whispered. Before she could protest, his fangs sank into her.

Cyn cried out as the best orgasm she'd ever fucking had tore through her. Her legs trembled, barely holding her up. She clung to him as the pleasure went on and on.

Oh, hell yes. This really is the Big O.

The unbelievable taste of his mate filled his senses. Cyn shuddered in his arms and groaned. The knowledge that she was finally, *finally* his sank into him. No one could take her from him now. Even in death, he would follow where she led.

He was hers.

He carefully pulled his teeth from her skin, licking the wounds closed. He picked her up, her shuddering driving him nearly insane with want. He carted her off to his bedroom, hoping against hope she wouldn't protest what he needed to do next.

Those gorgeous eyes of hers opened as he settled her on the bed. "Julian?"

The husky, needy sound of her voice nearly ended things before they began. Julian had never come in his jeans before, but just the sound of her voice post-orgasm was enough to almost send him over the edge. He bent and took her mouth, not at all surprised when she tried to take over the kiss.

He smiled, his lips still on hers. *There's my girl.*

Her hands tugged on his shirt. "Naked."

"Hmm?" He pushed the edge of her shirt up, sighing happily at the expanse of golden skin. God, she had a belly button ring! How come he'd never seen *that* before? The pretty little bit of gold dangling from her belly button was the most erotic thing he'd ever seen.

"*Now,* Julian."

He blinked. "Now, Julian, what?"

She huffed out a frustrated breath. "Why is it that when I want you to get naked you're not, but when I don't want you to—mmph!"

He didn't hear the rest of what she wanted to say. Her shirt was blocking her face, after all. Julian had her clothes off her so fast a Cheetah would have missed it. Then he was kissing her again, tugging at his own clothes in a frenzy to get his skin against her skin. He barely got his jeans down to his knees when her legs wrapped around his waist and he was flipped onto his back.

He stared up at her, startled. How the hell...?

She grinned down at him and took his painfully erect cock in her hands. "Too slow!"

And then she was sliding down him, gripping him inside her, and it no longer mattered that he was too slow, or that his jeans were around his knees. His mate was riding him, her breasts bouncing, her face pinched in a way that told him she was riding the thin edge of her own orgasm.

Damn, she had the prettiest breasts he'd ever seen. He cupped them, thumbing her nipples into hard little points, grunting when she tightened around him. He let her set the pace, watching the way she took him. This first time, for him at least, had to be all about her. Whatever she needed, however she wanted to love him, he'd accept.

But later, it would be his turn.

Soft sighs, the creak of the bedframe and the slap of flesh against flesh filled the room. Cyn's eyes were unfocused as she chased her orgasm, her hips snapping faster and faster. She clenched his shoulders, the small bite of pain barely registering as his spine began to tingle.

Julian grabbed and pulled her down, kissing her savagely as his body erupted. She cried out into his mouth, spasming around his cock as her orgasm took her.

Julian softened the kiss as they both came down from their high, breathing her in as she panted above him. Finally she tried to pull away, only getting as far as the end of his nose. He refused to allow her any further away.

"Wow."

Julian grinned in sleepy satisfaction. "Yeah."

She chuckled. "You're still wearing your boots, cowboy."

"Yup," he sighed, happier than he could ever remember being.

Cyn shook her head, but couldn't hide the small smile curling the edges of her mouth. "Next time we need you completely naked."

He hugged her tight, ignoring her squawk of surprise. "Yeah, we do."

She shook her head, but allowed him to keep her close. He breathed in her scent, and decided that today had to be the best fucking day ever.

This had to be the worst fucking day ever. Cyn walked along the rocky dirt path and wondered what the fuck was going on. She'd thought she was dreaming at first. After the incredible sex she'd had with Julian, she'd pretty much passed out.

Then she'd stepped on a sharp stone and the pain had been excruciating. She was even bleeding. She'd never done that in a dream before.

"Freaky ass Kermode. Super Bear my butt." She glared at the scrub on either side of the path. "If I see even *one* dead person I am so out of here!" She blew her bangs and renewed her embarrassingly naked march down the road, hobbled by her bloodied foot. "Guess what, Cyn? There are a few things I forgot to tell you. For instance, when I bite you I'll chuck your soul into the middle of a B horror movie. Enjoy!" She clenched her hands. "He is in *so* much trouble when I get back."

She wandered down the road for what seemed like hours. The one time she even considered going back, she rejected it immediately. Every instinct she had declared that if she did turn back, what she sought could never be found again. She had to go forward. She had to succeed if she was going to protect those she loved, even the stupid Bear who'd done this to her.

Eventually the road forked, but that wasn't what surprised her. What did was the simple glass sitting right at the juncture, half full of what appeared to be water. Cyn stared at it. "The glass is half full, huh?"

Fuck it. She was thirsty. She shrugged, sniffed it to make sure it really was water, picked it up and drank it, then carefully placed the glass right back where she'd found it.

She took a deep breath and studied the two paths. One seemed similar to the one she was already on, rocky and dirty with the occasional scraggly tree to add some visual interest. Bland, sort of boring, in no way like the *other* path.

The *other* path, if you could even call it that, appeared chock full of thorn bushes and sharp rocks. Even the air down that path appeared different, full of menace.

"Gee, Captain Obvious. I wonder which path I should take." She'd been a fearless adventurer in her Dungeons & Dragons days. She was pretty sure she could guess where this little side trip was going. She gritted her teeth and covered her boobs with her hands. There were some places she really didn't want scratched all to hell and gone, thank you very much.

The moment she set her foot on the dark path, she realized she'd made the right choice. "OW! *Mother puss-bucket!*"

After an eternity of painful steps, her flesh gouged in places that would make sitting down very difficult, the path finally opened up. Blue skies and a meadow full of wildflowers greeted her weary gaze. In the middle of that meadow a child knelt, crying. Over her stood a man, his hands at his sides, his expression pinched. The child cringed as the man raised his voice, his words muffled by the distance between them. He raised his fist into the air and shook it.

Cyn's eyes narrowed. That man was bullying the child. Without even having to think about it she reached behind her and grabbed hold of a thorny branch, breaking it off the bush. She darted in front of the child and held the branch in front of her like a sword. "Hold it! Leave the girl alone."

The man's searing white eyes burned into hers. "You do not believe I justly chastise her?"

Cyn shifted her stance, ready to defend the girl. "It's possible. But if I'm wrong, you'll have hurt her, and I can't allow that."

"What if she were the danger, and not I? An innocent face can hide a monster just as easily as an ugly one."

Cyn shook her head, certain of one thing. "Her posture. She was down, kneeling. Defenseless. Her hands were on her face, so unless she's got daggers up her nose I don't think she was hiding a weapon."

"So you put your back to her, hoping I was the threat."

"No. To protect a child." She waved the stick at him. "Are we done with twenty questions now? I have places to be." *Bear butt to kick.*

The man smiled, his teeth blindingly white, and held out his hand. The child took it, using her free one to wipe away her tears. "Look behind you. The path continues on. Know that the one you have set your feet upon will be difficult, but I believe it suits you."

The man and the child both smiled at her and disappeared.

She turned and stared at the path. It was remarkably similar to the one she'd just left. "Peachy."

God, part of her just wanted to lay down in the meadow and sleep, but she couldn't. Again, if she faltered here the elusive something she needed would be lost. She had the feeling she would wake up in the real world, puking and completely human.

There was no real choice to make. Cyn put her foot on the path and cursed at the top of her lungs in both English and Spanish.

Hours, perhaps a day, passed, as more of Cyn's skin was stripped away by the thorns. She was bleeding so badly now that if it hadn't been a dream she was sure she would have died from the wounds. She ignored the few side paths that opened up to her, her only goal to move forward. Sheer determination kept her on her feet when she should have faltered.

The path opened before her and she sighed in relief. Too much more and she *would* have gone down, willing or not.

Her bare, bleeding feet met stone and she gasped. The feel of the cool stone was a balm to her sore soles. She wiggled her toes, almost wishing it were grass instead of stone.

When she was able to focus again, she almost sobbed. There, on a pedestal, was a shield, a sword, a set of leather biker gear, complete with boots, and the kind of staff she'd seen martial artists use.

"Gee. I wonder which one I should pick up." She rolled her eyes and limped to the pedestal, the thorny branch she'd been clutching this entire time falling with a clatter to the ground. She sighed over the leather clothes, because, *damn* those were pretty. Too bad she couldn't take more than one item. It was weird, the certainty she had that the moment she made her choice, all the other objects would disappear.

She reached for the staff as soon as it was within reach. As nice as the clothes were, all they would do was cover her nudity and protect her skin. That wouldn't be enough, not against a shifter. The shield would keep her from being damaged, but that was all. She supposed she could ram someone with it, but

136

she risked having it taken from her if she did. The sword was designed solely to do harm, with very little defense unless you were a professional fencer. Something Cyn definitely was not.

The staff, on the other hand... The staff could be both weapon *and* shield, and was just what she needed.

The clearing disappeared in a brilliant flash of light as the staff practically leapt into her hands. When she blinked her vision clear she found herself at the top of a cliff, overlooking a rocky sea. All of her wounds were healed, but she was still covered in her own gore.

Obstructing her view was a very large, very white bear.

Cyn clutched her staff. If this was the final test, she was in big trouble. "Hi."

The bear snorted as if amused.

Right. "So. I'm here. Now what?"

The bear stared at her.

She leaned on the staff and stared right back.

The bear's nose wrinkled ever so slightly. She would have missed it if she hadn't been staring so hard.

Cyn lifted her foot and scratched the itchy, healed wound on the bottom.

The bear just sat there, blinking, as if it had all day to wait. If only she could figure out what it was waiting for, then they'd be golden.

"You want me to find you some honey? A cookie? Maybe a small, furry animal? You could hug it and love it and call it George." She scratched at some of the dried blood on her stomach. "I could really use a shower."

Water drenched her from a little black cloud that appeared over her head. She pushed her soaked hair out of her eyes and glared at the bear. "You're funny. I should call you Baloo."

The bear's left shoulder twitched. She was willing to bet tomorrow's lunch that it was laughing at her.

Julian grimaced as Cyn twisted painfully beneath the sheets. Shit. This wasn't going at all the way he'd expected. She was reacting as if she was in pain, her body shuddering and sweating. His hands itched to heal a wound that wasn't there. For the first time in his life Julian battled his Bear. There was nothing he could do for his mate. She was on her own.

A low moan drifted from her lips and his Bear turned frantic, striving to break through Julian's control, to heal the damage that *had* to be there.

Shit. What the hell had Cyn done now?

"Thirty-six bottles of beer on the wall, thirty-six bottles of beer," Cyn sang under her breath. She was lying on her back, staring at the clouds drifting lazily overhead. Her hair was almost dry, and she'd gotten most of the blood off her skin.

At her feet was the white bear. It still sat there, unmoving. Staring. It no longer creeped her out. Now it just...bored her.

"Julian is much quieter when he comes to visit me."

Damn. I still had thirty-five bottles to go. "I bet. Super Bear isn't much of a talker." She leaned up on her elbows and blew her bangs out of her eyes. "Okay, that's wrong. He *talks*, it just takes a while to get anything out of him that means something."

The bear huffed out something that sounded suspiciously like a laugh.

"See? You get what I'm talking about."

"Yes. I understand more than you think." The bear lumbered to its feet, its massive head hovering over her.

Suddenly Cyn didn't feel so much like a warrior as a late-night Taco Bell snack. "There are many things in store for you, Cynthia Reyes-DuCharme, and not all of them will be pleasant."

Big bear head in the way or not, Cyn was on her feet, the staff in her hand, before the bear could blink. "Is Julian in danger?"

The bear was looking at her with approval. "Yes."

Her heart stuttered. "Shit. I *knew* it."

"So you did." The bear's head lifted; it sniffed the wind. "Change is coming, whether it is wanted or not. Two becomes one, one becomes three. Bear knows the way, but Fox holds the key." Its eyes focused on her again. "Guard my child well, warrior. He will need you in the days to come."

She nodded. Guarding Julian was a given. "Can you tell me what's going on?"

"It is not permitted for me to tell more than I have. There are decisions that must be made on your own, decisions that will influence those that others will make. Your strength and courage will take you far, but do not dismiss what your heart tells you."

"I'll try." It was the best she could offer.

"You will." The bear began to glow. "It is time for you to return. Your mate is frantic with worry. He fights his Bear, fearing you are injured."

Suddenly it all made sense. She'd heard Julian discuss Bear as a person rather than some amorphous concept. "Wait. You're—"

She was hurtled into the darkness, her question unasked and unanswered.

Chapter Twelve

She took a deep, gasping breath, and Julian sagged with relief. She was all right.

Her eyes opened, and it was the most beautiful sight he'd ever seen. They were deep brown and frightened. He wrapped himself around her cold body and breathed in her scent.

She smelled of Bear. She'd been accepted. He peppered kisses across the mating mark. "You're all right."

She tugged his braid before stroking his back. "You're shaking."

He just hugged her tighter. She'd terrified him. He'd thought Bear had taken a dislike to her and ripped her soul to shreds.

"I feel like I went a few rounds with that big-ass bear. Ow."

He flinched. "Did you?"

"Did I what?"

"Fight Bear."

"No." She tugged on his braid again, harder this time. "We sang the beer bottle song and had a cozy chat. All we needed were s'mores and a campfire."

He laughed, the hysterical edge to it surprising him. "I bet he loved you."

"Oh yeah. He invited me back for tea, once the bleeding stopped."

Bleeding? His Bear wailed, but Julian could sense no real damage had been done to her. If there had been spiritual wounds, Bear must've healed them. That was beyond even Julian's power. "Tell me everything."

"That might take a while."

He settled in more comfortably, cradling her close. She rested her head against his chest and he damn near howled like a wolf at the feeling of *rightness*. "We have time."

"Let's see. There was a long, dusty road with sharp, pointy rocks. I expected a Gorn to pop out any minute and challenge me to a duel. And did I mention I was naked?"

Julian chuckled. Only his Cyn would think of a classic Star Trek episode while wandering in the spirit world.

"I came to a crossroads and saw a glass of water that was half full."

Interesting. He'd found a book on his first journey. "What did you do with it?"

"Drank it."

He blinked. "Oh." He shouldn't be surprised. He'd picked the book up and tried to read it. It had surprised him when it disappeared out of his hands.

"What? I was thirsty. Anyway, one branch of the path seemed pretty much the same as the one I was already on. The other was chock full of thorns and stones."

He winced. "Let me guess which one you took."

"Hey, I played Dungeons & Dragons. You never take the easy path. There's always a trap at the end of it."

"This wasn't a game." If only she'd taken the other trail...

She rolled her head until they were eye to eye. "You took the easy way, didn't you?"

"Not easy. Different." Who the hell would willingly walk down a path full of sharp stones and thorns? It seemed like a remarkably stupid thing to do, deliberately inviting pain that way. The other path might have been longer, but it was no less challenging.

Wariness crept into her expression. "I didn't have to go down the thorny path?"

"Nope." First decision made, first crisis met and overcome. Something told him the outcome was going to be exactly what he'd expected. "Then what?"

"A meadow with a man standing over a crying girl, yelling at her."

Uh-oh. Julian remembered something similar. He'd watched for a few moments to discover the problem, and then had done his best to bandage the child's leg. "What did you do?"

"Grabbed a branch and protected the girl."

Yes, that sounded like his Cyn. "What happened?"

"The man asked me if I was sure he was the threat and not the child. I pretty much told him to shove off, and the two pointed me toward my next path and disappeared."

"Another thorny one, I assume."

"And worse than the last one. I almost didn't make it."

He froze. Those who didn't make it on *that* path... Best not think about that. He was going to have nightmares as it was.

"I got to the end and there was this table with four objects on it."

"A book, a chalice, a healer's kit and a dream catcher."

She looked at him like he'd grown snakes on his head. "A sword, a shield, biker leathers and a staff."

"Oh." Yeah. That pretty much summed up what he'd thought would happen. No way was Cyn a Spirit Bear. Damn. He tamped down the disappointment. It wasn't that big a deal. At least she was Bear now, rather than Puma, like she'd threatened more than once.

"I want those leathers."

His eyebrow quirked. "Have a thing for leather, do you?"

She grinned. "You have no idea. But I took the staff."

"Why?"

"Protection and a weapon in one convenient package."

"Ah." He was beginning to see the pattern, and while it wasn't adding up to Spirit Bear, it wasn't adding up to Black Bear, either. A Black Bear would have gone for the leathers or the shield. What was going on?

"Then BAM! I'm sitting in front of this huge white bear who's just...staring at me. Sitting and staring. It was creepy, especially since I was naked."

"I meditated."

"I sang the beer song. I still had thirty-five to go when he decided I was a Chatty Cathy, unlike *some people*."

From the glare she was shooting him he could guess who those *people* were. "So? What did he say?"

"Other than how quiet you are?" She took a deep breath. "Two becomes one, one becomes three. Bear knows the way, but Fox holds the key. Oh, and that change is coming."

Great. Wonderful. That was three times the message had been delivered. He hoped the spirits considered it received. "What aren't you telling me?"

Those beautiful eyes widened. Her left eyebrow twitched. "Nothing."

He shot her a look that had gotten more than one reluctant patient to admit something they didn't want to.

"I'm serious." She frowned. "Okay, there is one thing."

"Hmm?"

"He called me warrior."

Julian stared at her. That couldn't mean what he thought it did, could it? He buried his nose against her neck and breathed in her scent again. When he finally understood exactly what he smelled he laughed so hard he fell off the bed.

She leaned over the edge and glared at him. Then she lifted her arm and sniffed her pit. "Do I offend?"

He'd never understood the laughing-so-hard-until-you-cried thing before, but now he totally got it. Alex was going to be tickled pink.

And Eric was in for a serious shock.

Cyn woke to the feel of a heavy arm across her middle and the sensation that she'd had a really rough night. Her body ached in ways it hadn't in a long time. She moved her leg, ready to climb out of bed and answer a rather urgent call of nature when the arm tightened.

"Don't go."

Damn. Julian's sleep-roughened voice made all sorts of things quiver inside her. "I will go if you don't let me up."

He snorted a laugh and rolled over, releasing her to run for the bathroom like a bear was after her butt. After she was done she helped herself to his toothbrush and combed out her hair, which was sticking up in all sorts of new and interesting ways.

She took a good, long look at herself when she was done. She didn't *look* any different. She certainly didn't *feel* any different. Maybe it had all been a crazy, sex-induced dream?

Fingers brushed over the bite mark on her neck and she darn near fell to the floor in a puddle of goo. "Morning, Cyn." His lips brushed the mark and her knees gave out. "Whoa!" He caught her before she fell, strong arms wrapped around her waist. "You okay?"

"What the fuck was that?" She brushed her fingertips across the mark. The sensation was still there, but not nearly as strong. It was like someone was gently stroking her clit, just enough to interest but not enough to arouse.

"Well..." Julian licked the mark, and she moaned. Now *that* was the touch of someone determined to arouse her. "That's the mark you begged for last night."

How could someone look so innocent and so evil at the same time? It seemed Glory hadn't cornered the market on that particular look after all. "That's it? That's the bite?" He nodded. "Fine. How long until it fades?" There was no way she was going to be able to go through her day with *that* on her neck. What if someone touched her there while she was doing a tattoo? A simple pat on the shoulder from a guy with big hands could cause an accidental orgasm.

He smirked. "Who said it would?"

She turned in his arms and glared at him.

Julian looked utterly pleased with himself as he stroked a finger across the mark. "This tells anyone who looks at you that you're claimed. You belong to me." He must have realized his mistake almost immediately, because he dodged out of punching range, his expression turning wary. "Now, Cyn—"

"I belong to you?" She crossed her arms over her chest. "Since when?"

He tugged on his braid. "Since I bit you?"

She ground her teeth. Fine, he'd given her the mating mark, but since when did that mean she *belonged to him*?

"When you bite me, I'll belong to you."

"Oh really?" She kept the bite of anger in her voice, but a strange sensation was running through her. The thought of sinking fangs into Julian, leaving a mark on his body that would warn away all other females, was oddly appealing.

He took a cautious step forward. "When you bite me, the only thing I'll care about is making you come."

She blinked, memories of last night dancing through her head. "Really?"

"It won't be that much different from how I feel right now, except I'll *have* to make you come at least once before my Bear will let me have you."

She swallowed hard. She could feel her nipples beading. "Oh."

"You'll be able to do whatever you want with me." He breathed the words against her mark, and it was only then she realized how close he'd come.

She bit her lip, fighting the arousal crashing through her. "Will I get you to...?"

"Hmm?" He nibbled her earlobe and she shivered.

"...make me..."

He kissed her jaw. "Anything."

"...waffles?"

He froze, but she could feel his smile against her skin. "You're evil."

She patted his ass, amazed at how firm it was. "But you like me that way."

"Much to my shame, yes." He grinned down at her. "Do I at least get a good morning kiss?"

She cocked an eyebrow at him. "Have you brushed your teeth?"

"No."

"Then no."

He shook his head and reached for the toothbrush. "The things I do for you."

"Oh yeah. Getting rid of the dragon breath is *such* a chore."

He pinched her hip. "If I'm making waffles you might want to get dressed. Borrow one of my T-shirts and scrub pants for now. We can wash your clothes while we eat."

"Wow. A practical man." She looked up at the ceiling. "Nope. Sky's still up there."

She didn't appreciate it one little bit when he shoved her out of the bathroom and closed the door. She settled on the bed and waited for him to come out. When he did, she hopped up and brushed past him to head back into the bathroom.

"What you doing?"

"I'm skuzzy and gooey and I want to shower."

His dark brows rose as he leered at her. "You... Hot water... Soap bubbles... I'm in!"

She held up her hand when he tried to push past her into the shower. "I thought you were going to make me waffles." He whimpered and made puppy-dog eyes at her. She rolled her eyes and sighed, secretly delighted that he wanted to hop in the shower with her. "Fine, but that means you're adding chocolate chips to my waffles, got it?"

His answer was to reach around her and turn on the water. "There's something I'm interested in other than waffles."

From the way his cock was bouncing she could guess what it was he wanted. "Really?" She reached out and grabbed hold of him, loving the soft hiss that escaped his lips. "I can't imagine what that might be."

He brushed his fingers across her mating mark. "I think you can guess." Julian turned off the water and led her back to the bed.

"What do you have in mind?" She didn't mind the thought of one more round before she ate. Hell, the way Julian was eyeing her she bet she was the only thing on his menu.

He lay down and tugged her on top of him. "Turn around. I want a taste."

Oh, hell. Yeah, she could go for that. She wiggled around until his cock was right before her, swallowing him down. He grabbed hold of her hips, pulling her in to position. At the first swipe of his tongue, she gasped. It was almost too much to bear, warm and wet and perfect. He licked at her clit like she was the best thing he'd ever tasted, driving her insane with need. She moaned around him, the sensations rocketing through her. She'd never had a man taste her the way he did.

God, he was *good*. She was on the verge of coming and they'd barely started.

Something nudged at her opening and she spread her legs wider. His beautiful, talented tongue began fucking into her, his fingers rubbing her clit.

Cyn couldn't take much more. Damn, she needed, almost as badly as she had last night. But there was something missing, something that would take it that extra step from really good to incredible. She sucked on the tip of his cock, stroking the head with her tongue, trying to figure out what that special something was.

She pushed her hair out of the way, accidentally hitting the mating mark. *That* was what she wanted, what had been missing. She needed him to stroke her there, to bite her, and sink his fangs into her until she screamed.

She pulled away from him and turned, sinking down on his cock in one smooth motion.

"Cyn?" He was breathless, his pupils dilated, his irises pure silver.

She leaned over him and grabbed the headboard.

"Now what?" He grabbed hold of her ass, thrusting into her hard enough to raise her up.

She smiled and stroked the mark at her neck, shivering as the sensation quivered down her body right to her clit. "Fuck me."

His gaze went right to the mark, his expression one of conquest and need. He licked his lips, his fangs descending. "I'm going to bite you again."

She hoped the fuck so. In fact, she was counting on it. She tightened her muscles around him, groaning with him as his cock jumped inside her. He dragged her head down, tilting her to the side.

Oh yeah. Bite me, Jules. She rocked on him, anticipating the feel of his teeth against her skin.

Instead, he licked the mark.

Oh. Shit. She nearly came then and there. It was like he was fucking her and licking her at the same time. Over and over he licked that goddamn mark, driving her closer and closer to the edge. She began to ride him hard, the sound of skin slapping against skin loud in the quiet room.

"Wait."

She whimpered. He wanted to wait? She was *this close!*

He rolled them over, spooning against her. He lifted her leg and slid back inside, his mouth fastened to her neck, his tongue working over the mark.

She moaned, coming before he'd gone two strokes, the orgasm washing through her in a tidal wave.

"Good. So good." He sucked on the mark again, the feel of his teeth scraping her skin bringing her right back to the brink. "Come again for me."

He rolled them again, this time putting her on her stomach. He entered her again, fucking her hard and fast, his mouth pure magic against the mark, pinning her down. Not that she wanted to go anywhere. The man was a fucking *god.*

His hands were everywhere, stroking her skin, pushing her hair aside, wrapping around her to cup her breasts. Her nipples were hard little points against his palms, twisted and pleasured until they ached. She threw her head back, forced to take what he gave her, unable to gain the leverage she needed to thrust back into him.

He was taking her and making her love it.

The combination of his hands on her breasts and his mouth at her neck was just too much. She whimpered as her orgasm crested, the electric slide of his skin against hers dragging her under once more.

"Fuck, yes, Cyn. More. Give me more."

He began doing something, rotating his hips or some weird shit, kissing and licking the nape of her neck to her unmarked shoulder. He tasted her skin, whispered naughty things in her ear, insistent things that made her blush, that had her writhing under his hold, desperate to feel that intense pleasure only Julian seemed able to give her. She'd never look at him the same way again. Her loveable, geeky boyfriend had morphed into a conquering barbarian, demanding she surrender once more. She was surrounded by him, part of him. Owned by him, by her consent.

From what he'd told her, she owned him too, so maybe it wasn't such a bad thing.

"Going to come, Cyn. Going to make you come with me, come so hard." His teeth sank in, breaking the skin. Cyn screamed out a pleasure so intense her vision turned black, her breath catching in her lungs. Her whole body seized, her toes curled. Her fingers scrabbled for purchase in the sheets. He grunted behind her, warmth flooding into her as he came, her name a broken, reverent whisper.

Chapter Thirteen

"So, how did it go last night?"

Cyn propped her chin on her hand and sighed dreamily. "He makes the best waffles."

"So...you guys made waffles last night?" Glory tilted her head, her expression turning sweetly innocent. "Did he get butter in all the nooks and crannies? Did he heat your syrup just right? Did you order some sausage on the side?"

Tabby began to giggle. "Do you think he toasted her muffin before he ate it?"

"I hate you guys." But even their stupid banter couldn't wipe the stupid smile from her face. Julian had been everything she'd ever hoped for and more, but no way was she sharing that with these morons.

Glory squealed and clapped her hands. "He did! He did toast her muffin." She leaned across the counter until she was nose to nose with Cyn and gave a wide, toothy grin. "Deets, please!"

Cyn snorted and pushed Glory's face away. "Get your own Bear. Oh, wait..."

"Aw, come on. Just one little tidbit of information? Please?" Glory batted her baby blues, but Cyn was immune to her ways.

"Fine. He has a really..."

"Uh-huh..."

"Big..."

"Uh-huh, uh-huh!" Glory's eyes had gone so wide Cyn thought they might pop out of her head.

"Toaster."

Glory blinked, trying to make something dirty out of that in her head, no doubt.

Cyn held her hands about a foot apart. "Seriously, he's got one of those big industrial suckers that can do, like, six bagels at a time."

Tabby's giggles turned into outright laughter as Glory growled at Cyn.

"You should see his kitchen. It's like Martha Stewart's wet dream. Emeril would walk in and say 'Dayum'."

Glory glared at her, but Cyn could tell she wasn't really angry. The corners of her lips kept twitching upward, a sure sign she was holding back a laugh. "Did you do it on the counter?"

"No." Although that was something she wouldn't mind testing out at some point. Did Julian like the thought of sex in the kitchen? She'd have to ask him when she saw him later. Some of those counter-height stools would be perfect for—

"Then why do you think I care about his kitchen?"

"You guys are the ones that brought up muffins." Cyn shrugged and yawned. She was still tired after her ordeal in the spirit world and the incredible sex she'd had. Maybe she should've listened to Julian and just stayed home today, but she'd been too worried about leaving the girls alone. What if whoever was trying to hurt them came back and Cyn wasn't there? She had to be there to protect them whether they liked it or not.

The door to the shop opened, the bell tinkling merrily. Cyn stood up straight and grinned at their customer. She recognized him as the college kid who'd come into the shop to get a tattoo of a wolf a few months before. Little had he known that it had been a picture of Gary, Tabby's stalker, in his Wolf form. Tabby had talked Tim into getting a different tattoo, and they'd formed a friendship that day. This was his third trip into the shop, probably to get the tattoo touched up again. "Hey, Tim. Come back for some color on that dragon of yours?"

Tim grinned and shrugged, his cheeks flushing bright red. Really, he was just too adorable. "No, I like it just in black. I think it's perfect. But I *was* thinking of getting something on my other arm." He was staring at Tabby with something akin to hero worship.

Tabby smiled gently and took Tim by the arm, leading him over to the flash books. "Why don't we take a look and see what you'd like?" She settled him on one of the chairs by the window. "Do you want something to drink?"

"Can I have some water, please?" Tim shot her a bashful grin, and Cyn prayed Alex didn't come back too soon with lunch. If he got even a whiff that someone else was sniffing after his mate he'd go ballistic on the poor boy.

Tabby headed into the back room to get Tim's water. Glory wandered over to see what tattoo Tim was thinking of getting. She started to bend over the book, her long blue hair obscuring her face. Suddenly there was the sound of shattering glass and she was thrown back. Tim hunched over the book and fell to his knees, his arms covering his head.

Cyn smelled blood.

Without even having to think she raced over to Glory and threw herself on top of her. She glanced over at Tim to find him looking back at her, his face filled with horror and glass glittering in his hair. The window behind him was shattered.

"I think she's hit."

She looked down at Glory and saw that she'd passed out. Blood poured from a wound in her chest, soaking the bright paisley of her shirt.

"Holy shit." Tabby crawled over to them, her face pale. "Tell me somebody didn't just shoot one of us."

"Call an ambulance." Tim crawled over to them and pulled off his T-shirt. He pulled up Glory's paisley shirt and mopped up some of the blood. "I'm pre-med. I have to do something."

"Call Julian." Tabby, hands shaking, drew out her cell phone.

Cyn couldn't speak. She could barely breathe. Someone had tried to kill Glory right in front of her and she hadn't been able to stop him. She hadn't been able to protect her friend.

"Cyn!" Tabby's sharp voice almost cut through the haze of rage surrounding her.

"Holy fuck, what are you?" Tim was staring at her, his eyes wide and filled with fear, but the T-shirt remained right where it was.

"Stop it, Cyn, for Glory's sake. She needs you calm and in control."

Cyn managed to pull her gaze from Glory's wound and met Tabby's. Golden Wolf eyes stared back at her. There was a spot of blood on Tabby's cheek, and her eyes were filled with tears.

Tabby smiled weakly. "You're claws are showing."

She looked down to find six-inch black claws sprouting from where her nails should be. She took a deep breath and tried to calm herself, but all that did was intensify the scent of blood until it filled her head.

"I'm calling an ambulance. You have to calm down, Cyn."

"Yeah. Please calm down, you're scaring the straights." Tim's voice shook, but once again, his focus seemed to be on Glory's wound and not Cyn's freakiness.

Cyn tried to will her claws away, but something fought her, something that desperately wanted to come out, find the being that had hurt her friend, and beat it to death with its own arms.

It wanted to roar out her rage and her grief until the very building shook.

She heard Tabby speaking on the phone. The ambulance was on its way, but the information didn't help. She had to do something.

She reached up and placed her hand on the bloody T-shirt, almost crying out at how soaked it already was. Blood was bubbling from Glory's lips as she breathed. That couldn't be a good thing. She took a deep breath and let it out slowly, trying to calm herself down. If she was going to try this, she couldn't be in a killing rage.

If her Bear was already with her enough to sprout claws, then he was with her enough to help her heal.

Cyn closed her eyes and mentally reached for the presence she could feel in the back of her mind. It wrapped itself around her like a furry, loving blanket, a living hug inside her head. She'd never be alone again, would always have someone who believed in her. Her Bear understood her in ways no one else did or ever would, not even her mate. It loved and accepted her anyway, and Cyn could do no less. She opened her heart to her Bear, joining them together forever.

Once her Bear understood what it was she wanted, it eagerly showed her the spiraling, healing path she'd need to take. It wanted to save Glory too, and lent her its strength. The power trickled forth from her palms and into Glory's wound.

It wouldn't be enough to heal Glory. But she didn't need to. All she had to do was keep Glory alive long enough for either Julian or the ambulance to arrive. She wasn't certain why she didn't have Super Bear's healing powers, but she couldn't take the time to question it now. She could feel her strength waning almost immediately and prayed they'd arrive quickly.

The world around her was quickly graying, her vision darkening at the edges. When the paramedics finally arrived they pushed her out of the way, quickly assessing the damage to Glory's chest. IVs went in and bandages were wrapped around the wound. Cyn knew something was wrong with Glory's lung, and it scared her. Alex arrived just as they strapped her onto the gurney and wheeled her out to the ambulance.

"What the fuck happened?" His hazel eyes had gone dark brown. He rushed to Tabby's side, checking her over for wounds.

Cyn scooted back, uncaring that she was in broken glass. Her hands and arms were covered in Glory's blood and she was so dizzy she was afraid she would pass out at any moment. She'd never been so tired in her life. "Someone took a shot at us and hit Glory."

"No offense, but I think I'll skip the tattoo today." Tim was pale. He watched Alex check Tabby over with a pained expression. The poor kid had it bad.

She tilted her head and tried to smile at Tim. "You okay?"

His answering laugh was shaky. "Oh yeah. I'm peachy. What the hell is with the claws, by the way?"

"He saw your claws?" Alex muttered under his breath. "And I thought I had control problems."

She flipped him the bird. "Do you really want to know the answer to that, Tim?"

He nodded slowly. "I think I do."

She looked up to make sure that they were alone in the shop. "Okay, but don't ever say I didn't warn you."

He blew out a shaky breath. "Just tell me."

"Fine."

"Cyn." Alex shot her a warning glance, but what was she supposed to do? Tim had seen her claws, and she doubted he'd buy a bad manicure story.

"Do you believe in werewolves? I mean, I'm not one of them, but do you believe in them?"

"Shit." Alex sighed and hugged Tabby close. "I hope you know what you've just done."

"Werewolves, huh?" Tim stared at Alex and bit his lip, pondering God only knew what. He then looked down at Cyn's hands, his expression distracted. "I do now."

Julian raced to the hospital corridors, his only thought to see his mate. Was she all right? Had she been hit?

Someone had shot at Cyn.

He could have lost her.

Those two thoughts kept cycling around in his head. She could have *died*. As it was, Glory was in critical condition, the bullet having pierced one of her lungs. Ryan had raced ahead of him, desperate to get to his mate. If Glory died, Ryan would follow her. Despite the fact that they hadn't shared mating marks, Ryan had somehow already linked their life forces. Julian had never seen anything like it. Ryan had known even before the phone call came in that Glory was badly hurt. He'd been pounding on Julian's door, frantic, as Julian's cell phone rang. When Cyn told him what had happened he'd been equally worried.

Ryan had come for him rather than going straight for the hospital. He'd made it clear that he hoped Julian would be able to save Glory when the doctors might not be able to. Julian was more than willing to try. As frustrating as it was to watch her yank Ryan's chain, Julian would do anything to save his mate's best friend. Ryan had taken off in a cloud of burning rubber when Julian had taken too long to get dressed. Julian, watching the Grizzly peel away, had actually been glad he wasn't in the car with him. He didn't have a death wish.

He skidded around the corner into the ICU nurse's station. "I'm looking for Glory Walsh."

"Are you family?" Julian shook his head no. "I'm sorry, sir, no one's allowed in unless they're family. You'll have to go to the waiting room."

He ground his teeth together. "Is Ryan Williams here?"

The woman gulped. "I'm afraid we had to have him escorted out. He was far too disruptive."

Oh, shit. They had no idea what they'd done. They were lucky they didn't have a rampaging Grizzly in the parking lot.

"You understand you just kicked out her fiancé. He had every right to be here."

The two nurses exchanged a worried glance. "He didn't tell us he was her fiancé."

"I'll go find him and bring him back. I'll do my best to keep him calm, but I'm sure you can understand why he was upset." If he didn't get to Ryan soon he had no idea what the Grizzly would do.

He'd also have to figure out a way to get into Glory's room. He pulled out his cell phone and dialed Jamie Howard's personal number. He sniffed the air as discreetly as he could, hoping to catch Ryan's scent. He followed it to the elevator and stepped in just as Jamie picked up.

"Hey, Julian. How's Glory?"

"They won't let me in to see her." He'd called Jamie on the way to the hospital to inform him of what had happened and that he wouldn't be in the office for a day or two. Jamie had told him to stay at the hospital until Glory was out of the woods. "Worse, they kicked Ryan out for being disruptive."

"Shit. Let me make a few phone calls. I'll get you in to see Glory, you keep Ryan calm."

"I'm tracking him down now. I haven't seen Tabby or Alex yet, and I haven't found Cyn." He ran his fingers through his hair. There were just so many things to worry about; it was starting to give him a headache. "I wonder if anyone has called Glory's parents."

"You concentrate on Ryan and Glory. Let Alex protect Cyn and Tabby."

He stepped out of the elevator and followed Ryan's scent out of the hospital. "Not good enough. I need to find out if Cyn is hurt."

"She would've called and told you if you she was."

Julian stopped and pulled the ear from his phone, staring at it in disbelief. "You don't know her very well, do you?" He put the phone back to his ear in time to hear Jamie chuckle. "Her fucking jaw was broken and she didn't call me because she didn't want me to be bothered about it."

"Point taken."

Julian sniffed again and began walking toward the parking lot. He wasn't catching a lot of rage in Ryan's scent. It could simply be the hospital smells of worry, despair and sickness, but what he *was* catching off of Ryan was a strange calmness. That concerned him more than any amount of rage would have. "I think we have a problem."

"What?"

He watched as Ryan drove sedately out of the parking lot. Even at distances he could see the five-inch claws wrapped around the steering wheel. "I think Ryan's hunting."

"I'll call Gabe, so don't worry about that. You get back in and see what you can do about Glory. They should let you in now."

"Thanks, Jamie."

"I'm curious about one thing, though."

Julian stepped back into the hospital. "What's that?"

"Is your life ever boring?"

Julian sighed. "Not since I came to Halle." Hell, it had been downright somnolent before he came to Halle. He hung up the phone and stepped into the elevator, heading once more to ICU. This time, when he requested access to Glory's room, it was granted right away.

The sound of life support machines disturbed him more than he was willing to admit. Glory had tubes down her throat helping her breathe. Another tube stuck out of her chest, indicating a collapsed lung. She was pale, and almost as blue as her hair. They were giving her blood to replace what she'd lost. The sounds coming from the heartbeat monitor were far too slow for his liking.

He could tell she was stable, but barely. A nurse was prepping her for surgery. How long had it taken them to get her stable enough for it? It wasn't that far from Living Art to the hospital, but it had taken him an hour to get there. He could feel his Bear reaching for her, anxious to heal her. To see such a vibrant woman so wounded troubled him.

"Julian."

Just one whispered, tear-laden word eased his heart. Cyn's face was swollen from crying, her eyes red and damp. She reached for him, and he pulled her into his arms. He stroked her hair as she collapsed in his arms, all her strength deserting her. She sobbed against him like a broken child, and Julian understood why Ryan had gone hunting. He never wanted his mate to hurt like this again, and he would do anything to make sure it never happened a second time. "I'll fix this, I swear."

She stiffened and lifted her head. "Can you leave us for a minute?"

The nurse nodded briefly and left the room.

Cyn took his face in her hands and glared up at him. "I won't lose either one of you. Do you understand me? You only heal her to the point where she'll survive with surgery, and let the doctors take it from there. You *don't* risk yourself. *¿Entendido?*"

"I understand." He pressed a kiss to her forehead, healing the swelling from the crying and the headache that was beginning to build behind her eyes.

Already he could feel his Bear pulling him back toward the bed. Glory needed him. Ryan and Cyn were counting on him. He sat on the edge of the bed and took hold of Glory's hands. With a deep breath he focused on the healing path, his instincts and his understanding of anatomy blending together as he began to repair the damage done to Glory's body. The harm to her lung was severe, and by far the most traumatizing injury. He began the slow process of knitting together the wounded flesh, the torn blood vessels. The bullet had glanced off her ribs and entered her lung, deflating it like an overblown balloon. He was surprised she wasn't in surgery already. Things must've been truly bad if the doctors said it would be better to wait. As it was, odds were good she'd lose the lower lobe of her lung and require months of therapy. Even if Ryan bit her now, the change wouldn't repair the damage done.

Julian did what he could to stabilize her condition and improve her chances in surgery, but unless he wanted to tip his hand or risk his own life, there wasn't much more he'd be able to do. So he made sure she had the best odds possible before he pulled back from the healing path. He sighed as he pushed bone white hair out of his eyes. "She'll live."

Cyn smiled and popped a baseball hat on his head, hiding the thick white streak in his hair. "Good job, Super Bear."

He allowed her to pull him to his feet just as the nurse walked back in. He smiled wearily at the poor woman. "Thank you."

The nurse's answering smile was sympathetic. "You're welcome."

Hours had gone by, and still there was no word on Glory's condition. Cyn looked ready to tear her hair out in frustration. Gabe had called and told him he couldn't find any sign of Ryan, which could be a good thing or bad thing. Good, because Gabe's Hunter instincts hadn't kicked in, meaning Ryan had not yet gone rogue. Bad, because nobody had a clue where Ryan was or what he was up to. Tabby and Alex had remained behind to close up the shop and get some plywood taped over the shattered window. A few policemen had come by to talk to Cyn and some kid named Tim about what had happened, but there wasn't much she could tell them. None of them had caught sight of the shooter.

"I thought you could use some caffeine." Tim, the young man who'd been in the shop when Glory got shot, handed Julian the cup of coffee. Julian took a sip and grimaced at the bitter taste. Tim leaned closer, his expression somewhere between curious and concerned. "Can I ask you something?"

"Go ahead." He could guess what the boy wanted to ask him.

"Why doesn't one of you bite her and change her? Wouldn't that heal all of her wounds?"

Julian rolled his eyes. "Why does everyone think it works that way? Stupid Hollywood movies." He leaned on the arm of a hard plastic chair and kept his voice low. He didn't want any of the humans to hear him. "Look. Whatever injuries, diseases or

162

other problems, physical or mental, that you had as a human will still be there when you get changed. If you have cancer as a human, you'll have cancer as a Bear. If you have scars, they'll still be there." He took another sip of the really bad coffee and wondered if he could sneak out to Starbucks. "It's nice to think that something as simple as a bite can cure everything, but this is the real world. Problems just don't magically go away because you get bitten by a shifter."

"Oh." Tim grimaced in sympathy. "That sucks."

"On top of that, it takes days for the change to fully manifest itself. Most people can't change into their new animal form until about a week after getting bitten. I've heard of cases where it goes faster, but those people are incredibly strong-willed."

"So Cyn got bit almost a week ago?"

Julian froze, coffee cup halfway to his mouth. "She got bit last night."

"Then how come she had claws?"

Julian's gaze darted over to where Cyn was resting. She was half asleep, her head resting on Alex's broad shoulder. His mate was exceptional in all respects, and he couldn't be more proud of her. "Because she's Cyn."

Chapter Fourteen

Cyn stared at the plywood over the window of her dream shop. What was she supposed to do now? Without Living Art, she'd lose not only her livelihood but her independence. She'd be forced to rely on Julian for everything. No matter how good a man Julian was, she'd never be able to tolerate that for long. They had to find whoever was targeting her and her friends and end this.

Glory had been in the hospital for two days. Thanks to the damage the bullet had caused, part of her lower lung had been removed. She was in a lot of pain and cranky as hell. The two tubes in her side were driving her crazy, but the doctors had told them that they'd be removed tomorrow. The physiotherapists were encouraging Glory to cough, something she wanted to do about as much as she wanted to shove red-hot pokers up her ass.

They were no closer to finding the shooter. Cyn knew at least some of Glory's crankiness came from fear rather than pain. Alex and Tabby were practically living at the hospital while the entire Williams-Bunsun clan hunted for Ryan, who was still missing. Gabe had told her in private that something was rattling the Hunter within him. If Ryan had gone feral from Glory's injuries nothing would save him from Gabe.

"We'll find him." Julian wrapped his arms around her and propped his chin on her shoulder. He'd left his hair down, and the strands were cool against her cheek. She could smell the coffee he'd had prior to driving her over to the store on his breath. They were sitting in his car, Julian unwilling to allow her out of it, or anywhere closer to Living Art than they already were. She understood his concern. If the shooter was keeping an eye on LA then she'd be a prime target. She still wasn't certain whether Glory was the one the shooter intended to hit or not.

If he'd hit Tabby she could have lost the baby.

The low growl that reverberated through the car startled her. What surprised her even more was that it came from her. "I want to play hacky sack with their nuts."

He snorted a laugh. "That's the best you could come up with? I'm disappointed."

"Did I mention they'd still be attached?"

"Mm. In that case, I know a couple of Grizzlies who should be more than happy to play with you."

"If you can find them." She sighed wearily. "I think part of the reason Glory is so pissy is because Ryan's not there. No matter how much she squirms and complains, she cares about him."

"Do you have any idea why she's fighting their mating so hard?"

"Her father was an absolute jerk. I mean, my mother didn't say boo without my father's permission, but he was never abusive toward her. He just ran her life like it was a military operation. To him, it probably was."

"And Glory's father was abusive." Julian's tone was thoughtful, as if he was trying to figure out a unique puzzle and didn't have all pieces.

"Her father was extremely conservative. He was a firm believer in spare the rod, spoil the child, and was exceedingly possessive toward his wife and children. If anyone showed an interest in any of his daughters he would run them off. I'm not certain all the methods he used were legal."

"I'm thinking he's no longer around?"

"He may be. I'm not sure. He and Mrs. Walsh left the area about two years after Hope disappeared. He took Faith and Temp with them, but left Glory behind. I think they'd argued, and she refused to go with him. Since she was eighteen, he couldn't force her, but he could make her life hell. He left her with the clothes on her back and whatever was in her wallet at the time. Thank God my mom let her live with us until we could get an apartment together." She winced, remembering how Glory had looked that day. "She had bruises all over her, Jules."

He winced, but didn't question her about that. "I didn't know Glory had a missing sister."

"She was the oldest daughter, and Glory's twin. She claimed she was going to the library, but she never came back. The police weren't able to find anyone who had seen her. They never found a trace. All the Walshes were devastated, but Glory most of all. They were sixteen, and did everything together."

"Wow. Has she told Ryan about any of this?"

If she did, he never would have disappeared the way he had. Ryan just didn't have it in him to hurt Glory like that. She was willing to bet that was why Glory was flipping out. It was like losing her sister all over again. "None of us talk about it, especially in front of Glory. Hope's disappearance is still an open case."

They were quiet for a few moments, each absorbed in their own thoughts. "Glory, Hope, Faith and Temp?"

Cyn rolled her eyes. Poor Temp. "It's short for Temperance."

"That's a horrible thing to do to a little girl."

"It's a worse thing to do to a little boy. Especially when he's the oldest child and gets to watch his sisters get fairly normal names."

Julian whistled and tugged on a lock of his hair. "So how many black belts does he have? He must've gone through some major ass kicking's in school. His butt must still be black and blue."

He had the uncanny knack of making her smile even when she was at her worst. "He always said he would've felt better if the girls were named Chastity, Prudence and Patience."

"I could totally see Glory rockin' the name Prudence. It suits her to a T." She could hear the faint hint of laughter in his voice. "We could call her Prue, Prude or just plain Dence."

"I vote for number three." And dammit, there it was, that stupid little giggle. He always managed to get one out of her.

"Was Temp anything like their father?"

"That's the strangest part. I would've said no, but he went with his father rather than stay behind."

"He might've been trying to protect Faith."

"Maybe. Mr. Walsh was a mean S.O.B. Faith was only twelve when they left; she'd be eighteen now. None of them have tried to contact Glory since they left."

"Was she supposed to go with Hope that night?"

"Yeah, I think she was."

She stared at her shop, weary to the bone. It would be quite a while before the authorities would allow her to open up again. While she understood it, it still broke her heart. As it was, she was pretty sure her insurance was going to go through the roof. She ran her fingers through her hair. "Good-bye, lease. I will miss you."

"Your landlord is going to kick you out?"

Her place had come under fire far too many times for any landlord to let it go. "I've received notice to vacate the premises, and I won't be getting my security deposit back." She sighed. "At least I own all the equipment."

"Then you start over, somewhere else." Julian touched her cheek in an attempt to soothe her.

She shrugged. Cyn was a fighter. She would mourn her lost dream, but she wouldn't let it keep her down for long. She'd start a new dream. "I'm going to look into a new place nearby. I love this neighborhood, but I'm not sure they'll love me when this is all over."

"You'll be fine. None of this is your fault."

She shrugged. It might not be, but that wouldn't matter. If the other landlords blacklisted her she'd be forced to move.

Damn it. She *really* loved this neighborhood.

"I want to meet your parents."

She should've expected that request, but for some reason it still startled her. "My father is dead. He died when I was sixteen, of a heart attack."

His arms tightened around her briefly, hugging her close. "I'm sorry to hear that, sweetheart. It must have been rough for you and your mom."

She relaxed back into him, letting him take her weight. There was no sympathy in his voice, just calm acceptance. She would've brushed off any hint of pity. It was over and done with a long time ago. "It was harder on my mom than on me. She couldn't function without my father. Bills didn't get paid, groceries didn't get bought. Trash started to pile up because she couldn't bring herself to clean. I learned how to cook so we didn't starve to death. I also learned to use the Internet to pay our bills."

"I always knew you were strong." He pressed a soft kiss to the side of her neck, right above her mating mark. "That strength will get you through what's going on now."

She stroked his cheek. "I still want to play Jenga with their bones."

He grinned against her neck. "I love vicious women."

"Vicious?" She laughed bitterly. "My best friend is in the hospital after being fucking *shot*, I have no idea how I'm going to pay my rent and I'm going to turn fuzzy any day now. And the fuzzy thing is the *good* part of my week. You're lucky I'm not rocking back and forth, sucking my thumb and mumbling like a crazy person."

"You're doing better than most would. Glory probably would have died if you hadn't healed her. You should be proud of yourself." He shook her shoulder, emphasizing his point. "It takes most Bears months to learn how to do that. You did it a day after being marked."

"But I couldn't heal her the way you can."

He sighed gently, his warm breath tickling her mating mark. "That's because you're not a Spirit Bear."

He turned her so that she was staring at him and not the shop. He hadn't told her yet that she wouldn't be a Spirit Bear. "Then what am I?"

He bit his lip. "Don't you like surprises?"

Her brows rose. Why didn't he want to tell her what she'd become? "Jules."

"I told you we're different."

"Julian. What did you turn me into?" His reluctance to answer was beginning to scare her. What the hell had he done?

"Me? You're the one who decided to walk the thorny path."

"What does that have to do with anything?"

He looked over her shoulder, his eyes widening. "Is that Ryan over there?"

She whipped around to see what he was looking at, to see if it really was Ryan. He let her go so abruptly, she almost fell to the car's floor. He put the car in gear, and peeled away as if the hounds of hell where after them. "I'm in the car with you, numbnuts."

He had the grace to look sheepish. "It works in the movies."

"You forgot the whole *shove her out of the car first* part." She poked him in the arm. Hard. "What am I going to turn into, Julian?"

"So, where does your mother live?"

"Julian DuCharme, you answer me right this instant or no sex for you!"

"Kodiak."

She gaped like a fish. "Um… Say what now?"

He shrugged. "What can I say? Apparently Bear thinks you need to be really, really big. Look on the bright side, he didn't turn you into a Polar."

"*Jules!*"

"Although, come to think of it, Kodiaks are comparable in size to polar bears. They've even interbred. Or am I thinking of Grizzlies again?"

She opened her mouth, but nothing came out except a squeak. She was going to be a motherfucking *Kodiak*?

He darted a sidelong glance at her but quickly turned his attention back to the road. It was enough for her to notice that he was trying to hold back his grin. "I'm betting you'll be able to kick Eric's ass."

"I'll be able to kick yours too."

"Female Kodiaks might actually be larger than female polar bears. I'll have to double check, I'm not sure."

Well, shit. Wow. She was going to be *huge*. "So when Tabby tells me I have a fat ass—"

"I refuse to answer on the grounds that I may be eviscerated."

She growled again, not at all amused when he laughed so hard he had to pull over.

Julian sighed in relief as he escorted a much calmer Cyn back into the hospital. The shock of finding out she was a Kodiak had left her practically speechless. Well, for Cyn anyway. She'd mumbled to herself the entire way to the hospital, unaware he could hear every single word.

He really hoped she wasn't serious about the rotating pineapple attachment. That might sting.

He spotted Gabe before Cyn did. Julian hoped he had something that would ease his mate's mind, but from the look on Gabe's face he doubted it.

"Cyn. Julian. I need to speak with you alone." Gabe gestured for them to follow him right back out the double doors of the hospital.

"I'll go to check on Glory." Cyn looked back over her shoulder, but allowed Julian to tug her along in Gabe's wake.

"Tabby and Alex are here. They'll let you know if there's any change in her condition." Unless Julian was wrong, she was going to want to hear first-hand what Gabe had to say.

Gabe led them over to his squad car and leaned back against the hood. He crossed his arms over his chest and sighed wearily. "The bomb squad took care of the pipe bomb. They managed to safely explode it, and we're looking into whether or not we can get fingerprints or DNA off of it. Once we have it, we'll send it off to the Senate investigators to see if they can make a match to any rogue shifters. But I should warn you, there was no smell of Cheetah on the pipe bomb."

"What did you smell?"

"Wolf." His frown was confused. "It was almost buried beneath the scent of deer, though."

Julian swore under his breath. "You think whoever hired Gary and his goons have sent others to finish what they started."

Gabe shrugged. "I spoke to the Senate representative in charge of their case. He hasn't been able to get much more out of them. Since Gary spilled the beans that they weren't the ones who attacked Chloe they've kept their mouths shut. I've told Max that there might be a rogue Wolf in the area, as well as a rogue Cheetah, and I called Rick Lowell as well."

"Rick Lowell? As in the Poconos Pack Alpha?" Cyn darted a look back toward the hospital. "Someone had better tell Tabby that both of her Alphas will be in town soon."

Dr. Max Cannon, the Halle Puma Alpha, had granted Tabby, Cyn and Glory his protection when Gary had threatened them, and accepted Tabby as part of his Pride, despite the fact that she was a Wolf. Not long after, Rick Lowell and his Luna, Belle, had arrived from the Poconos and also included Tabby in their Pack. Max had even been willing to change both Glory and Cyn into Pumas right up until he heard they had Bear mates. Then he couldn't leave Living Art fast enough.

Max had good reason to run. While a black Bear like Julian would walk away from a fight with a Puma, a brown Bear like Alex or Ryan would maul even someone as strong as Max. If anyone other than Ryan changed Glory, the fallout had the potential to be disastrous. Not even the Senate would be able to ignore a direct attack on an Alpha by a Bear. Despite the unique circumstances, Ryan would be declared rogue and Gabe would be forced to hunt him down.

"We were thinking of asking his Marshall to assist Adrian and me in hunting the Wolf down." Gabe shook his head, his expression confused. "There's more going on here than I can guess at."

"In other words, your Hunter senses are tingling?" If so, Julian would have to make it a priority to find Ryan before Gabe did. He was the only one who would be able to talk Ryan down. If he could get close enough, he could calm Ryan. Once he understood that he'd been granted access to Glory's room and that she was on the road to recovery his Bear would back off. Ryan would once more be in control of his instincts.

Cyn tapped her foot, her hands on her hips. "We need to find Ryan."

"I'm being pulled in multiple directions. And I'm not entirely certain that Ryan isn't one of them." Gabe tipped his hat to Cyn and shook Julian's hand. "I'll give you both a call when I have something. In the meantime, now that you're mated—congratulations, by the way—I highly suggest the two of you live together. With Glory in the hospital Cyn is alone in the apartment, and that just makes my butt itch."

"I'll make sure she's not alone." Even if it meant he had to give up his job with Jamie's practice. He'd rather force her to move back with him to Canada than risk her life.

"I can't believe I'm saying this, but if Julian and I get married wouldn't he automatically become a citizen? He's worried about missing work, since he's here on a work visa. If he's with me around the clock, that jeopardizes his visa, doesn't it?" Cyn bit her lip, her expression a combination of concern and determination.

Gabe's brows rose in surprise. "I'm not sure."

Julian shook his head. "Marriage to a US citizen would allow me to apply for a green card on our third anniversary. I can then apply to become a citizen, but it's still no guarantee. And while I have every intention of doing just that, I'll have to double check with Jamie and make sure that what's going on right now counts toward my vacation time. That way, my visa should be safe."

"The other option is I go to work with you. I should be safe enough in Jamie's office, right?" She scowled, but the expression was far too adorable to be intimidating. "It's not like I can open the shop."

"And I'm betting Alex will keep Tabby close, so she should be safe." Having Cyn around while he worked wouldn't exactly be a hardship. "If Jamie okays it, we'll go for it."

"In that case, I'll leave you to check on Glory. I've already spoken to her, but unfortunately she didn't see anything." Gabe walked off with a wave, but stopped before he reached the patrol car. "Do me a favor, Julian. Talk to Tim. Find out if certain steps need to be taken." He drove off, leaving Julian behind to explain to Cyn exactly what *steps might need to be taken* meant.

He wondered if, given the choice, which option Tim would choose.

Chapter Fifteen

"I'm exhausted." Cyn flopped down on the sofa with a groan.

Julian flopped down next to her and pulled her close. "Me too." His dark hair caressed her as he leaned over and kissed the top of her head. "Any idea what we're going to do?"

"About?" She began stroking the length of his hair that had fallen across her chest. It always amazed her how soft it was.

"Ryan and Glory."

She smiled. "Steal their clothes, lock them in a room together and let nature take its course."

"Huh. I should have tried that with you."

She smacked him in the stomach. Like that would have worked with her. It would have only pissed her off.

"That is why I don't think it will work with Ryan and Glory." He nibbled on her ear. "You keep caressing your breasts with my hair and I'm going to get ideas."

She blushed as she realized he was right. She *had* been stroking her breasts with his hair. "Good ideas or bad ones?"

Julian smiled against her neck as he licked the mating mark. "Definitely bad."

Cyn shivered and brushed his hair over her nipple.

"I think that would work better if we take your clothes off." Before she could suggest they move to the bedroom, he was tugging off her T-shirt. "Bra too."

She moaned as his hair brushed against the tops of her breasts. Shit. She couldn't believe they were going to do this.

She'd never had any kind of weird fetish before, so what was up with the feel of his hair?

Her bra hit the floor, and her nipples were exposed to the air. God, she ached, and he'd barely touched her.

Julian kissed her, tasting her mouth in slow, sensual strokes. All the while he was undoing her jeans, sliding them down her thighs, exposing her hot-pink panties. "Take them off the rest of the way."

She pushed off her jeans and panties, eager for what he had planned. He had that wicked gleam in his eye, the one that promised they were both about to have some fun.

She could use some damn fun.

Julian straddled her thighs, careful to keep his weight off of her. He put his hands on top of the sofa, effectively caging her. "Now. About my hair." He shook his head and the ends of his hair tickled across her nipples. She arched her back, unable to stop herself from reaching for the pleasurable sensation. "Like that, hmm?"

"Oh God." She covered her face with her hands. "I'm a perv."

He laughed and pulled her hands down. "Nope. You've just given me another reason to never cut my hair."

She glared at him. "You'd better not." She loved his hair. She whimpered as he stroked the long, silky strands across her breast. *Maybe a little too much.*

"Don't worry, Cyn. Everyone has a thing."

She stared down at his crotch. "I hope not."

He chuckled and leaned forward, nibbling the side of her neck. "Not *that* thing." He arched his hips, brushing his hardened *thing* against her. "Something that turns them on. Yours is my hair."

She leaned her head to the side to give him better access. She wanted to wear a different mark there, one everyone would understand. "What's your thing?"

Julian bit down gently and sucked. Cyn wove her hands in his hair and cupped the back of his head, holding him to her. She wanted his mark good and dark. She bucked her hips, the sensation of him sucking up a mark on her going straight to her clit.

"Still want to know my thing?"

She nodded. If he reacted like that, she'd give him anything he wanted.

"Wait here." He hopped off of her and raced out of the room. Was he going for whipped cream? Chocolate? Maybe...no, he was running up the stairs. What was up there? Dildos? Did he have a box of vibrating fun he wanted to play with?

He came back down with his hands behind his back, completely naked. His dick bobbed as he walked, rock hard and mouthwatering. "Want to see?"

"Yeah." Now she was curious. She sat up straight, eyeing him with some misgiving. He looked guilty as hell.

He held out a red bit of fabric. "Put it on for me?"

She stood and took the fabric from him. It wasn't until she held it that she realized what it was. "I'm going to need more *kanji*, aren't I?"

"That depends on where you want to stick it."

She stifled a laugh and slid the red satin Sailor Mars skirt up her thighs. When it was at her knees, he held up his hand. "Wait!" She paused, wondering what the hell he was up to.

When he moved behind her she knew. *And I thought I was the perv.*

"Okay. Go."

She teased him, sliding the skirt up slowly, giving him the show he so obviously wanted. She even made sure to wiggle her ass as the skirt slid up those final few inches, causing it to sway enticingly.

He moved in close behind her, lifting his hair and sliding it over her shoulders until it cascaded over her breasts. "Hold still, sweetheart."

Cyn did as he asked, wondering what he was going to do next. She didn't have to wait long. He slid his hands under the skirt and palmed her ass. He began nibbling on her neck again. "You like this?"

It had potential. "You going to do anything besides feel me up?"

"I was thinking of fucking you. If you don't mind, that is."

"Oh. No. That's okay." He was suddenly stroking her pussy, his fingers playing with the curls. "Fucking's good."

I have got to stop sounding like a squeaky toy when he touches me there.

He licked another spot on her neck. "Walk forward."

Forward was the stairway. Were they going upstairs? She was so ready to be fucked into the mattress.

Cyn took a tentative step forward and Julian moved in sync with her, the two of them awkward in all the right ways.

Suddenly she was pushed forward, her hands landing on one of the steps. "Have I mentioned how much I love your ass?"

She squirmed as he stroked the round globes. "You're not going there." Not now, anyway. If they ever did that, she was going to be well prepared, well lubed, and well and truly drunk. He wasn't about to go where no man had gone before without making sure both her inside and her outside were greased.

He laughed. "That's not the hole I'm looking for."

She glared at him over her shoulder. "So what are you looking for?"

He grinned that evil, Grinchy grin, and got on his knees behind her. Within seconds his tongue was in her pussy and she was nearly on her knees herself. She went up on her toes as he found a *really* good spot to suck. "Oh God. Jules." Her hands clenched in the carpet. The pleasure was overwhelming. She folded her arms on the step and rested her head on them, watching her red skirt sway gently as her mate ate her out.

She began to push back against him. She needed something larger than his tongue in her. "Fuck me, Jules."

He gave her one last swipe before he stood. "Sure you don't want to come first?"

She growled, low and inhuman. If her mate didn't get his dick in her in the next two seconds she was going to jump his ass and do it herself.

Julian grasped her hips in a firm grip and pulled her back. He slid into her with a moan, his hips slapping against her ass at the force. He leaned over her and placed his hands on either side of her head, his hair a curtain around them, locking them in their own little world.

"Tug on my hair. Play with it. Do whatever you want," he whispered in her ear. She shivered as he gave her shoulder a gentle bite, not strong enough to break the skin. He ground his hips against her, driving his cock even deeper. "I wanted to do this the minute I saw this skirt."

She shifted position until she was kneeling on the steps. She spread her legs wider, wanting him as deep as he could get. "Give it to me." She tugged his hair hard and was rewarded by his Bear growl.

Fuck. She never thought hearing him growl like that would be such a turn-on.

She tugged on his hair again and Julian went wild, pulling upright to pound into her with such force she had to brace herself on the step. He kept pulling her toward him as he fucked her until she got the message and began thrusting back, making them both work for it. She stroked her clit furiously, ready to come. "Jules. God, Jules."

With a strangled groan he came, pouring inside her in a hot wave.

Shit. She was so. Damn. *Close.* Just two more seconds. That was all she—

Razor-sharp fangs sank into her and she screamed, coming in a white wave of pleasure so brutal she nearly passed out.

Julian draped himself over her and panted in her ear. "I love this skirt."

Damn it. There went those stupid, happy giggles again. One of these days she was going to have to admit why he made her so happy all the fucking time.

He kissed the side of her neck and helped her to her feet. "Bed."

"Bed," she agreed, and staggered up the stairs with him. Snuggling down with him in the warmth of his bedroom both scared her silly and made her yearn to say three simple words. She snuggled up against him as they drifted off together, her last thought one of self-preservation.

But not today.

Finding Ryan was turning out to be harder than she thought. It was like the man had fallen off the face of the earth. The amazing Super Bear said he couldn't sense Ryan, even when they left the town limits. They'd spent two whole days just combing the campus, only to come up empty-handed.

Today, Julian was returning to work and Cyn was going with him. She was looking forward to seeing him do what he loved. And it was obvious he loved helping people. He put on those blue scrubs, and his whole face lit up. His smile was brighter, his walk lighter. There was a sparkle in his eye that had been missing for the last few days. Just listening to him chatter about his upcoming day while they ate breakfast together was enough to drive home one simple fact. There was no way she'd ever be able to take this away from him. She would do better to just pluck his heart from his chest and have done with it.

Cyn understood. She missed Living Art like she'd miss an arm or leg. Her fingers were itching to get back to work, to make the art that she loved. He'd bought her some sketchpads and some pencils, but it just wasn't the same. When they weren't hunting for Ryan or sleeping, she was drawing new flash for the display cases. She had one in particular that she thought she might want to ink on Julian, but she'd have to run it by him first. He was the only man she'd ever been with whose skin was ink free, and she longed to change that.

"You're going to be a good girl today, right, and let Daddy work?" She glared at him, but all he did was chuckle. "You'll sit quietly and eat your cookie and drink your juice?"

"Only if the juice has vodka in it," Cyn muttered. She held up her sketchbook. "Do I get to color too?"

"Only if you're coming up with a tattoo for me." He shot her a cheesy grin. "Remember, it has to say 'Property of Cyn' in big, bold letters."

"I've told you before that I am not tattooing that on your ass."

"I bet I could get Tabby to do it."

"You really want Alex to find out that Tabby saw your naked ass?"

He frowned, but he was having a hard time keeping it in place, the smile he was holding back threatening to break free. "Good point. He's mean when he's pissed."

"Yep. And since you've proven you know how to use this—" she patted his cock through his scrubs, "—I'd hate to lose it to a Grizzly mauling."

"You and me both." He pressed her hand closer. "Hold that thought, would you?"

Aggravating man. She was giggling again despite herself. She swatted at him with the sketchbook, delighted when he laughed. Who knew something so simple as a man's laughter could make her feel so good?

"I spoke to Tim."

There went the good mood. "What was his decision?"

"He wants to meet Rick Lowell."

Cyn blinked. The Poconos Pack Alpha was a scary fucking dude. If Tim was thinking of going that route, he had bigger balls than she thought. "You think Rick would go for it?"

"With Tabby and I to vouch for him, I don't see why not. And Rick has been muttering about wanting a nurse or doctor up at the Lodge for some time. Tim might be just what the Pack needs."

"Has Rick tried to get you to move up there?"

"Yup."

"And your answer was?" She was pretty sure what it had been, but it wouldn't hurt to have it confirmed.

"Nope."

"Good. I don't think the Red Wolf Ski Lodge needs a tattoo artist."

There was a soft smile gracing his lips. "Haven't you figured it out yet? I go where you go. If that means I live the rest of my life in Halle as an illegal immigrant, so be it. If you choose to move to Hawaii or Alaska? I pack my bags. My only request is that we not move to a big city like New York or Los Angeles. I don't think either one of us would be very comfortable there. Besides, our Bears would have no place to roam when we wanted to shift."

The thought of Julian in a place like New York or Los Angeles, with so many people in pain, sent shivers down her spine. He would literally kill himself trying to heal the world. It was now her job to see to it that her Super Bear would be around to save those who truly needed it.

She picked up her sketchpad and began to draw.

"We're here." He pulled into the parking lot attached to the doctors' office and parked in the employees' only area. "Alex told me that if you and Tabby want to go out for lunch he's willing to take you. The only thing I ask is that if you do, don't leave his side."

It would be nice to go out to lunch with Tabby. "Maybe Alex could take us to the hospital, see how Glory's doing today."

"I could meet you there if you wanted to. You and Tabby should be safe in the hospital." He pressed a soft kiss to her lips. "Promise me you'll be careful. It would literally kill me to lose you now."

She paled. She'd forgotten that. When she asked Tabby about her mating with Alex, Tabby had told her that when two shifters mated their life forces were intertwined. That meant if anything happened to her, Julian would die.

"Cyn?"

She took a deep breath and tried to calm down. She could freak out later, maybe with Tabby. Or better yet, Alex. She now understood why Alex reacted the way he did every time his mate was threatened. She'd almost forgotten about Tai's words, the vision he had of Julian lying in a pool of his own blood. "I'm fine."

He pushed her hair back behind her ear. "You sure?"

"Yeah." She'd have to be. She didn't stand just to lose Tabby and Glory now. She had a whole fuzzy family, the most important of which was the fuzzy sitting next to her. She offered him a smile, cursing to herself when it trembled. "Just a whole lot of shit going on."

He nodded as if he understood, but she sincerely doubted it. She barely understood it herself. "Let's go in then." He waved to someone over her shoulder, and she turned to find Dr. Howard, waving back from his own car. Climbing out of the car with him was Marie, and Cyn smiled to see her. Since the lunch they'd had together Marie had gone out of her way to email Cyn, slowly building a friendship with her. They might never have much in common beyond their men, but Cyn respected the hell out of her. "Good morning!" Marie gave a wave of her own, beaming at Julian and Cyn. "I hear you'll be spending the day with Jamie." Jamie and Marie wrapped their arms around each other's waists, leaning into each other like they'd done it a thousand times before. They probably had.

"We thought it was a good idea. Do you have any problems with it?" She didn't want Marie to worry about Jamie's safety. Had anyone told Marie what was going on? Jamie already understood, and was willing to stand by them.

Marie waved her hand dismissively. "Not a one. Just do me a favor and make sure he actually takes those breaks he's supposed to." She gazed fondly up at her husband. "I'm off to get my hair done. Have a good day, sweetheart."

"You too." The pair kissed good-bye and Marie walked away, a spring in her step. Watching the two of them together gave her ideas on the way she and Julian would be once they settled into their own mating. Marie was her own woman, part owner in several of her father's businesses, and a major contributor to at least two local charities. She was busy being who she wanted to be, and shared that with Jamie, just as he seemed to share his life with Marie.

Maybe saying those three little words wouldn't change anything at all. Maybe she *could* have it all with Jules.

A bright shimmer on the ground caught her attention. She bent down and picked up an earring off the ground. "Pretty. I wonder who it belongs to?"

"Shit. That's one of Marie's favorite earrings." Jamie reached for it.

Cyn was already moving, the earring clutched in her fist. She had something she wanted to ask the other woman, out of hearing of the men. "She's right over there. Just wait a second before you go in."

"Cyn, don't you dare." Julian strode after her, his expression alarmed.

Cyn rolled her eyes. "I don't think anything bad can happen to me in the next five feet." She held out her hand, earring in her palm. "Marie, I think you lost your earring."

Marie started to turn. "Thanks—" She pitched forward, landing in a sprawled heap on the ground. Barely a second later Cyn heard the reason why.

Gunshot. The crack echoed loudly and seemed to come from everywhere at once.

"Down!" Julian shoved her behind the car before racing back to Jamie. She risked a quick peek and saw the Jamie lay on the ground as well. His skin had taken on a waxy, bluish tinge.

He wasn't breathing.

She risked crawling to Marie. The shooter could still be out there, but Cyn was compelled to check on the fallen woman. She touched Marie's wrist.

She was already dead. From the way the back of her head looked she'd been dead before she hit the ground. And if Marie was dead...

She got to her feet and raced toward Julian. Fuck the sniper. Super Bear was going to try and save Jamie, no matter what. If Jamie was too far gone, Julian would be taken with him. He would pour everything he had into keeping the man alive until there was nothing left to save himself with.

Cyn placed her hands on Julian's shoulders and concentrated, harder than she had when Glory had been shot. She couldn't allow Julian to go. Love, lust, freaky shifter hormones; it didn't matter what she wanted to call it. If Julian died here there would be four bodies for the undertakers, three without a mark on them.

His hair was pure white, his eyes closed as he battled death itself. She followed him down the spiral of the healing path, lending her own strength to his, little though it was. She kept him tethered to his body as he somehow pulled a miracle out of his ass and got Jamie breathing again, got his heart to start. He repaired what little damage there was from Jamie's body being deprived of oxygen. Jamie rewarded them with a whimper, but he didn't wake up. When Julian slumped over, exhausted and unconscious, Cyn was there to catch him.

She was still sitting there, body bowed protectively over him, when Gabe Anderson pulled up. Lights and sirens blared from all three patrol cars, and in the distance she could hear an ambulance. She caressed Julian's cheek, uncaring that her claws were out. "Cavalry is here, Jules."

He didn't stir. There was not a single strand of black in his wild mane of hair.

Chapter Sixteen

God damn, he hurt. He couldn't remember ever hurting this badly in his entire fucking life. His eyelids felt like they were weighted down with stones, and he'd swear before the ancestors even his toenails ached. What the hell had he been doing? More importantly, where was Cyn?

He finally managed to wrestle his eyelids open, only to find he was in a hospital room. Hell, it even looked familiar. Maybe he was in the same one he'd been in last time he'd—

Shit. *Marie.* They'd lost Marie, and nearly lost Jamie.

He hoped he hadn't been foolish to save Jamie. How was Jamie supposed to survive without his mate? Would he spend the rest of his life pining, tortured by mate dreams that could never be realized? One thing was certain; Jamie would never be the same again.

The squeak of a sneaker on linoleum had him forcing his head to turn. Cyn was pacing back and forth, her sneaker squeaking with every turn she made. She was snarling, the sound inhuman. Her Bear was close to the surface, trying to escape her control.

He tried to whisper her name, but all that came out was a soundless exhalation. She must've heard him anyway because she faced him, his name a breathless whisper. He could see the wildness in her, but he was too weak to calm her.

She took a step toward him, reaching for him, when the door behind her opened. Gabe stepped in, followed by his mate Sarah, the Halle Puma Omega. Both looked weary to the bone, their eyes red-rimmed. Julian could make out the scent of recent tears.

Cyn took hold of Julian's hand and turned to face them. "Gabe. Sarah."

Sarah ran her hand through her hair. "How are you two?"

Julian couldn't roll his eyes, but he could think about it.

"Jules just woke up. He's still weak as a newborn kitten and he can't speak yet. He…" Cyn gulped, and only then did he realize how close to tears she was. "He almost died."

Sarah's eyes filled with tears. "I'm so, so sorry."

Gabe took his mate in his arms and held her tight as she broke down. "Adrian collapsed in the middle of the office. He's got the world's worst migraine right now. He's home, allowing his mate, Sheri, to pamper him. Max is beside himself. He's declared the sniper a threat not just to you but to the whole Pride. He's officially asked me to Hunt." Gabe shrugged. "I've contacted the Senate and I might get some reinforcements. I might not, depending on how large the threat turns out to be."

"The shooter is a shifter. I'm positive." Sarah wiped her eyes. Her voice was shaky but determined. "The rage behind his actions was overwhelming."

"How could you tell?" Cyn settled down on the bed by Julian, still firmly grasping his hand.

"Omegas can sense the emotional well-being of the Pride. When Marie fell, Sarah sensed Jamie's suffering." Gabe grimaced. "Due to some…unfortunate misunderstandings, Sarah's power is exceptionally strong. When she experienced Jamie's loss, she touched something out of the ordinary."

"When I connected to Jamie I felt the rage of the shooter. Whoever this is, it's personal."

"So they *are* after me." Cyn tightened her grip and Julian gasped. She was nearly pulverizing his fingers. She'd gotten stronger. "We need to lay a trap for this son of a bitch."

"I don't think I can track him. He's not one of us; I'll only feel it if he targets one of you again." Sarah bit her lip and stared at Cyn, her expression sympathetic. "He's not after you, per se. I think he's after *all* of you."

Cyn tilted her head. "Huh?"

"You, your friend Glory, and Tabby. I think all three of you are the target."

"So the shot that killed Marie was meant for me, and he got pissed when he missed."

"I think so, yes."

Shit. Julian needed to get his strength back as fast as possible. Cyn was in greater danger than he'd thought. The heartbeat monitor picked up his distress, blipping faster than it had been.

"Shh." Cyn stroked his hair, smiling at him as if she didn't have a care in the world. Too bad he could clearly see her fangs. "It'll be all right, Jules."

Bullshit. His beautiful, strong mate was going to go out there and make herself a target while he was strapped to a fucking hospital bed. There were only two other people who could stop her, and one of them was in the same damn hospital.

He struggled to sit up, trying desperately to find the strength to hold her to him.

"Jules, I'm not going anywhere. Not until you're out of here. I'm not stupid, *querido*."

He stilled. She'd never used an endearment with him before. He'd have to ask what it meant later, when he could speak again.

"We'll sit down together with Gabe and figure out the safest way to do this. I'm the best candidate. Glory is still too injured, and with Ryan gone I'm not risking her. Tabby is pregnant. That leaves me." She grinned down at him savagely. "Besides, I want to see the look on that fucker's face when he finds out he's been messing with a Kodiak."

"You're a *Kodiak*?" Gabe choked out a laugh when Cyn nodded. "Holy shit. How the hell did that happen?"

Julian did manage to roll his eyes this time, but his voice still wouldn't work. What came out sounded more like a croak.

"Ask Super Bear some time. I think it had something to do with thorny paths and the beer bottle song."

"Okay." Gabe had the same half-confused, half-amused expression a number of people sometimes had around Cyn. "Julian, to help you feel better, there are guards on your door and Glory's. We're not taking any more chances. Adrian has given orders that none of you be left alone."

"If we aren't left alone how are we supposed to catch this asshole?"

"He has to be aware that he's being hunted." Gabe stroked Sarah's hair; whether he was attempting to soothe himself or his mate, Julian wasn't sure. "The fact that he was willing to take a shot at you with others around makes me really uneasy. I don't think it will matter to him if I put a hundred guards on you, he'll still come after you."

Then how were they supposed to keep the girls safe? Alex had to be going out of his mind with worry. Julian wouldn't put it past him to pick up Tabby and cart her off to Oregon, where the rest of his clan lived. If Julian thought it would keep Cyn safe, he'd encourage Alex to take her with him. It was going to take Julian days to heal the damage he'd done to himself saving Jamie.

"I think you should put a guard on Jamie." Cyn sat on the edge of his hospital bed with a weary sigh. "Now that he's lost Marie he's going to..." She scrubbed her hand wearily over her face. "Hell, I don't know what he's going to do, but I have an idea. I've only been mated a short time, but I don't think I could live in a world without Julian in it."

Julian squeezed her hand as tightly as he could, which admittedly wasn't very. He could barely muster up the strength to do even that. The fact that she was willing to say such a thing, especially in the presence of others, warmed him straight through.

Whether she wanted to believe it or not, she was coming to love him. He liked to think she would've loved him even without the mate bond, but it sure didn't hurt. At this point he'd take any advantage he could get. His mate was a stubborn woman. She would have fought any permanent connection to another person other than the one she had with Tabby and Glory.

Does that make me a bastard or just a man desperately in love?

"Tell your guards I've moved in with Julian." She stared down at him, her expression savagely protective. "I'm not letting him out of my sight."

He would've had no problem with that if he hadn't noticed the fur sprouting from her arms.

"You're changing." Gabe cursed softly. "You can't do that here."

"Really? You think?" Cyn was staring at her arm with something akin to horror. "What the fuck do I do?"

Call Alex. Julian still couldn't speak. *For fuck's sake, call Alex!*

191

Gabe's phone rang. He grimaced when he saw the caller ID. With a guilty look at his mate, he answered the phone. "Hi, Chloe. What's up?"

Sarah stiffened, but didn't pull away from her mate.

"I'm sorry. Could you repeat that?" Gabe was giving Julian a strange look. "Right. I'll do that. Okay. Yeah. Take care, vixen. Talk to you later." He hung up the phone and pulled Sarah tightly to his side. "That was Chloe. She says you want us to call Alex."

Julian sighed his relief and relaxed. For the first time he thanked his strange bond with the little Fox.

"I'll take that as a yes." Gabe opened his phone again and began dialing.

"Don't worry, Super Bear." Cyn kissed his forehead, her fangs cool against his skin. "Everything will be all right."

It was not all right. It was so far from right it was almost left. Who the hell had she been kidding? Julian or herself?

"It's a lot easier than you think it is."

Cyn rolled her eyes and wondered how the hell she'd gotten into this situation. Here she was, standing naked in the woods with her best friend's lover, who was also naked (and yummy-looking, not that she'd tell either Tabby or Julian that). Worse, she was standing butt-naked out in the woods with Alex and six other men, half of whom carried guns. The other half were in their puma form, scouting the area as quietly as only a cat could. All of them were Halle cops, and each and every one of them had checked her out before going to their assigned tasks. Brown fur kept sprouting in the oddest places, and her claws refused to retract. Her fangs were so stinking long she was beginning to lisp. Julian, who was supposed to help her through her change, was still in the hospital. He barely had the strength to speak, let alone defend himself. According to Gabe and Sarah, that was half the reason her Bear was coming out early. Between Glory's wounds and Julian's weakness, the need to defend her loved ones was just too strong. Her Bear was reacting to her emotions and forcing its way out. She was going to change today whether she liked it or not.

And her best friend's naked mate was going to help her. In front of witnesses. Joy. Thank God Tabby wasn't here to see her humiliation. She was safe, sound and dressed, keeping watch over Glory and surrounded by guards.

"Do yourself a favor and just relax." Alex demonstrated by taking a deep breath, pushing out a truly impressive pair of pecs. No wonder Tabby always had a smile on her face. "Now you."

Cyn rolled her eyes and took a deep breath, blowing it back out noisily.

Alex grinned. "Now you're getting it."

Yeah, right. The only thing she was getting was frozen boobs and sideways looks. This was her teenage hell come to life. All that was needed was for somebody to start belting out *Oklahoma!* and her day would be complete.

"Now, let your Bear out. She wants to come out. Close your eyes and scent the wind."

Cyn closed her eyes. She lifted her face to the breeze, trying to smell the things Alex did. Amazingly enough, she could detect things she never had before. She had no idea what they were, but she was sure Julian would be able to help her figure it out once he was well enough to shift with her.

"A bear's sense of smell is much stronger than that of a bloodhound. We can track prey over miles, and our mates even further than that. Our night vision is better than that of a human, but we get the same color vision."

193

Her nose twitched. She tilted her head, trying to catch a strangely alluring scent.

"Bears are omnivores. What you smell is a squirrel, racing across the treetops to get away from us."

Well. That was disgusting. She was salivating over a squirrel? Maybe she should've had Alex take her to McDonald's before coming out here.

Mm. Big Mac. Her stomach rumbled. She prayed it wasn't for two all-squirrel patties on a sesame seed bun. That was just...ew.

"Look down at your hands."

She opened her eyes to find her hands had become paws.

"Let it flow. You've followed the spiral of the healing path before. This is almost exactly the same, except instead of you drawing strength from your Bear it will draw on you."

It was the strangest thing she'd ever experienced. Her skin rippled, flowed over muscle and bone that was suddenly bigger. There was no ugly, painful crunching as her bones realigned, never mind what the horror movies showed. It was more of a pins and needles feeling, electricity dancing along nerve endings that were abruptly in different places. Her hands—no, her *paws*, landed on dry leaves and dirt.

The change was almost complete.

She looked up from her hands to find herself nose to nose (Snout to snout? She really had to look this shit up) with a Grizzly that smelled remarkably like Alex. She jerked back, landing on her furry rump, woofing in surprise.

Who knew bears could laugh? Alex's shoulders shook as he wheezed. Cyn stood back up and growled softly, almost laughing herself when Alex hid his face under his paws. He was such a goof that it was hard to remember sometimes how dangerous he could really be.

Alex stroked his nose under her chin, and then lumbered off into the underbrush. It startled her that they were roughly the same size. She'd thought he would be bigger, but they really were snout to snout. He paused momentarily to look back at her as if to say, *Well?*

Cyn lumbered off after him, content to play follow the leader. She did chuff out a laugh when her posse of Pumas scrambled to keep up, the ones who'd chosen to stay human having the hardest time. But even her bodyguards couldn't distract her from the whole new world that had opened up to her senses. Her sight didn't seem to be any different than her human form, but her heightened hearing and sense of smell were almost overwhelming. It was going to take time to sort out everything she was experiencing. She just hoped the next time she changed Julian was at her side. As cute as Alex was, she missed her mate.

Chapter Seventeen

Julian groaned as Cyn helped him settle on the sofa. "Thank fuck. I fucking *hate* hospitals."

She lifted his feet up onto some propped up pillows and covered him with a throw he'd never seen before but smelled distinctly of her. "You were only allowed out as soon as you were on the condition that you would rest."

"I will. I promise." Hell, he could barely walk. What did she think he was going to do, juggle chainsaws? They'd managed to keep him in the hospital for two days, and if he'd stayed any longer than that, he would've lost his mind. There was no way he'd be able to recuperate around all those people.

She muttered something under her breath, something in Spanish that ended in *cabrón,* and stalked off toward the kitchen. She'd been stubbornly opposed to his leaving the hospital until he'd explained to her what staying there was doing to him. She still wasn't sure she'd made the right decision in helping him convince the doctors to release him, but she'd see. Already he was stronger, his Bear calmer. Getting away from all of the sick and the wounded would help his recovery immensely.

The doorbell rang, startling him, but he didn't even bother trying to stand up to answer it. He wouldn't be able to make his way to the door anyway. Not without falling flat on his ass. Cyn stomped by him, still muttering in Spanish. He pitied anyone on the other side of the door. His mate was spoiling for a fight.

He heard Cyn gasp as she opened the door. "Oh, hi."

"Hello, Cyn." In breezed Emma Cannon, Curana of the Halle Puma Pride. Her dark brown hair was tied up in a long, bouncy ponytail. Her crimson V-neck shirt and dark gray jeans hugged every curve. In her hands were three pizza boxes, the rich scent of spicy meat, melted cheese and ripe tomato sauce making his mouth water.

She was followed swiftly by her mate, the blonde haired, blue-eyed Halle Alpha. Max had five more pizza boxes, and from the scent Julian could tell at least one of them was his favorite Hawaiian style. Max followed his tiny mate right into Julian's kitchen, smiling cheerfully at Cyn and nodding to Julian. "Hey, Julian. Sorry about this."

The doorbell rang before he could respond.

"Did I mention the others will be here soon?" Max glided, catlike, right over to Julian's favorite chair. He settled himself in and immediately pulled his mate onto his lap.

Julian frowned at Emma. "You haven't been getting enough iron."

Emma's eyes went wide with a clear message that, if Julian valued his balls, he'd stay quiet.

"Emma?" Max's attention was completely focused on his Curana, barely acknowledging Simon and Becky Holt as they carried even more pizza into Julian's kitchen.

"I'm fine, Max." She wiggled her butt, clearly trying to distract him. From the way Max's nostrils flared it was working.

"You've been tired a lot lately." Max stroked a hand over Emma's hip, stilling her. His golden gaze suddenly stabbed into Julian as a white mist surrounded the Alpha pair. "Tell me what's wrong with my mate."

He could hear Simon and Becky groaning as their Alpha's power washed over the room. Cyn actually went to her knees, unable to hold under the weight.

Julian smiled, and yawned.

Emma slapped Max's arm. "Knock it off, Lion-O."

The white mist dissipated, along with the weight of Max's displeasure. "I'm sorry, but if it was your mate what would you do?"

Julian stared at Emma for a few moments before answering Max's question. "I'd let her tell me when she was damn good and ready."

Max sat up a little straighter, comprehension slowly beginning to dawn in his expression, when the doorbell rang again. "Emma?"

"Shh." She stroked Max's cheek, her gaze tender. "We'll talk when we get home. I promise."

Poor Max looked dazed as Adrian and Sheri walked in the front door, carrying enough soda to drown the Pittsburgh Steelers. Or rather, Adrian was carrying it. Sheri had her seeing-eye dog, Jerry, guiding her through the house. She waved to the room in general. "Hi, everyone. Gabe and Sarah are right behind us."

Sarah dashed into the house and right up to the Alpha pair. "What's wrong?"

Max smiled into his mate's eyes and caressed her stomach. "Absolutely nothing."

"Think you have all the answers, don't you, Lion-O?" But Julian noticed Emma wasn't pushing her mate's hand away. On the contrary, her fingers stroked across the back of it as she gazed fondly into blue eyes still speckled with gold.

Max's answering grin was chock full of lazy arrogance. "I do."

Julian yawned again. This time it wasn't faked. "Not that I'm not thrilled to see all of you, but why the hell are you here?"

"Because you couldn't come to our house." The look Emma shot him said that answer should be obvious.

"Rick and Belle should be here in about fifteen minutes, and Tabby and Alex are on their way." Gabe began dragging chairs from the kitchen and dining room into the living room.

"So we're having an impromptu pizza party because...?" Cyn crossed her arms and began tapping her foot. She had that stubborn look on her face, the one that said she'd better get answers and soon.

"Pride meeting. Well, Pride and Pack, since Tabby's technically both." Emma patted Max's arm and stood, heading straight for the kitchen. "Do you guys have any paper plates and cups?"

"But we're not Pride." Cyn looked as confused as Julian.

"Not yet," Becky giggled.

"When I told Gary that you, Glory and Tabby were under my protection, I meant it." Max crossed his arms over his chest and practically dared Cyn to question him further.

Her gaze landed on Julian, and an unholy grin crossed her face. "Does that protection extend to my mate?"

Max's answering smile was as full of evil as only a cat could manage. "It does now."

Julian thumped his head on the sofa with a groan. Wonderful. Now he was being protected by Pumas and Foxes and Bears, oh my. He wondered if he could sell tickets to this little three-ring circus.

"I had forgotten about that." Sarah stared thoughtfully at Cyn. "Maybe that's why I could feel the shooter so clearly."

"Because there were three Pride members there." Max nodded sagely. Julian figured the man was bullshitting. Max liked to pretend he was the uber-wise Alpha, but Julian—

Wait. When did Cyn become Pride?

Alex and Tabby walked into his house as if they owned it, not even bothering to use the doorbell. Any thought of irritation vanished when he saw who was with them. "Glory!"

Glory was immediately surrounded by overly solicitous kitties. She was settled into Julian's favorite chair, which Max rapidly vacated, and handed a drink and a slice of pizza that had her wrinkling her nose. She set the plate aside on the side table and turned watery baby blues toward Max. "Where's Ryan?"

Wow. Talk about an uncomfortable silence.

"We haven't got a clue." Gabe shared a long, uncomfortable look with Adrian, the Halle Marshall. "It's like he just disappeared."

Julian winced. That was probably the worst thing Gabe could have said. Glory took a deep breath as if to yell, but instead wound up in a long, painful sounding coughing fit. She was instantly surrounded as everyone but Julian tried to soothe her. He hadn't seen so much guilt in the room since his mother caught him and his friends covered in Christmas cookie crumbs two hours before the relatives were due. All of them were talking at once so none of it made any sense. It got so loud that only Julian noticed when the front door opened again. A massive, scowling redhead and a dainty, China doll blonde stopped and stared at the chaos before the blonde reached into her purse and pulled out—

Ancestors have mercy that was *loud*. But effective. All of the Pumas stopped and stared at the smiling woman holding the air horn. The redhead shook his head like a dog in the rain. "I hate it when she does that."

The blonde, who just had to be Belinda "Belle" Lowell, shook the air horn enticingly at the Curana. "Come on, you know you want one."

Max scowled at the gleam in his mate's eye. "Don't even think about it, Emma."

"But Max, it's so shiny." Emma pouted up at her mate and batted her ridiculously thick lashes.

"*Emma.*"

"Fine."

Out of the corner of his eye Julian saw the Poconos Pack Luna make the universal sign for *call me*.

"Oh no, you don't." Rick Lowell picked up his mate like she weighed less than a kitten. "Let Max keep the illusion he runs things around here."

The Pumas laughed at Belle's indolent grin, easing the tension left over from Gabe's earlier remark. Soon everyone was settled with pizza and drinks, some on the floor, some nudging at Julian until he sat upright. Cyn sat at his feet, her back resting comfortably against his legs. Next to him sat Belle, her mate on the floor between her legs. She leaned down every now and then and fed him bites of her pizza, never once breaking the stream of gossip between her and Emma. Their favorite topic seemed to be two men named Ben and Dave who were planning a commitment ceremony sometime around Christmas. Apparently, Dave had sent Emma some images of drag queens in wedding dresses. He wanted her opinion on which one she thought would look best on him.

Belle didn't even laugh. Hell, she had a favorite, and planned to tell Dave so when she got home.

Once everyone was done eating, Max rose to his feet, ready to begin the meeting. "Thank you for coming, everyone. I think we all know why we're here."

Rick held up a hand. "I'm extending an invitation to Tabby, Alex and their friends to come up to the Lodge until the shooter is caught."

Julian blinked in surprise. He hadn't been expecting that maneuver from the Wolf alpha. "How will we be safer up there than we are here?" If Rick could guarantee Cyn's safety, her furry butt was going up that mountain whether she liked it or not.

"Don't even think about it, Super Bear." Cyn glowered up at him, which looked really odd, considering she had to do it upside down. "They need me to catch this son of a bitch."

"Unfortunately, I think she's right." The few times in the past when Julian had met with Adrian Giordano the man had seemed easy-going. He looked anything but as he sat forward on the coffee table and leaned his elbows on his knees. He was trading stare for stare with Cyn, but the Marshall wasn't backing down. "Since you're the one he's targeting, I think he'll just follow you." He nodded to Julian, the concern in his expression newly overshadowed by sheer determination. "I'm sorry, but the only way I can see to catch him is to use your mate as bait."

"Unfortunately, I agree." A man Julian had never met before held out his hand. "Ted Pedroza, the Poconos Pack Second, here to keep my alphas out of trouble." Ted laughed out loud as Rick snorted in amusement. "Nice to meet you."

"Nice to meet you too." Ted had super-short, nearly black hair, eyes so dark Julian couldn't make out the pupils, and the warm skin tone of someone of Latino origin.

"If you don't mind my asking, how long has your mate been living here?"

Julian wasn't fooled for a moment by Ted's easy smile and relaxed stance. To be a Marshall's Second you had to be one hell of a fighter. "Not very long at all. Why?"

"There's no scent marking around your place."

Everyone stared at Ted, confused. Everyone except Rick and Tabby.

Rick turned his piercing, pale blue gaze on Tabby. "He's right. You check for scent marking as soon as you get home."

Tabby nodded as if she understood exactly what he was talking about.

Emma's hand rose in the air. "Um, for those of us of the non-canine persuasion, can you explain that please?"

"Dogs mark their territory." Belle yawned daintily behind her hand.

"I'm not a dog."

"You keep telling yourself that, Fido." Belle patted her husband's chest, laughing when he growled. "From what you say, he's been watching them, kind of stalking them."

"That means he's going to be feeling territorial." Tabby was practically curled around Alex, but her worried gaze was glued to Cyn. "He'll have marked the places we tend to hang out, like Living Art and the apartment."

"And your new house," Cyn snarled. "I've just about had it with this fucker."

"You've gone through your first change?" Cyn nodded, and Max sighed in relief. "Good. That means we're not throwing you defenseless to the wolves."

"Did she tell you what she turns into?" Gabe's grin was viciously pleased.

"I thought she'd be a Spirit Bear, like Julian."

"It doesn't quite work that way." Julian tugged on his braid, unsure how to inform the Halle Alpha that he had a Kodiak living in his territory.

"I'm a Kodiak." Cyn shrugged. "It's a Bear thing. You wouldn't understand."

Alex didn't quite manage to muffle his laugh. Tabby didn't bother trying.

"Oh." Max blinked, his expression blank. "That's... Large."

"And mean." Gabe rubbed his hands together gleefully.

Adrian was staring at Cyn with an expression of unholy delight. His wide, evil smile reminded Julian of the Grinch. "Can I watch you turn that bastard into furry origami?"

This had the potential to become a nightmare. Cyn might be big for a Bear, but a bullet would still kill her. "I think we need to worry more about how we're going to keep her safe." Julian winced as he tugged a little too hard on his braid, his nerves getting the better of him.

"We'll have people watching her around the clock. Living Art is going to remain closed in order to protect its clientele."

Cyn couldn't hide her unhappiness over Gabe's pronouncement. She was itching to get back to work, but she had to agree with the Hunter. She was just too vulnerable when she was in Living Art. He just hoped they could resolve this swiftly. She ran the risk of losing her business entirely the longer she stayed closed.

"Julian, until you're stronger, you'll have to trust us to protect your mate." Adrian's gaze was sympathetic but uncompromising. "This man is guilty of murder and attempted murder. We need to catch his ass before anyone else gets hurt."

"Are we so certain it's a man?" Sheri's hand was clenched so hard it was white knuckled.

"It's okay, sweetheart." Adrian immediately reached for his mate and pulled her close. "Sheri was the victim of a stalker attack."

Sheri patted Adrian's knee. "I'm all right, I promise."

"It's definitely a man, Sheri." Sarah stole Gabe's drink and took a sip. "I could feel his rage at missing his target."

"Is he sane?"

Sarah wiggled her hand in a so-so motion. "That depends on your definition of sane, Max. What I sensed was anger, and lots of it. But it didn't feel manic, if that makes any sense."

"The real question is, why is he doing it?" Adrian stared at Tabby as if she had a red targeting dot on her forehead. "Why is he focusing on the three of you?"

"One theory is that it could have something to do with Gary." Gabe pinched the bridge of his nose with a sigh. "Although I'm not entirely sure of that. Gary's orders were to watch Chloe, not Tabby. He has something to do with whoever is targeting half breeds, even if he's not talking about it. Tabby, Cyn and Glory were just a side bonus. They're both human, or were. Their mating won't produce half breeds like Alex and Tabby's will."

"Do we still have to worry about that? I thought now that Gary is in prison it was all over with." Tabby rubbed her stomach. The little peanut growing there was only a few weeks old, but Tabby already loved the child.

"There was the Cheetah that attacked me. Is he working with the Wolf or is he working alone?" Cyn stood and began to pace. "What if the incidents are unrelated?"

"I can't see a reason for those going after half breeds to attack you. It has to be something else." Julian couldn't figure out what it was they were missing.

"This is *personal.*" Sarah took hold of Gabe's arms and wrapped them around her waist, something Gabe allowed with an indulgent smile. "He wanted you dead."

"If that's the case, we have to figure out who the three of you have pissed off recently." Belle reached into her oversized purse and pulled out a tablet PC. She tapped a few buttons and then looked up with an expectant look. "Names, people."

"I can't think of anyone specific. Other than Gary and his goons, I mean." Tabby bit her lip. "What about Gary's family? Didn't he refuse to name his Alpha when he got arrested?"

"The goons have family too." Cyn turned and stared at Glory.

"Don't look at me. I got nothing."

"You got shot."

"Well. Other than that."

Cyn's pacing paused as she shot Glory an apologetic glance. "There's Hope."

Glory flinched at the sound of her sister's name. "I doubt it would have anything to do with her after all these years."

"Still, it's a possibility."

"Any little tidbit of information will help." Gabe knelt in front of Glory and took her hands in his. "Tell me what you think happened to your sister."

"I think..." Glory lowered her head, looking so tired Julian just wanted to scoop her up and put her to bed. "It doesn't matter what I believe. Hope is gone."

"The one who did it left town." Glory jolted at Cyn's quiet statement. "Your father did it, didn't he?"

"I'm not sure. I've never dared say it out loud." Glory wrung her hands together until the skin turned red. "He went insane when she didn't come home that night."

"He blamed you." Sarah moved behind Glory and placed her hands on her shoulders. It looked like the Omega was attempting to use her powers on the human.

"He did. I was supposed to go with her that night. I didn't want to go and I had an argument with him." Glory relaxed beneath the Omega's hands. "When she didn't return he beat me till I couldn't move."

When Ryan found out about this he'd flip. If Glory's father ever returned to Halle he wouldn't be alive for long.

"Do you think your father is back in town?" Gabe kept his voice low and soothing, working in tandem with the Omega to keep Glory calm.

"Even if he is, he has no reason to go after Tabby and Cyn."

"She's right. Mr. Walsh was an asshole, but he wasn't stupid. He'd have no reason to shoot us. It's not like we've been looking into Hope's disappearance."

"And he has no idea that shifters even exist." Glory frowned. "At least, I don't think he does."

Cyn shook her head. "Everything we've discovered points to shifters, not humans."

"Which brings us back to square one. Why you three?"

"My father is dead, but he died of natural causes." Cyn resumed pacing, her hands on her hips as she thought out loud. "My mother is still alive, but she's a complete ditz. I don't even think she's dating, and he's been dead for years. She adored my father, would have done anything for him."

"Any pissed off customers?" Belle's fingers were tapping rapidly across her PC.

"If I have a customer who is dissatisfied with a tattoo I either offer to fix it for free, or give him a partial refund. So far I haven't had any complaints about that policy."

"So no pissed off customers or past enemies. What we do have is a missing sister, a person or persons unknown targeting half breeds, a ragey bastard who's tried to kill you three and not much else." The Luna turned her bright green gaze on Tabby. "What about your old alpha, Tabby? Could he have something to do with this?"

"I suppose. But he should still be in Marietta."

"His son, Micah Boyd, has been trying to contact you." Cyn and Tabby exchanged an enigmatic glance. "And Dennis Boyd is no longer the Marietta alpha. It's possible he's left Marietta all together."

Tabby looked utterly confused. "What the hell would that have to do with me?"

"I have no idea, but she did ask about past enemies." Cyn waved her arms in the air. "Not like any of this makes any sense."

"Is he *still* calling? I thought he gave up on you." Alex plucked Tabby's phone out of her pocket and began scrolling through her missed calls.

"I think we should spam him with Nyan cats until he stops." Glory giggled when everyone turned to stare at her. "What? Look it up on YouTube. That shit's annoying." The giggles turned to wracking coughs, but at least she was smiling.

"She's right. I ticked her off once and she made that my screensaver. I still can't eat cherry Pop Tarts." Cyn shuddered. "And I had no idea how many different versions of it there were."

"The scariest was Nyan Cat 3-D."

"Bitch. I still can't believe you made me watch that."

"You got even with me." Glory winked at Cyn. "You made me play it on Guitar Hero. My fingers still haven't recovered."

Cyn winked back, and Julian knew they were pulling someone's leg. "You're just ticked because my Nyan streak was higher than yours."

Tabby was gaping at them in disbelief. "How the hell did you get Nyan cats on GH?"

Glory sniffed. "See what you miss when you move out?"

"Ladies." Gabe shook his head, amusement warring with disbelief. "We have a killer to catch. Worry about your star power later, okay?" He grinned. "Besides, there is no Nyan cat for GH."

"Are you sure?" Cyn challenged Gabe.

"Yup." Gabe's grin turned sheepish. "I'd own it."

Tabby glared at Cyn and Glory, who were giggling like loons. "Y'all suck."

Julian couldn't give two shakes of a rat's ass about videogames just then. His focus was still on the most important thing. "There's got to be another way to bring this guy out into the open. Using Cyn to draw him out is unacceptable."

"Do you have a better idea, Super Bear?" Cyn crossed her arms and smirked at him. She thought she had him.

She was wrong. He turned to the one person in the room who should be out there hunting a killer, not sitting in his living room scarfing pizza. "Gabe, what were you able to find out about the shooter?"

"Not a hell of a lot. He took the shot at Marie from an empty apartment. I'm just glad the inhabitant had already left for work that day. As it is, she's scared to death to go home."

"Puma?"

"No, but she is a shifter and has requested sanctuary. Max has granted it. That's all I can tell you." Gabe pulled Sarah close again and rested his chin on the top of her head. "He left behind no fingerprints. The lab reports are starting to trickle in, but from what we can tell he didn't leave behind a single hair. The only thing he did do was smash parts of her apartment to bits. He punched a few holes in her walls, broke some of her knickknacks. It looks like when he missed Cyn he had a tantrum and then booked."

"What about the other crime scenes?"

"We'll probably get more information out of the pipe bomb than anything else. I got my guys working on that, tracing where the components were bought. It's going to take time, though. We just have to be patient."

Julian wanted to snap at Gabe. If it were his mate would he be so patient? He turned to Rick, hoping the Wolf Alpha knew where he was about to go. "Would it be easier to hunt him up on your land?"

"If I had his scent, yes." The Wolf Alpha sounded absolutely certain of that. "Those woods are mine. There's no way the fucker would be able to hide there."

"Then we split up. Tabby, Alex and Glory head up to the Poconos where Rick's Wolves can protect them. I stay down here and try to draw the shooter out where the Pumas can take care of me." Cyn held up her hand as Tabby opened her mouth to object. "Alex, take some of your relatives with you and leave some here. That will help Julian and Tabby feel better about all of this."

Alex shared a look with Tabby. No matter what Tabby wanted, she'd be visiting the Poconos, in-laws in tow. "If the Foxes pick up the scent, they'll make useful scouts."

"And I'll finally get to answer the age-old question." Belle tilted her head, her expression more vapid than Julian had ever seen on anyone outside of Paris Hilton. He heard tales of the Poconos Luna. Perhaps the rumors were true. Maybe she really was Psycho Barbie. "Does a Bear shit in the woods?"

Alex returned her look with a bland one of his own. "Only if there's a roll of toilet paper on a convenient nearby branch."

Julian nodded sagely. "And it has to be the kind that doesn't leave toilet paper dust on our poor furry behinds."

"Yup. That is a total breach of Bear etiquette."

Rick clamped his hand over Belle's mouth before she could respond. "Do we have a plan, then?"

Glances were exchanged. After nods all around, some reluctant, some not, it was agreed. Alex would be taking Tabby and Glory into hiding while Cyn played tag with the killer. Julian damn near growled out his frustration. It had *not* gone the way he'd planned.

Fuck a duck.

Chapter Eighteen

Cyn opened the front door as quietly as she could, hoping Julian was taking that nap she'd ordered him to. When she didn't see him loitering around in the front hall she sighed in relief. He'd been adamantly against her being bait, but what else were they supposed to do? It had been over a week since Marie's death and they hadn't found more than where the sniper had been hiding. None of the lab work had come back, and even Cyn's new sense of smell couldn't track the killer. She'd tried following the scent only once, but Gabe had stopped her before she'd gone too far.

At least Tabby and Glory were safely away. Alex had whisked her friends away so fast Cyn had barely had time to say good-bye. But that was all right, as long as she got to say welcome home when it was over.

She hung her coat up with a sigh, rubbing her neck wearily as she closed the closet door. She was so tense she could probably be used as a tuning fork. "The Amazing Cyn, vibrating in C minor."

A low chuckle had her whirling around. Julian sat halfway down the stairs, a smirk on his face. "I could take care of that for you."

Shit. He was awake. "Hey, Jules." She tried her best to smile for him, but knew she failed when his welcoming smile dimmed.

"You're hurting. Let me help."

Her muscles were one tight knot, but no way in hell was she going to allow Julian to heal her. "No. You just got out of the hospital." He'd only been home for six days, and already he was trying to act as if nothing had happened. It was like it didn't matter to him that he almost died. Meanwhile, Cyn was having nightmares about Julian lying in a pool of blood.

When she met Tai Boucher she was going to kick his ass. The leader of the Spirit Bears had never called Julian back, and it was driving both her and her mate crazy.

She rotated her shoulders and tried to hide her wince. His eyes still had silver flecks in them. There was still more white in his hair than black. Did he really think he was fooling her?

"I could give you a massage."

She didn't trust him. He'd try and sneak a healing in, she just knew it. "No."

He sighed. "I give you my word I won't use my powers."

She eyed him warily. "You promise?" He'd break his word in a heartbeat if he thought she was in serious pain.

"I promise." He even crossed his heart, the silly Bear.

She studied him, but he was the picture of innocence. He was definitely up to something. "Fine."

The wicked grin that crossed his face worried her. "Get naked, then get on the bed."

She took off her clothes quickly, not wanting this to turn into something sexual. Julian wasn't up to any antics. She lay down and pulled the sheet up over her butt, hiding herself from him. Her butt didn't hurt, after all, her shoulders did.

"Aw. There went the view." He laughed when she gave him the finger. "Close your eyes and try to relax."

She did as he asked, wondering why she heard him rattling around. She expected to hear him removing his clothes, but instead she heard what sounded like...glass?

The snick of a lighter startled her. One of her scented candles was placed on the nightstand. Next to it was a bottle of lavender massage oil. Julian dimmed the lights and finally stripped off his shirt. "Like what you see?"

She closed her eyes again.

"You are so mean." She heard more cloth rustling, then the sound of a cap snapping. Within seconds the soothing scent of lavender filled the room. His warm, oiled hands began to rub up and down her back, spreading the self-heating oil. "You like that?"

Already she could feel herself relaxing under his touch. "Mm-hmm."

He began to massage her back and shoulders, varying hard, almost bruising kneading with almost ticklish butterfly touches that had her squirming. She moaned when he hit a particularly bad spot, the tension in her shoulders melting away under his skilled hands. She could have sworn he was using his powers, but when she opened her eyes his were still vaguely speckled with silver, his hair still tinged with black.

His hands wandered down to her ass, massaging her just above the globes. It felt surprisingly good, and damn arousing. "Julian."

"Hmm?"

"Are you hoping to get laid?"

His hands didn't even pause. "The thought did cross my mind."

She growled. "You're not up for it."

He chuckled. "I beg to differ." He moved to the side and took her hand, placing it over his straining erection. "I'm very much up for it." She watched as he poured more oil into his palm. "I'm fine, Cyn. Better than fine, now that you're home."

She grimaced. It had been her idea to roam Halle, waiting for the bad guy to strike. Gabe had been against it, but he'd agreed once she allowed him to give her more than one tail.

Julian's hands began massaging her thighs, and she groaned. She hadn't realized how tight all her muscles were until Mr. Roamy Hands got started, but damn, it was so good. She didn't even realize the sheet had been pulled down until his hands reached the soles of her feet. *So much for discouraging him.*

He began massaging her ass once more, spreading the cheeks apart. "Julian."

Shit. His name came out more a moan than a warning. She was so screwed. Literally.

"That's my name." He patted her ass. "Roll over."

She lifted her brow at him. He expected her to move? After turning her muscles to Jell-O?

She managed to get onto her back, flopping ungracefully back down. "Make with the oil."

"Yes, ma'am. Your command is my wish." He massaged the top of her shoulders, his fingers deliberately stroking the mating mark over and over again before sliding down to her breasts. He spent an eternity just oiling and playing with them. Her nipples were so hard they hurt worse than her muscles had.

"Jules." She squirmed, aching for him.

"I have you." He took hold of her arms and lifted them over her head. His bright silver eyes were heated as he placed her hands on the slats of the headboard. "Hold these for me."

She grabbed hold, not that she'd be able to move anyway. She was one limp, aroused woman, accepting anything he wanted to give her.

And give to her he did, sinking his fingers into her in one smooth stroke, the oil warming inside her body. Her pussy tingled as he fucked her gently, bending over her to take one oily nipple into his mouth. He suckled her hard, the combination of the easy finger inside her and the hard tongue on her nipple sending her over the edge.

Gods above, she was *amazing.* Just looking at her as she came nearly had him following her, spending his seed on her stomach. But he had other plans for his mate, ones that involved riding her until she fell asleep, warm and sated and no longer hurting.

He could feel it, the pain still hiding under the pleasure, her muscles still not completely cured. He'd broken his promise in little bursts, removing as much of the pain as he dared, but he doubted she'd noticed. She'd been too busy writhing under his hands, coming on his fingers.

He especially liked that last part.

So he slid down her body, taking that pretty little clit into his mouth, his fingers still inside her. He wanted her mindless, dancing under his tongue. He watched as she clenched her hands around the spindles of the headboard. Her hips lifted against him, forcing him to lick where she wanted him. Even half melted, she still tried to rule their passion.

He almost laughed. If she told him to jump, he'd probably ask how high and in what direction. Then she'd probably yell at him for not jumping fast enough.

He sucked and licked and fucked her till she trembled, ready for him. When he pulled away she whimpered in protest, a sound she'd deny to her dying breath. She wanted him, and that was enough for him.

He slid his cock into her, shuddering when her legs wrapped around his waist, pulling him in deep. "Cyn, hold still."

Gods, he was such a liar. The last thing he wanted was his beautiful mate to hold still. He wanted her to fuck him into the damn mattress. But he was determined to be gentle. She hurt, and he didn't want to add to her pain. She'd feel it after the high of two orgasms wore off.

Her eyes opened, and she snarled at him. "If you don't fuck me right this instant I *will* get even. You won't like it if I get even."

"I don't want your muscles to get tight again."

She grinned up at him. "You could always massage me again."

This time he was the one who whimpered. Her legs tightened around his waist, demanding he do as she demanded. He did what any man would do in that situation. He began fucking her hard, loving the moans that poured from her lips. He could see her toes curling out of the corner of his eye. Her pussy began to tighten around him. She grabbed handfuls of his hair and dragged his head down, stealing a kiss before sinking her fangs into his neck.

Oh. Oh fuck. She'd marked him. The urge to feel her come on his cock overwhelmed him as the mating hormones raced through his system. He extended his fangs and leaned down, biting her as she'd bitten him.

She screamed, her pussy tightening around him so hard he couldn't move. Her whole body bowed off the bed. When she collapsed back onto the mattress, spent, he began fucking her again, gentler this time. She was going to come at least one more time before he was done.

"Jules." She tugged on his hips, encouraging him to go faster. "Need it."

"Want to come again?"

Her nails raked down his back, scoring him. He hissed, the pain driving him deeper into her. She'd drawn blood, and he refused to heal it. Let it scar. If his mate wanted her claw marks in his flesh, so be it.

He lifted her legs, automatically healing the muscles she'd overworked that day hunting for a lunatic. Julian saw the way her eyes narrowed but didn't care. She wanted to be fucked hard, then she had to be able to take it. He rested her calves on his shoulders and began to pound her so hard the bed shook. This time, he was going to come with her.

Her skin glistened from the oil in the light of the candle. She clenched the sheets in a white-knuckled grip. Her head tossed from side to side, and the sweetest little moans were pouring from her mouth. "Come on, Cyn. Come for me."

She brushed her fingers across the mark on her neck over and over, driving her closer to orgasm. He held on to her legs, waiting for her to fall.

Cyn shuddered. "Oh fuck. Fuck." She gave off one choked off cry and came, so tightly wrapped around him that he followed her over that glorious edge. His vision went black as pleasure roared through him, white-hot and molten, pouring from him in waves. It took everything in him not to collapse on top of her, but it was close. They were nose to nose when he regained his senses.

"Wow."

He smiled wearily. "Like your massage?"

Her expression was full of lazy satisfaction, like a cat that had gotten not only the cream, but the bowl too. "Enough to offer you one the next time your muscles are sore."

"Ah, so this was a sixty-eight."

She giggled. "You do me and I owe you one?"

"Damn straight."

She pulled him close and cuddled him, stroking his hair. "Let me know when you want to collect."

Chapter Nineteen

It was killing him. It was fucking killing him that she was out there, risking her life, and he was stuck in the house, healing. He should be out there with her, protecting her. What if that son of a bitch got a shot off? Julian didn't think he would be able to live with himself if anything happened to her and he wasn't there to prevent it.

Julian ran his hands wearily through his hair. Who the hell was he kidding? She'd already been damaged and he hadn't been there to take care of her. He tugged on his hair, frustrated beyond belief. Sometimes it seemed like since he'd moved to Halle there had been nothing but one huge fuck up after another. He hadn't been able to protect Tabby when Gary had gone after her in the woods. He hadn't been there to save Glory when she'd been shot. He sure as fuck hadn't been able to save Marie, and Jamie… No one knew if Jamie would ever be the same again. Jamie still hadn't woken up and it'd been three weeks since Marie's death. Her father had flown in, heartbroken over the loss of his only daughter, and made the funeral arrangements. Jamie's parents and brother had attended in her mate's place.

Jamie's brother, Grayson, had come to see him and had quietly thanked him for saving Jamie. Gray had been the complete opposite of Jamie, quiet and reserved. It wasn't just because of the tragedy. Gray was like a deep, still pond, where Jamie had been more like playful ocean waves. Gray stayed, making Julian lunch, commiserating with him over Cyn's role in finding the killer.

He'd offered to be one of her shadows, protecting her where Julian couldn't. Julian thanked him, but declined. He couldn't allow Gray to risk himself. Jamie's family had been through enough. Gray had accepted with quiet graciousness, but Julian wasn't certain whether or not Gray had gone hunting anyway. He sincerely hoped not.

He shivered, chilled to the bone. The restless itch that had been under his skin since Cyn had walked out of the house that night was getting worse. He began to pace, rubbing his arms as goose bumps rose all over them. Something was seriously wrong, and all of it centered on Cyn.

He closed his eyes and tried to focus on what it could be, but he was too restless. He settled down on the floor and crossed his legs, settling down into the pose he used for meditation. He wasn't planning on heading into the spirit world to speak to Bear, but if he could calm his racing heart he might be able to sense the threat to his mate. If he were truly lucky, Bear would send him a vision. Even if his spirit visions weren't as in-depth as Tai's, they were always accurate.

Deep, soothing breaths helped to relax him. He focused his mind on the color white, the color of snow, the color of Bear. His breathing began to even out, his thoughts settling, his heart rate slowing down. He let the color white go, waiting patiently to see what would come to him.

Blood began to drift down the white. As he watched, the simple, flat white took on texture and form. His view drifted back and up until he was staring down at a prone body, it's white hair streaked with red. Beneath the body a pool of blood spread. But what truly terrified him was a familiar mop of blond, pink and black hair. Cyn was lying beneath him, one arm flung out to the side, the T-shirt she'd been wearing that night when she left the house soaking wet.

It was then he realized it wasn't his blood on the ground. He blinked, shattering the vision as memories of Marie's blood splattered hair superimposed themselves over that of Cyn.

He stood, his hands automatically braiding his hair so it would be out of his way. Changing into jeans and a T-shirt, he shoved his bare feet into his sneakers and raced out the door. He barely remembered to grab his car keys and his wallet, and he was sliding into his car, ready to take off to where Cyn had said they were laying their ambush for the night.

"Julian DuCharme?"

Julian turned to see who called to him, and stared at a strange Wolf. The Wolf exuded an aura that he'd only sensed in the presence of Max Cannon and Richard Lowell. He had a thick southern accent reminiscent of Tabby's. His light brown hair and eyes practically glowed under the streetlight. "Who are you?"

The man held his hands at his sides, indicating he was unarmed. "My name is Micah Boyd."

Why was that name so familiar? A trickle of unease shivered down Julian's spine. Whoever this man was, he was somehow connected to what was happening to the girls.

"I'm the Alpha of the Marietta Pack. I'm looking for Tabitha Garwood."

Oh, shit. This was the man Tabby had been exiled from her birth Pack over. At the age of fifteen she'd been Outcast while dating him, the old Alpha accusing her of robbing his home when she'd simply been trying to escape Micah's bedroom unnoticed. If he was here Alex was going to shit a brick. "Tabby's not here."

Micah lowered his arms and shoved his hands into his front jeans pockets. "I know that. She's refusing to take my calls." He scowled. "And she sent me these *really* annoying videos of a cartoon cat dressed like a Pop Tart." He shook his head, the scowl lightening to a simple frown. "Look, she has no reason to trust me, but I just want to tell her it's safe for her to come home now."

Julian couldn't stop the rumbling growl, even if he wanted to. "She *is* home."

Micah shifted, his stance changing from defensive to proud. "I Outcast my father." He stared straight into Julian's eyes, and Julian could see how this man had become an alpha. There was strength there, and determination. Julian could sense the desire to make amends in the other shifter, and it was bothering the hell out of Micah Boyd that Tabby wouldn't let him.

"Why?"

Micah's gaze filled with rage and sorrow, an odd combination. "Tabby wasn't the only one he hurt."

That cold, twitchy feeling was stronger than ever. "When did you Outcast him?"

Micah frowned. "It was my first act as the new Alpha."

Julian cursed under his breath. "How long have you been alpha?"

"A little over two years."

Tabby had been living as a human in Halle for less than a year. She'd spent years as a Wolf, avoiding Packs due to being made an Outcast by her former Alpha for a crime she didn't commit. He tugged on his braid, praying he was wrong. "Please, for the love of the ancestors, tell me that son of a bitch is being watched."

"Honestly, I hope he rots in hell. I told him I never want to see him again, and he left. I don't know if he's still in Georgia or not, and I don't care."

"Shit." He waved to the passenger seat. "Get in and help me clean up your family's mess."

"What are you talking about?"

Julian did something he'd never done with a non-Bear shifter. He used his shaman's voice, allowing his power as a Spirit Bear to flow over the other man. "Get in the car, Alpha Boyd."

Micah's eyes went wide, but he stood his ground. "What the hell? What did you just try to do to me?"

Well. Hopefully curiosity would win out over the ass kicking Micah was probably going to try and hand him. "I'll explain if you'll just *get in the damn car!*" He didn't care that he was shouting. He just needed Micah to either get in the car or get out of his way. Didn't he understand? Cyn was in danger. He let his eyes go silver, his hair white, and glared at the alpha. "Did you get permission from Max and Rick to be here?" When Micah cursed Julian almost laughed. According to Pack protocol, the Marietta Alpha had royally screwed up. He'd stepped onto another Alpha's territory without clearing it with that Alpha first, and if Max didn't hand him his ass Rick would. "If you get in the car, I'll cover for you."

Micah grumbled but got his ass in the car. "Now will you explain it to me?"

Julian dove into the car and took off in a squeal of rubber and smoke. "Have you ever heard of a Spirit Bear?"

Micah shrugged. "They're the mystical, magical, legendary priests of all shifter kind. My father used to tell stories of them, but I never believed in it. I mean really, Spirit Bears? Who believes in that kiddie kind of shit?"

Julian was tempted to start singing the Care Bear theme song. He'd looked it up and learned the lyrics to make Cyn laugh, but he hadn't had the guts to sing it to her. Yet. "We prefer the term shaman over priest." He took a turn so sharply he almost ran up on two wheels.

Micah was staring at him as if he lost his damn mind. "Are you telling me you're some kind of legend?"

"Only in my own mind," Julian muttered. He ignored Micah's chuckle. "If you don't believe me, you can call my leader, Tai Boucher." Wouldn't he love to be a fly on the wall for that conversation? Tai would take the young Alpha and have him spinning in circles within minutes.

He screeched to a stop right outside of Living Art Tattoos, just remembering to turn off the engine before he was out of the car, Micah hot on his heels.

"Are you going to tell me what's going on?"

Julian ripped open the door to LA, ignoring the startled look on Cyn's face. "I think your father is trying to kill my mate."

Cyn damn near jumped out of her skin as Julian raced into the shop, a strange man hot on his heels. She crouched, her claws extended, ready to defend her mate from danger. Julian shouldn't even be out of bed, let alone running anywhere. The doctors still hadn't cleared him to do anything more strenuous than eat a sandwich and pee.

In two strides Julian had her in his arms, his face buried in her hair. "You're all right."

She allowed her claws and fangs to recede. Julian would never hug her in front of a dangerous stranger. "Jules?" He was shaking like a leaf. She tugged on his braid, stroking his back when he shuddered. "What's wrong?"

The relief in his silver gaze was overwhelming. "Nothing, I just had a bad feeling."

Cyn froze. Tabby had once told her that Julian's *bad feelings* were almost as good as a prophecy. Something was about to go down, and her mate was smack dab in the middle of it. Without letting go of Julian, she pointed toward the stranger. "Does he have anything to do with it?"

Julian loosened his hold on her and turned to look at the stranger, keeping one arm around her waist. "Yes, but not the way you think." He nodded toward the stranger, but she could tell Julian was uneasy around him. "This is Micah Boyd, Alpha of the Marietta Pack." Julian tugged on the end of his braid. "He's here to hunt down his Outcast father."

She absolutely hated it when Julian lied to her. "Sure he is."

"His father, Dennis, is the one who Outcast Tabby. One of Micah's first acts as the new Alpha was to Outcast him. He's been gone from Marietta for two years now. He also wants to reinstate Tabby's position in her birth Pack."

Tabby had told her a long time ago that Outcasting was a huge deal to Packs and Prides. She remembered Tabby's constant skittishness, her fear that Max would drive her from Halle without any warning, simply because he could. An Outcast had no one they could rely on, nowhere they could turn to for help. Outcasting was supposed to be used for those who committed a crime against Pack or Pride, but Alpha Boyd had used it to hurt a little teenaged girl who'd never done anything wrong other than dare to be different. Tabby still carried the emotional scars of having lived her life in her Wolf form for eight years. Only now that she'd been accepted into both the Halle Pride and the Poconos Pack did she finally feel she had a safe harbor. "You think your father is capable of seeking revenge?"

"I wouldn't put it past him." Micah was staring at them, looking utterly confused. "Can someone please tell me what the hell is going on?"

"Someone's been trying to kill us." Cyn didn't see any reason to beat around the bush. If it really was his father doing these things, Micah deserved a shot at him. "One of Max's

Pumas has already died." She still felt guilty as hell over losing Marie, even though there was nothing she could have done to save her. It was stupid, but that didn't stop her from wanting a do-over. If she hadn't gone to give Marie the earring, perhaps Marie would have survived.

"Why would my father be trying to kill you? If he was going to go after anyone I'd think it would be Tabby."

"*¿Está loco en la cabeza?*" Both men were looking at her like she was the one who was *loco*. She shrugged. "He's one wave short of a shipwreck."

"Tabby and Alex are still in the mountains?" Julian was still tugging on his braid, his gaze glued to the front door.

"I think so, yes. Why?" She blinked. "Shit. If it really is Alpha Boyd, and he's after Tabby—"

"—and Tabby isn't here—" Julian darted a quick, horrified glance at her before plucking his phone from his pocket.

Cyn pulled her cell phone out and quickly dialed. Gabe answered on the first ring. "Cyn, my guys just radioed me. Who the hell just ran in there with Julian?"

"Tell them to stay calm. Alpha Micah Boyd is with us out of Marietta. He thinks his father is the one who's been targeting us." She began to pace, her Bear restless and ready to tear someone apart. "Dennis Boyd is the one who Outcast Tabby all those years ago, and now he's been Outcast for his crimes. We think he's going after her."

"Calm down. They aren't alone. I'll warn my men to keep a lookout. You three need to sit tight. If Dennis Boyd is in town, he might decide to take out his son instead of running after Tabby. Stay there where you're being watched over, got it?"

"Will do," Julian said loudly, replacing his phone in his pocket. "Rick is aware of who we think the shooter is. He's going to take Tabby and Alex on a little hiking trip to see if she can catch his scent. Hopefully they won't find anything."

She growled at him. "We need to protect Tabby."

Julian's silver eyes glittered. His Bear was close to the surface. "No. We stay put, like Gabe told us to."

She opened her mouth, ready to argue, but closed it when she saw the way he was still shaking. "What happened? What has you so scared?" Hell, the way he was reacting, her Bear was trying to scramble its way out. She'd seen him silly, scared, upset, even angry. But this was the first time she'd ever seen him terrified.

His lips compressed, his jaw clenching so hard she could feel the pain of it.

"Jules? Just tell me. I'll find out anyway."

He sighed and leaned against the counter, his arms folded over his chest. He refused to look at her. "I had a vision."

"A bad one, I'm guessing." Whatever had scared her mate so badly would be dealt with. She didn't even realize her claws had extended until they dug into her palms.

"I need you to stay safe." He finally looked at her, those bright, beautiful eyes of his dull with pain. "I can't..." He bit his lip and turned away again.

Shit. This was worse than she thought. She barely noticed Micah watching the two of them closely, her attention centered solely on Julian. "Tell me about the vision."

He ignored her, staring out the front window at the dark street. He was so tense she thought he might shatter with a breath.

She took a step toward him, needing to soothe him. "Julian, tell me so I can deal with whatever—"

"No!"

She gasped as his power rolled over her, the strength in him stunning her. She hadn't realized how strong he was until her Bear bowed her head in submission, accepting Julian's right to rule her actions. She would've been pissed as hell if his fear hadn't been steamrolling over her, nearly dragging her to her knees.

"I cannot lose you." He was practically panting, his eyes wild with fear.

She had to force herself to walk toward him. It was like being thigh high in the ocean, trying to force herself to move forward while the waves of fright kept pushing her back. She could barely keep her balance, both emotionally and physically. "You aren't going to lose me."

"I can't." Her beautiful lover began to cry, and Cyn knew she wasn't going anywhere. Not when his vision was affecting him this badly. "I waited so long for you. I can't lose you now."

"Shh." She reached up and brushed away a crystal tear, the heavy weight of his fear receding at the touch of his skin under her fingertips. "I'm not going anywhere. Not without you." She hugged him tight, almost crying herself as he shook in her arms. His tears were wet against her neck. "You need to tell me about this vision of yours, okay? So we can both be safe."

Julian took a deep, shuddering breath, and nodded.

She stroked his hair, undoing his braid so she could finger comb the long strands. There was still far too much silver in the black for her comfort. "So how long exactly did you wait for me?" Her voice was shaky, but at least she'd managed a light tone. She had a pretty good idea what he must have seen, but she was more scared for him than she was for herself. She had to find out exactly what he'd seen, but first she had to get him to calm down.

"Since the first moment I saw you."

She pulled back and stared up at him. Julian had met her almost a year ago. Alex had been right. Julian *had* been suffering before they mated. "Was I worth it?"

His thumb stroked over her cheekbone as he smiled down at her. "You're worth everything."

"Y'all are so cute together. You should be a Hallmark card."

Cyn and Julian turned as one to glare at Micah.

"Sorry." He gave them a sheepish grin. "I haven't found my mate yet. I'm not sure whether I should be jealous or vomit from the sugar overload."

Julian patted her on the behind, still a little teary. "Well, my sugar needs to get her ass behind some nice, thick walls." He eyed the plate glass window with disfavor. "Seriously thick walls. Maybe underground."

Cyn rolled her eyes and hid her grin. "I'm a Bear, not a mole."

Julian wiped his eyes dry with the heels of his hands. His answering smile was shaky. "Because weremoles are just silly."

"Um. What?" Micah's brows rose. "What the hell are y'all talking about?"

Cyn giggled as Julian began counting on his fingers. "There are no weremoles, werevoles, wererats, weremice…" Her Jules was sounding more like himself and less like the half-crazed maniac that had run into her shop a few minutes before. She would get to the bottom of his vision, one way or another. But for now, she was content that he was safe.

"…but we're still not certain about weredolphins and wereorcas. What do you think?"

Julian knew he'd scared the hell out of Cyn, but it was all just too much. First Glory was shot, then Marie, but the vision of Cyn lying dead in his arms had been the final straw. He just couldn't contain his fear.

Hell. If Ryan and Alex found out he'd cried he'd be forced to turn in his man card. He'd be getting Judy Garland movies every Christmas for the rest of his life.

"Are you serious?" Micah's jaw seemed to be permanently unhinged if the way his mouth remained open was any indication.

Julian barely heard the shattering of glass, the cracking sound of the gunshot. All that registered was the sudden flaring pain radiating from Micah. The Marietta Alpha staggered and grabbed his bleeding shoulder. Without thought Julian extended his power toward the wounded man, beginning the process of healing. It was a through-and-through, thank the ancestors. The only concern would be infection.

"Down!" Cyn grabbed him and tossed herself on top of him, breaking his connection to the healing path. Micah fell to the ground as outside the shop the world erupted, cops shouting for the shooter to show himself. All the cops surrounding Cyn were Pumas; Julian didn't think he'd be getting away.

"Jesus. You weren't kidding when you said someone was trying to kill you." Micah crawled toward them, his expression a mask of pain.

"No shit." Julian pushed Cyn off of him. Where the hell did she get off covering him? It was his job to protect her, not the other way around. "We need to get out of here." He began crawling on his belly toward the back of the shop, heading for the employee area and the back door.

"Aren't you the one who said 'sit tight'?" Cyn was following him closely even as she questioned him.

"The shooter has to be out front still. No way can he get past the Pumas guarding you. But in front of those windows he can take more shots at us."

"He's right. My dad was always one hell of a hunter. Don't trust that he'll stay put, either. He'll be running for the hills, hoping to get another shot at you on a different day."

Julian pushed aside the curtain and made his way into the break room. "Do you think he'll go after Tabby?"

"If he figures out she's not in town? Yes." Micah held the curtain open for Cyn, dropping it when she was safely inside.

"Rick can keep her safe. Ben and Ted won't allow anyone to touch her, especially since she's a Pack mate." Julian listened, waiting for the cops to come in the shop. Eventually they'd have to tell them whether or not they'd caught the son of a bitch.

"Who are Ben and Ted?" Micah stood and brushed his jeans off.

Julian followed suit but held his hand out to assist Cyn to her feet. "Ben is the Poconos Pack Marshall and Ted is his Second."

Micah's hand froze on his knee. "She's joined another Pack, then."

"And a Pride," Julian added.

Micah stared at him, astonished. "A *Pride?* How the hell did a Wolf wind up in a Pride?"

Cyn shrugged, her gaze darting around the break room as if the shooter were hiding in the cupboards. "Max likes her."

"And she proved herself to him. He had no problems accepting her, and neither did Rick."

Cyn grinned. "They share her."

Micah looked horrified. "How do their mates feel about that?"

Cyn and Julian gaped at him. He could not mean what Julian thought he did. "Are you nuts? Emma and Belle would eviscerate anyone who touched Max or Rick."

"They share her as a Pack mate, not a fuck toy." Cyn snarled. "What kind of Pack do you run, anyway?"

Micah had the grace to look sheepish. "Sorry. It's just...some of the things my dad forced us to do were horrible. Sharing a female, whether mated or not, wasn't uncommon."

Forcing someone to have sex with a person who wasn't their mate wasn't possible for a male, and tantamount to rape for a female, once the bond was established. The old Alpha had to be one sick son of a bitch to do that. "Your father wasn't mated to your mother, was he?"

"How did you know?"

"Lucky guess." Julian flinched at the sound of another gunshot. "Shit. They have to catch this asshole."

"At least this isn't a residential area. Even the restaurants close down by six." Cyn rolled her eyes at him as she stepped around him. She peeked around the curtain, pulling back as another shot was fired. "Yeah. I think we need to stay in here."

They hunkered down in the break room, keeping out of sight. At least Julian was certain Cyn was safe. She was whistling and tapping her fingers, restless as she never was. She was hating the fact that they were pinned down, helpless to stop the man who'd shot Glory.

Micah frowned curiously at Cyn. "Why are you whistling the Hawaii Five-O theme?"

Cyn blinked and stopped whistling, but her fingers continued to twitch restlessly. "No reason."

After a few minutes, Micah held up his hand. "Shh. Hear that?"

Julian cocked his head, trying to hear what had Micah quivering with tension.

"No sound." Cyn closed her eyes and tilted her head. "I can't hear anything."

Julian slipped out of the break room. Something was very wrong. "Stay put."

Cyn took a step toward him. "No."

"Cyn." He pressed a hard kiss to her lips before shoving her back into the break room. "You have to stay safe."

"Ditto."

He glared at her. No way was she leaving the protection of the break room. "Don't make me use the voice."

She blew her bangs out of her eyes and glared back. "Give me one good reason why I shouldn't follow your ass."

"Because I don't want to watch you die."

Chapter Twenty

She watched Julian stalk out of the break room and out through the curtain at the front of the shop. "What is he doing?"

"Checking things out, I'd assume." Micah leaned back against the break table and sighed. "Look, as much as I'd like to get my hands on my dad and kick his ass again, if he's somewhere with a rifle we won't get to him before he can take us out. Let me guess. You've been playing bait?"

"Yup." She leaned against the doorjamb. She might not go chasing after her mate, but hell if she was going to cower in the room. "Do you have any idea why your dad would go after Glory and I? If he's after Tabby, why not just shoot at her?"

"He's a vindictive son of a bitch. To tell you the truth, I've been waiting for him to come after me all this time." Micah shrugged. "How close are you to Tabby?"

"We're family." Cyn shot him a glance. "You're kidding me. That's why?"

Micah nodded. "He'll want her to hurt before he kills her."

She stared at him, appalled. "He's done this before."

"And I found out, took his Pack from him, and Outcast him for it."

"Why didn't anyone stop him?"

His answering grin was sour. "He was *Alpha*. No one was strong enough to stop him. Hell, I'm not sure his Beta wasn't in on it, but without proof I couldn't Outcast him. I constantly have to watch him, make sure he isn't stirring up shit. The

Omega was kept constantly drugged, and is just now getting over it with intensive therapy. He'll never be who he was before he became my dad's Omega. They broke him. The only thing I can do for him is keep the old Beta away from him, just in case. And the Marshall was a sadistic son of a bitch who died shortly after I Outcast my dad. He challenged me for the Pack and lost."

"Wow. Makes me glad I'm not a Wolf."

"Sometimes I wish I wasn't. Being a Tiger sounds really good some days. No Pack politics, just big-ass teeth and a pissy attitude." He stood and made his way to the door. "He's been gone a long time."

"The front of the shop isn't that big."

His brows rose. "Want to check things out?"

"Hell yes." Cyn pulled aside the curtain and stepped into the main part of the shop. "Julian?"

Julian turned from the front door where he was speaking to one of the cops. "Get back in the break room, Cyn."

"Did they get him?"

Julian shook his head. "No. They're following his trail now." He gestured toward the curtain. "Now get your ass back there, okay?"

"Fine."

"Yes, it is. It's a very fine ass. Now keep it behind the curtain."

Micah snorted a laugh as he followed Cyn back into the break room. "Is he always like that?"

"Nope. He's having an off day. Usually he's much worse." Cyn stared around the break room, restless to be doing something, *anything*. Fuck, she'd inventory stock if it meant she got to move. "I'm heading in the back for a bit. Let Jules know where I am." There were no windows back there so Super Bear couldn't get upset over it.

"Are you sure it's safe?"

Great. Just what I need. Another over-protective Alpha male. She was the Kodiak. She should be the one out front risking her hide, not Jules. "I think so. There are no windows, and the back door is locked."

"Maybe I should go back with you."

Cyn stared at the stubborn set of Micah's jaw. Nothing she said would dissuade him. "Follow me." She shook her finger at him as she led him into the stock room. "But I'm putting your ass to work."

"Fine by me. I'm feeling a little antsy anyway." He lifted a box off the nearest shelf and peered inside. "I hate sitting and waiting. I'd rather be out and doing."

"Ditto. I'm supposed to be a sitting duck, but sometimes I wish I was the one duck hunting."

Micah chuckled. "I know what you mean." He placed the box back on the shelf and followed Cyn further into the back room. "Do you mind if I ask you something?"

Cyn shrugged. "That depends on the question."

"Does Tabby's mate treat her well?"

Cyn stared at Micah and started laughing.

"What? It's a legitimate question."

"Tabby's mate is an overprotective Grizzly Bear who adores everything about her. Even the fact that she calls him sugar."

Micah paled. "Oh."

"Yeah. Look, I'd leave her one last message and let her decide if she wants to talk to you again. Because if you don't stop phone stalking her you're going to get your ass chewed off."

"Got it." He rubbed his face wearily. "Nothing is like I thought it was."

"Tabby had a rough time of it after she was exiled, but she's finally got her life together. You're not taking that away from her."

"I don't want to. I just want her to understand that she's got options. Her parents want to speak with her too."

Cyn frowned and started counting the crimson ink. She'd have to order more soon. "Her parents didn't say a word when she was kicked out of the Pack."

"That's not entirely true. After she left, they tried to find her. Like, almost immediately. They hired a private detective when they realized she wasn't nearby. But they never found her."

"Because she spent eight years as a Wolf." Cyn shook her head. "What would they have done if they found her?"

"Run with her. They wanted to chase after her that night, but the Alpha set some of his men to guard them, to keep them from following her. They've hated him from that day forward. Hell, they're my most vocal supporters, all because I promised I'd bring Tabby home to them."

Shit. Tabby needed to hear about this. If what Micah was saying was true then Tabby's parents deserved to repair their relationship with her. "I'll talk to her."

She hadn't realized how tense he was until that moment, when he practically slumped against the shelving. "I'd appreciate that. Even if she never speaks to them again, at least they'd all have closure. I think both sides need that." He tilted his head, listening. "It's pretty quiet out there."

She kicked the shelf, frustrated beyond belief. "He got away again, didn't he?"

"Probably." Micah winced and grabbed his shoulder. "Do you think your Julian could finish healing this?"

Cyn rolled her eyes. Like hell she was letting Julian heal anything bigger than a wounded gnat. "I'll do it."

He frowned. "I forgot you're a Bear like him."

She snorted out a laugh as she placed her hands over his wound. "Trust me. No one is like Julian." She began concentrating on his wound, calling on Bear to help her out.

Micah frowned. "Cyn?"

"Hmm?" She needed to focus. This healing crap was harder than she thought.

"Do you smell deer?"

Julian thanked the nice officer for telling him that the fucking asshole had gotten away from them. Really. He'd been *right there*, shooting at Cyn, and they'd lost him?

And they called themselves shifters. He bet a monkey with pneumonia could have sniffed the guy out, but no. He had to get Deputy Fife and Gomer Pyle. He hoped they were able to find they're fucking patrol car. After all, it was two whole cars down from the front of the shop.

Maybe he wasn't being fair, but enough was enough. Cyn was done. He wasn't going to allow her to play bait any longer. He was grabbing her ass and heading for the mountains, where he and Alex could take care of the girls while the Wolves played Marco Polo with the rogue. Let Dennis Boyd be the hunted for once. All he'd find was a couple of Grizzlies eager for a new chew toy.

"Cyn?" He stepped into the break room but it was empty. A cold shiver worked its way down his spine. "Cyn!"

He sniffed the air, then dashed toward the back room, following her spicy sweet scent. He tripped over something and landed flat on his stomach, his legs tangled in—

"Ugh." Micah sat up, rubbing the back of his head. "Shit."

Julian hauled himself to his feet. "Where's Cyn?"

"Huh?" Micah winced and pulled his hand away. His fingers were coated in blood. "Oh no."

Julian closed his eyes and tried to beat back the panic that threatened to engulf him. "Your dad."

"I think so."

"How could you not smell him?" Julian was screaming. What was wrong with everyone's noses?

Micah froze. "Fuck. He's masking his scent. He used to hunt deer all the time. He's adept at killing his body odor. He owns a whole bunch of hunting clothes with activated carbon in the lining and deer musk spray."

Jules took a deep breath and pulled out his phone. "Gabe, he got her."

A string of curses was broken by the sound of Gabe's cruiser, its sirens shattering the quiet night. "Stay put, I'll be there in a few minutes."

Bullshit. He'd heard *stay* one too many times. He wasn't a fucking dog. "I'll be out back. If they didn't go through the front, there's only one other exit." An exit he was currently running for.

"Julian, damn it. Sit tight. If anything happens to you Cyn will kill me."

"He's going to kill her. I've seen it." Julian burst through the back door, sniffing like an addict after a coke dealer. Cyn's scent pulled him to the right, mingled with blood. His mate was hurt, and once again he hadn't been there.

More curses poured from the Hunter. "I'm almost there."

"She's bleeding. I'm following the scent." He skidded in the gravel parking lot, muttering a few curses of his own as he realized Boyd had dragged her into a dark alley.

"I'm heading to the back of the shop. Don't do anything stupid, Julian."

Was Gabe kidding? Everything that could possibly go wrong already had. Murphy fucking owed him. "I'm following them down the alley."

"For fuck's sake, listen to me. I need you to stop for a minute and concentrate. Cyn is your mate. You should be able to sense exactly where she is."

That was news to him. Then again, he'd never had a mate before. Could every mate sense their other half? "I'll give it a try." He stopped, the scent of old Chinese food, rotting cabbage and dog shit almost overwhelming the scent of Cyn's blood. He closed his eyes and prayed Dennis Boyd wasn't doubling back. If he was, Julian would be a sitting duck. He reached out to his Bear, praying his mate wasn't far away. If Boyd got her into a car, it would be all up to Gabe and the shifter cops.

Julian reached out for Cyn's spirit, following the connection they had as mates. The connection was solid and thick, a brightly lit trail on a dark night, steady and strong. Without thought he was moving, following that radiant path. Gabe was right. It was like he had been following a shadowy figure in the dark, and now he could finally see where he was going. He didn't even bother switching his vision to his Bear's. He didn't need the extra low-light vision. That bright trail would take him straight to his mate.

"Got anything for me?" Julian was startled to realize how close Gabe had gotten to him without his knowledge. The Hunter was right next to him, matching him stride for stride. His dark blue eyes had shifted into his Puma's gold, allowing him to see better in the dim light of the alleyway.

Julian responded with a terse nod. "Follow me." Cyn was close and still alive. Either Boyd was holding a gun on her or she was unconscious, because his fiery mate would be struggling, fighting for her life. There was no sound except for their footfalls.

The trail was brightening; they were close to where Boyd had taken Cyn.

"I'm not telling you where she is." He almost stumbled at the sound of Cyn's defiant voice. The sound of a meaty thud was followed by a string of Spanish curses.

Julian began ripping off his clothing, preparing for the shift. He didn't care where any of it landed.

Boyd was about to find out what a pissed off Spirit Bear could *really* do.

Chapter Twenty-One

Cyn couldn't believe she'd allowed the asshole to get a drop on her. One minute she's healing Micah's shoulder, the next she's experiencing blinding pain. It didn't matter if the pain was Micah's or hers. Boyd had sure taken advantage of it. He'd used her disorientation against her and dragged her out of the shop, forcing her down the alleyway. But now he would have to shoot her ass to get her to go any further.

There is no way she was getting in that van.

"Don't worry little girl, you'll help me, whether you want to or not." Where Micah's light brown eyes had been filled with warmth, Dennis Boyd's were cold and dead. He had a huge pistol pointed at her with some kind of a hunting scope on the barrel. "I'm certain she'll come back for your funeral."

That is a really big gun. And it would leave a really big hole in her if she didn't move her ass out of the way now. "You could've just killed me in the shop."

"It's harder to drag a dead weight than you think. This way all I have to do is shove you into the van, pull the trigger, and we're gone."

"Gone to where?" She had a pretty good idea of what he had in mind, but she had to keep him distracted until Julian and Gabe arrived. And she had no doubt they were on their way. She could practically feel Julian chasing her down, pissed off because she wasn't where she was supposed to be. Scared because of who had her. *If I die he'll never let me live it down.*

His smile was chilling and creepy, and not just because he was going to shoot her. "I figured I'd dump it somewhere in the woods near the Red Wolf Lodge. How do you think that big, scary Alpha will feel when he finds out that I've killed someone he was supposed to protect?"

"I think his Luna will eat your intestines on toast." Because, if for some reason she didn't survive this, Tabby would hit Def Con One. If Rick or Alex didn't get to Dennis Boyd, Belle would, and it wouldn't be pretty. The Luna had a seriously wide streak of mean in her that scared Cyn a bit. But it was Alex's reaction that the man should be worried about. "And if they don't get you, her mate certainly will."

Oh how she wished she were one of those mystical Hollywood shifters. Then she wouldn't need to worry about things like clothing when she shifted into her Bear. She'd just shift and take this S.O.B. down before he could hurt anybody else. And then she'd magically be not naked when she shifted back. Unfortunately, she already knew that if she shifted in her clothes she would wind up hurting herself.

Hurry up, Julian!

"A mate, huh?" Boyd shook his head with a wry grin. "I'd wondered how she'd gotten into the Poconos Pack." Boyd didn't realize that Alex was a Grizzly and not a Wolf. She almost laughed out loud. She couldn't think of anyone who deserved an angry Grizzly mauling more than this man. "Richard Lowell is supposed to be a real hard-ass. I wonder what he did to make her prove herself?"

She'd done absolutely nothing but be herself, and that had been more than enough for Rick and Belle.

Boyd's gaze narrowed and he braced himself. It looked like her time was up. She closed her eyes, unwilling to watch him pull the trigger that would end not only her life but Julian's as well. "I love you, Jules." Why hadn't she been brave enough to tell him that when she had the chance?

A deep, gravelly roar sounded from right behind her, startling her. She'd never heard anything like it. She opened her eyes to see what fresh hell she was about to face and flinched as a wall of dark brown fur dashed past her. A deep, moaning wail sounded from the behemoth as it swiped at Dennis Boyd, shredding the man's arm from hand to shoulder. Screeching, Boyd dropped the pistol...but not before pulling the trigger.

The Grizzly reared up on its hind legs and roared once more in Boyd's face. Julian barely recognized the fact that Ryan was literally ripping Boyd apart despite Gabe's pleas to stop.

All he saw was that Cyn was on the ground, and she was bleeding.

It didn't matter that he was naked, that he'd never completed the shift. Her blood poured out from her chest and onto the ground. She was already unconscious, her eyelashes dark against her pale cheeks. He was going to take every ounce of strength he had to heal her, and it might not be enough.

If her soul fled her body, he would follow.

Julian dug deep, tapping into areas he'd never dared touch before, dancing further down the spiral of the healing path than he'd ever been. What he was doing should have been impossible, and would most likely cost him his life, but it was something that he would gladly give up to save her. Ancient prayers repeated over and over in his mind as he begged for the power to do what needed to be done. He battled death itself, and this time there was no one there to lend him strength, no one to save him from himself.

Beneath his hands torn muscles knit back together. Blood vessels repaired themselves seamlessly. The fragments of her shattered ribs drew together, whole once more. The bullet had been large caliber, bouncing around inside her rib cage before exiting and doing far more damage than he'd ever been forced to fix before. Her heart was nicked, forcing it to beat erratically. He mended the damage, making sure it beat properly once more. He moved next to her lungs, doing his best to be clinical and detached, and failing miserably. He wanted to scream at what had been done to his beautiful mate.

The damage was extensive. Cyn's right lung was practically torn in half. He knitted it back together piece by piece, repairing torn and inflamed bronchi. The pleural cavity had been breached, causing the fluid within to burst forth. He delicately repaired both the parietal pleura along her rib cage and the visceral pleura on the surface of her lungs, rerouting the pleural fluid in between the membranes back to where it belonged as he went.

He was beginning to tire, slowly losing contact with his body. He wasn't going to survive.

"Julian."

There was a minor risk of infection, but he boosted her immune system in preparation for that.

"Julian. You need to stop now."

But he wasn't done yet. He needed to repair the damage to the bones and muscles of her shoulder where the bullet had exited. If he wasn't careful, she would never again be able to use her right arm the way she had before. Her career, the living art she lived and breathed for, would be over.

"All right. I'll try and help, but if I cry I'm so haunting your ass."

Energy poured into him, feminine energy that was unlike anything he'd felt before. *"Chloe?"*

"That's me. Hang tight, Julian. I promise, you're not going anywhere."

It was just enough. He was going to be able to complete his work. He'd hurt, and hurt badly, but thanks to Chloe and their connection he'd live through it.

He'd just have to see if he'd live through what Cyn would do to him when she found out how far he'd gone. She wouldn't be too mad, right?

"You keep telling yourself that."

From somewhere far away he could hear the sounds of someone pleading with him to stop, but that was the last thing he planned to do. He was almost done. Her shoulder was almost completely repaired. All that was left to do was to repair the skin, make sure that not a single scar was left behind.

The only mark that should mar her skin was the mating one he'd given her.

"Jules."

Cyn's bleeding had become sluggish, almost nonexistent. No internal bleeding remained. Chloe withdrew with a quick, psychic hug, leaving him to his weariness and the last of Cyn's scrapes and bruises.

"Knock it off, Super Bear. I think I can put a Band-Aid on the rest of it."

Part of him recognized that voice, but he couldn't respond to it. It had gone dark where he was. He could no longer remember which way was up and out, and which way was down and in. The flesh between his hands was still knitting; he needed to hold on just a little bit longer.

He was going to sleep for a week when he was done.

"Gabe, knock his ass out."

What? No—

Cyn was going to kill him.

Okay, maybe not *kill* him. He was so good at trying to die all on his own. He certainly didn't need any help on that front.

"Thanks." Cyn took the spare clothes and, uncaring who saw, changed out of the shredded, bloody shirt she'd been wearing into the T-shirt.

"You're welcome." Sarah sat next to her and held her hand. "You're really angry."

Damn straight, she was. He could have stopped when he knew she'd live. Instead, he'd insisted on trying to heal everything down to the smallest scratch.

"Gabe risks his life every day, and not just as a Hunter. He's Marshall's Second, and a cop. I worry every time he walks out the door that it will be the last time I see him."

Oh hell. Another Dr. Phil moment was coming on. Cyn could feel it. "I understand Julian's obsession with healing. Hell, I encourage it." She shot Sarah a wry glance. "Mostly. It's when he pushes beyond what he should do that I want to tie him up and lock him in the closet."

Sarah laughed softly, not wanting to disturb the members of the Pride currently sleeping. It seemed all of the Pumas had arrived at the hospital to rally around Julian, ready and willing to lend a helping hand.

Emma, the tough Curana, was currently curled up on Max's lap, sound asleep. She looked young and innocent, and Max watched her with the same loving focus that Julian lavished on Cyn.

Becky was nibbling on some fruit Simon handed her, her eyes red-rimmed from either tears or lack of sleep. Possibly both. Simon barely looked away from his conversation with Adrian, until she stopped eating. Then he turned and frowned at her, pointing to the fruit, ignoring everything around her until she rolled her eyes and once again began to nibble.

Adrian was stroking Sheri's hair, her head pillowed in his lap, her dark glasses protecting her sensitive eyes.

Gabe was pacing, his gaze glued to a subdued looking Ryan. Ryan was staring at his hands as if he'd never seen them before, a haunted look on his face. Occasionally he would rub them together, a washing motion that made her wince in sympathy. He wouldn't be forgetting how he'd torn a man apart any time soon, no matter how justified he'd been. Gabe had told Cyn he wouldn't be arresting Ryan for defending her, but he was going to keep an eye on the Grizzly to see if he showed signs of going feral.

Cyn hoped not. As much as Glory protested, she would be devastated if anything happened to Ryan.

William and Barbara Bunsun, Alex's parents, had both gone into Julian's room to help his healing along. They'd both come out white-faced and exhausted. She still didn't know if they'd been able to help, but she was grateful nonetheless.

"Cynthia Reyes?"

Cyn stood as the doctor entered the room. With Jamie still out of commission, there was no longer a Pride doctor in the hospital. The very human doc smiled at Cyn and waved her over.

"How is he?"

"He'll be fine. He's exhausted and dehydrated. We've got him on a drip and a sedative for now. He keeps fighting us, wanting to get up and find you."

"Can I see him?" She clenched her hands to keep from wringing them like some weepy romance heroine. She wanted to see him so badly she was ready to burst into tears.

"Yes, but make it brief. He needs his rest more than anything right now."

"Thanks, doc." She practically ran into the room Julian was in, stopping dead at the sight of her mate hooked up to tubes and wires again.

This shit had to stop. She was ready to set up a bedroom in the hospital, she was here so damn much.

Julian whimpered, twisting in his sheets, fighting the medication that kept him unconscious. Cyn placed her hand over his, careful of the IV strapped to the back, and watched in astonishment as he immediately settled down.

It seemed Super Bear was still trying to save her, whether she needed it or not.

She settled in the bedside chair, prepared to fight to stay by her mate's side. If Julian needed her presence in order to rest, then she wasn't going anywhere, hospital regulations be damned.

It was hours before Julian stirred. Cyn had a cramp in her lower back, her arm was partially asleep from reaching for his hand, and her eyes were dry from lack of sleep. But when those beautiful brown-flecked silver eyes opened and focused on her, she smiled. "Hey, Jules." She swallowed around tears she refused to shed. "I love you. Moron."

He was too weak to say it back, but that was okay. He was alive. Nothing else mattered.

"No."

"Yes."

"No, damn it." Cyn's hands were fisted on her hips. Her foot tapped out an annoyed tattoo on the floor. "Fuck this, no."

Julian sighed and adjusted the flash he was hanging on the wall. In its new thick, black frame it stood out against the pearly gray walls of her new shop. "It's the best solution for everyone, Cyn."

Cyn set the box of ink she'd been carrying into the back room on the floor and growled. "You are not going to medical school, Jules." No fucking way. If he went back and became a doctor he'd have to do a residency in a hospital for at least three years. What the hell was he thinking? He'd kill himself! He'd been out of the hospital a month and now he wanted to go back? "Max and Rick are working on a solution. Let them deal with the shifter doc, please."

Julian made a face. "I just wish..."

She stroked his arm as he looked away, his expression one of guilt and regret. "I know, Jules." Saving Jamie hadn't been a blessing. The man had finally woken up, but he had become cold, and angry at the world. She'd never seen someone do such a personality one-eighty before in her life. She wouldn't be surprised if he turned into a serial killer.

Everyone agreed that if Jamie ever decided to take vengeance on Jules for saving him he would go after Cyn first. Even his family had told them to keep away from the former doctor, fearing that the sight of Cyn and Julian would trigger a need to kill in him. Gabe was keeping a watchful eye on him to see if he came out of the current funk or turned rogue.

He'd told her in private he was worried. Needless to say, she was keeping her distance, and making sure Julian did too.

"What do I do? There are people who aren't getting help because Jamie has his head up his ass." Jules flopped down in the turquoise chair by the window and watched the cars go by.

They'd kept the old chairs but had them reupholstered to match the new gray, turquoise and black color scheme. She liked the new color scheme even more than the aqua color of her old shop. It was soothing, yet modern. Tabby had talked them into buying a totally awesome chaise lounge in smoky gray that Glory had declared hers and a lighter gray sofa that Cyn had fallen into and in love with all at the same moment. The curtains at the window were white and black, in a modern floral print that Cyn wanted in her house.

Hell, even the floors here were nicer, a gorgeous dark oak that had sold her on the shop even without the added incentive of an awesome landlady.

"You're a Spirit Bear. If the Pride or Pack needs help, they can come to you. Otherwise, let the humans find a new human doc to deal with." Jamie's practice had been closed by the Howard family shortly before he woke up. He'd been in the coma for six weeks before waking up, raging and crying. He'd torn up his hospital room before being sedated. There was no way he was in any condition to deal with patients. "We could also have the shifters go to Doc Woods."

He rolled his eyes. "Jim Woods is a veterinarian, not a doctor."

"See? Perfect."

He snorted out a laugh, but it didn't last long. Julian looked pensive, never a good thing with her mate. He worried far too much in her estimation. "What do I do? If Immigration finds out I'm not working I could be deported back to Canada."

Cyn shrugged. "If that happens, I'll open a parlor in Manitoba."

"British Columbia." He turned and stared at her, stunned. "You'd go back with me?"

Was he really that stupid? "I can't believe you just asked me that." She'd follow her mate to hell. It was an odd feeling for someone who'd never wanted to be tied down to someone else's whims, but the knowledge that her mate valued her happiness above all else made the decision easy.

"Your family is here. All your friends." He stood and crossed over to her, caressing her cheek. "I can't ask you to give that up for me."

"Then marry me." Really, it was a no-brainer. Even if it took three years to get his green card, he'd be able to find a job and update his visa, she was sure of it. If not, she'd see if Gabe couldn't pull some strings with the shifter Senate and get Jules a permanent residency in the good ole US of A. Having one of the rare, elusive Spirit Bears on American soil should go a long way to getting Jules his citizenship, legally or not.

He laughed. "That sounds oddly familiar. Aren't you the one who asked me to mate you?"

"Because you take too long to get this stuff done." She wiggled her fingers in his face. "Make with the ring, Share Bear." She knew he already had one. Her Jules was thorough that way.

He closed his eyes and groaned, but the laughter still lit his face. "I'm not going to ask how you found out."

She cocked an eyebrow at him. "Ve haf our vays."

He wrapped his arms around her and pulled her close. "You were the one who wanted to go slow and date, remember?"

She shrugged. "I'm invoking a woman's prerogative and changing my mind." She wiggled her fingers again. It had irked her something fierce when the hospital nurses had tried throwing her out of Julian's room. She'd had to bring in Gabe to lie for her and say she was Julian's fiancée. She wasn't going without spousal privileges again. "Ring me."

He shook his head and pulled a ring out of his back pocket. It was gorgeous, a small but brilliant diamond flanked by emeralds, set in gold. "The diamond is my birthstone."

She grinned, loving it. His birthday was May 30. "And the emeralds are mine." She'd been born on April 5, and thanked God every birthday she'd been four days late.

He lifted her hand and kissed the back, his brown eyes twinkling. His dark hair had been left loose around his shoulders, just the way she liked it. "Thank you for agreeing to be mine."

She chuckled. "Agreeing, my well-padded ass."

He squeezed her butt and sighed happily. "I've come to enjoy that little extra bump in your grind."

She smacked his arm as Tabby walked, or rather waddled, into the room. The woman was barely four months along and acted like she was about to pop any minute. "I swear, I'm going to whelp triplets." She lowered herself into a chair with a groan. "My ankles look like Mama Leone's meatballs."

Julian immediately went to Tabby's side. He'd been concerned about her swollen ankles ever since she'd first complained about them, worried about gestational diabetes, but he hadn't found anything wrong with her when he checked her. Alex was threatening to toss all her high-heeled boots away, suspecting they were the culprit.

"Nice rock." Cyn jumped, startled when Glory picked up Cyn's hand from behind. "Hey, Alex. Check this out."

Alex sauntered out from the back and grinned at Cyn's engagement ring. "So he finally popped the question?"

Julian shook his head, his hands roaming over Tabby's tummy bulge. "Like she'd give me the chance." A small silver streak appeared in his hair as he worked on Tabby.

Glory dragged Cyn's hand, and Cyn, to the front window. She held the ring up to the Christmas lights they'd been hanging. "Oh yeah. We can so add this to the decorations."

Cyn smacked the blue-haired sprite upside the head, secretly tickled that Glory seemed to be back to her old self. Her breathing was still labored at times, but she seemed none the worse for wear. Even the fact that Ryan was constantly underfoot no longer seemed to bother her the way it had.

The bell over the front door jangled. She didn't even need to turn to see who it was. His timing was always the same. "Hey, Ryan."

"Cyn. Nice hand candy."

"Thanks." He stared at Glory with a look of longing that was quickly masked. He moved to her side, steadying her on the short ladder. "Let me get that, SG."

Glory snorted, hanging garland in the window of their new shop. "That had better stand for Super Glory, and not that blue furred freak of nature."

"If you say so."

Ryan, too, was mostly recovered. He'd told them how he'd gone and tried to hunt down the man who had shot his mate, but it wasn't until Cyn had become bait that he'd had any luck. He'd spent time roaming the woods just outside Halle, thinking the shifter was hiding there since it was the only place that Gabe hadn't checked yet. He'd been able to keep himself from going feral by focusing on Glory. The fact that his mate wouldn't be safe until he took out the shooter had been his saving grace.

When he'd found no sign of any stranger, he'd returned to Halle just in time to see Cyn get kidnapped. He'd quickly shifted, saving Cyn's life. Boyd had been aiming for her head; Ryan's intervention had knocked off his aim, giving Julian the time he needed to save her. When Julian had tried to thank him, he'd actually blushed. To him, Jules was family and, by extension, so was Cyn.

The bell jangled again, startling her. "Morning, Mrs. H.!" One of their best customers had become their landlady, renting them a place less than two blocks from their old one. Cyn had been grateful for what Evelyn Hagen had done, and promised her free tattoos whenever she wished. And Mrs. H. had no trouble with the security their Bears had insisted be added to the interior and exterior of the shop. In fact, she'd paid for it herself. Apparently Mr. H. had taken good care of his widow, because she got top-of-the-line stuff to keep "her girls" safe.

"Hey, girls and boys." She held up a couple of large white bags. "I brought barbecue!" Mrs. H. laughed as three large men descended on her and began to beg and whine shamelessly. Cyn had the urge to hang a sign over them: *Don't feed the Bears.* Mrs. H. had practically adopted all three of them, to the amusement of their mates and families. Mrs. H. had even paid Mrs. Bunsun a visit, and didn't Cyn wish she'd been a fly on the wall for that conversation?

Tabby sauntered over to Cyn and flung an arm around her shoulder. "Do you think they noticed the new sign?"

Cyn shook her head. She'd waited to unveil it until everyone was here, including Mrs. H. It had hurt, changing the name of the shop, but Tabby had insisted that they needed to change their luck. The best way to do that, she'd said, was to change the name. Glory had agreed. The three of them had sat down and hashed out what the new name should be. She still wasn't sure it was a good idea, but Glory and Tabby had overruled her. Since Tabby was now a full partner, she'd gotten a full third of the vote and had used it to bludgeon Cyn into submission.

She could admit it now, if only to herself. The name they'd come up with was somewhat flattering. However, when the boys saw it, she was going to be in for some ribbing, especially from Julian.

Glory hopped off the ladder, much to Ryan's obvious dismay. The Bear was frowning at her. He'd been treating her like a fragile china doll despite her clean bill of health from the doctor. If Cyn knew Glory as well as she thought she did, that wasn't going to fly for much longer. Glory was going to do something absolutely outrageous just to show how well she was. She still had trouble catching her breath, but all of the doctors assured them that her problems would resolve themselves with time. "I say we unveil the new sign now."

"New sign?" Julian smiled as he helped the other men lay out the food. "I thought you were going to use the old one."

Cyn shrugged, embarrassed. "We decided we needed a new name."

"We figured we could stand to change our luck." Glory twirled a powder blue curl around her finger.

"And we *love* the new name." Tabby's tone was so coy Cyn was surprised Alex didn't suspect something. Then again, the way he was sniffing the Styrofoam containers, she was even more surprised he hadn't started scarfing down ribs, Styrofoam and all.

"What's the new name?" Julian was the only one who was eyeing them with any suspicion. Ryan had sauce all over his chin and a blissful expression on his face.

Cyn exchanged a look with the girls. "Now?"

"Now." Tabby took hold of Alex's hand, ignoring his grumbly protest as she made him put down the beef brisket.

"Definitely." Glory stood by the door and waited. Sure enough, Ryan wiped himself off and ran to open it for her.

"Little princess." Cyn rolled her eyes and followed Glory out the door, smiling as Tabby joined them. Mrs. H. remained behind. They'd already told her what they were planning on naming the shop, and she'd laughed until she cried. But she did raise two thumbs up and, like the wonderful woman she was, began dishing up huge plates of food for the boys.

"Ready?" Tabby grabbed hold of the dangling rope that lead to the canvas cover over the sign.

"I am." Glory actually leaned back against Ryan, causing the Bear to freeze in place, a look of utter shock on his face.

Cyn nodded. "Do it."

"Yes, dooo eeet," Glory drawled, her teeth chattering. She shivered in the cold December air, the gauzy dress no barrier to the chilly wind. Ryan tentatively wrapped his arms around his mate, lending her his warmth.

Maybe it will be all right between them after all. Cyn smiled, happy that her friend was finally beginning to thaw toward the Bear.

"Here we go!" Tabby tugged the rope, but the canvas snagged on the corner of the sign.

"Wait. Why am I seeing C Y?" Julian tilted his head and squinted, as if that would let him see through the canvas.

"Stop trying to use your x-ray vision, Super Bear." Cyn blew her hair out of her eyes and tried to suppress her own shiver. "Any clue what it's stuck on?"

Tabby tugged again, but nothing happened. She walked to the other side of the sign, rope in hand, hoping to drag it along the sign and pull it down that way.

"I see," Julian whispered in her ear as the C Y N was revealed. "You named the shop after yourself, didn't you?"

"Sort of." She could feel her cheeks heating and knew she was blushing. She crossed her arms over her chest. "They outvoted me."

One dark brow rose as he stared at the sign. "Now I'm intrigued."

She rolled her eyes and snuggled up against him. Damn, it was cold out here.

"All right. I think I've got it." Tabby tugged one final time and the canvas fell. She backed up before she was covered in the falling tarp.

Julian burst into laughter as the sign was finally revealed.

Ryan's jaw dropped. He stared down at the powder blue head of his mate. "This was your idea, wasn't it?"

Alex shook his head. "Somehow it suits this place." He hauled Tabby into his arms with a huge grin. "Congratulations, Cyn."

Cyn stared up at the sign. "You don't think it's too much?"

Julian kissed the top of her head. "I think it's perfect." He chuckled. "I've always said you were sinful."

"No, Jules." She grinned up at the sign that bore her name...sort of. "I'm *Cynful*."

About the Author

Dana Marie Bell wrote her first short story when she was thirteen years old. She attended the High School for Creative and Performing Arts for creative writing, where freedom of expression was the order of the day. When her parents moved out of the city and placed her in a Catholic high school for her senior year, she tried desperately to get away, but the nuns held fast, and she graduated with honors despite herself.

Dana has lived primarily in the Northeast (Pennsylvania, New Jersey and Delaware, to be precise), with a brief stint on the US Virgin Island of St. Croix. She lives with her soul mate and husband Dusty, their two maniacal children, an evil, ice-cream-stealing cat and a bull terrier that thinks it's a Pekinese.

You can learn more about Dana at www.danamariebell.com or contact her at danamariebell@gmail.com.

Desire is the raw material. Lust is the spark...
and love will sculpt their destiny.

Artistic Vision
© *2011 Dana Marie Bell*
The Gray Court, Book 3

Akane Russo, one of the Hob's top Blades, can't wait for her current assignment to end. She's been tasked with protecting Shane Dunne from the Malmayne clan's scheme to kidnap him once again. But no one—not even her Seer half—warned her she'd have to protect herself from his heated gaze. Or that her dragon half would find him an irresistible puzzle.

Shane knew his destined bride would never come to him willingly, but she's stuck with him and he plans to use her predicament to his advantage. It's only a matter of time before she succumbs to what they both want. Their Claiming will be beautiful beyond even his wildest imaginings—and his wild, free dragoness will finally see herself as he sees her.

Then his unique, hybrid-borne visions reveal a new danger. The prophecy of the Child of Dunne can only be fulfilled down a path he must travel alone. To a place so dark and dangerous that even his truebond's flame may not be bright enough to lead him home.

Warning: Contains explicit sex, graphic language, a pissed-off dragon assassin and a smart-mouthed Nebraskan farm boy. Bet you can figure out who wins that fight! (Hint: It's not the dragon...)

Available now in ebook and print from Samhain Publishing.

The man who vows to protect her may be her biggest threat.

Savage Hunger
©2012 Shelli Stevens
Savage, Book 1

Being the daughter of a world-renowned scientist, Sienna Peters has struggled to carve out her own career in the field. But her world is sent spinning when she discovers a secret species being held in the lab where she works, and the horrible things being done to them. Compelled to do more than hand off an information-packed jump drive to her father, she sets out to free the creatures.

The minute his team enters the compound, federal agent Warrick Donovan knows their mission will have more trouble than they bargained on. Unfortunately, trouble comes in the form of Sienna Peters, the younger sister of his close friend. Now not only does he need to save her pretty ass, he needs to discover just how involved she is with the imprisonment of the shifters.

Sienna knows she should trust no one—not even the man she might still love. But as the danger escalates and past passion ignites, her heart has other ideas. Even when the shroud of mystery is ripped off more than one stunning truth...

Warning: Must love alpha males, be intrigued by federal agents who may or may not shift into wolves, and most importantly be prepared for intense action of the dangerous and sexual kind.

Available now in ebook and print from Samhain Publishing.

SAMHAIN

PUBLISHING

www.samhainpublishing.com

Green for the planet.
Great for your wallet.

PUBLISHING

It's all about the story...

Romance

HORROR

www.samhainpublishing.com

CPSIA information can be obtained at www.ICGtesting.com
Printed in the USA
BVOW07s1549180713

326318BV00003B/113/P